Return
to the
Stones

Return to the Stones

Jeremy Burnham

fantom
publishing

First published in 2013 by Fantom Films
Reissued in paperback 2015
fantomfilms.co.uk

Copyright © Jeremy Burnham 2013

Jeremy Burnham has asserted his moral right to be identified
as the author of this work in accordance with the
Copyright, Designs and Patents Act 1988.

A catalogue record for this book is available from the British Library.

Paperback edition ISBN: 978-1-78196-136-0

Typeset by Phil Reynolds Media Services, Leamington Spa
Printed and bound in the UK by ImprintDigital.com

Cover design by Stuart Manning

My thanks to astrogeologist Emma Evans and
Doctor John Reckless for knowing the unknowable

CHAPTER ONE

IT WAS GETTING REALLY scary.

For some time now, the avatar which Tom had created to explore the virtual reality model of Milbury had been behaving very strangely. It seemed to have started thinking.

He hadn't told his father, because there was bound to be some heavy parent stuff. 'Don't be ridiculous, Tommo,' he could hear him saying, 'avatars can't think.' And there was no answer to that: it was impossible.

But this one had certainly changed since he programmed it. He had given it his own sixteen-year-old face so that he could imagine he was there in person, part of the program which his father had helped him set up. At first, his digital image had done what it was supposed to do: explore the quiet English village and the circle of ancient stones which surrounded it. But now it had started to do things that weren't in the program. It would suddenly turn and wave at him, or point at something as if it wanted to draw his attention to it. And if he took no notice, it would glare at him angrily. Which was really spooky, because avatars didn't do anger. Or any other emotion, come to that.

Then there were the nightmares. Sometimes he would wake up in the middle of the night, with the weird feeling that the avatar had been watching him while he slept, trying to read his mind. And it was even worse when he was awake: he sometimes felt that it wasn't his own reflection in the bathroom mirror, but his other self.

Maybe all this detective work was driving him crazy. If he wasn't careful, he could end up like Lyman, the school nerd who was so hooked on video games he had to have therapy.

But this wasn't a video game, and Tom definitely wasn't a gamer. He thought of himself as a searcher after truth, like his father and grandfather. There were no 'wow' moments built into this program: no war games, no space invaders, nobody getting zapped. Just a stone circle, with a small village inside it. How could that drive anyone crazy? He still wasn't sure what had happened there almost thirty years ago, because his father never talked about it. All he would say was that when he was about Tom's age he and his father Adam, Tom's grandfather, had been caught in some sort of time warp from which they were lucky to escape. And that an evil magus called Hendrick had somehow managed to harness the magnetic energy in the stones to turn the other inhabitants into happy-clappy zombies.

It wasn't much to go on, and Tom knew that stuck here in Massachusetts he didn't have much chance of solving the mystery. His dad and grandpa were both Professors of Astrophysics, and if they couldn't come up with any answers, nobody could. Also, he'd never been to Milbury: never even been to England, his father's birthplace. But tomorrow, he would actually be there. He would be able to touch the stones, measure their magnetic field with his father's magnetometer, maybe even experience a 'wow' moment. So the avatar could misbehave as much as it liked: he wouldn't be watching.

But when he clicked the TURN OFF icon, the computer wouldn't shut down. Even the power button didn't work. The screen had frozen on the avatar standing by one of the stones, pointing to something carved on it... and strangely, the stone was lying on its side. This was odd, because it was the barber-stone, number nine in the south-west quadrant of the circle. And it shouldn't be lying on its side: it had been re-erected after the skeleton of a fourteenth-century barber-surgeon had been discovered underneath it.

The front door slammed. 'Dad!' he shouted. 'I need some help.'

'Can't it wait?' his father called back from his bedroom. 'I have to take a shower.'

'The computer's frozen. And there's something else.'

A moment later, he appeared, tying a towel round his waist. 'Quickly, what?'

'The avatar's gone off-program again.'

His father peered at the screen. 'What's that stone?'

'The barber-stone.'

'It can't be. It's horizontal.'

'Take another look. There's some sort of carving on it.'

'It's certainly in the right place,' said his father thoughtfully, 'and it's the right shape. But there's no carving on the barber-stone.'

'You're sure?'

'I told you – I know every detail of every rock in the Milbury circle. If it had a carving on it, I'd have built it into the construct.'

Tom hit the magnification icon. At least that worked. Carved into the rock was a strange winged creature, half-man, half-fish.

They studied it in silence for a moment. 'Maybe someone did that since you were there,' said Tom. 'Some kid who fancied himself as a graffiti artist.'

'No, it's primitive. Looks like cuneiform.'

'What's that?'

His father went into his lecturer's mode. 'It's a form of writing, consisting mainly of arrows and wedges, used by the Persians around 2000 B.C., at the time of Alexander the Great.'

Tom stared at the fish-man with interest. 'So what's it doing on the barber-stone? And who programmed it?'

'Well it certainly wasn't me.' His father peered closely at the screen. 'But I've seen that figure before somewhere...' Suddenly, the picture started to break up. The rest of the rock gradually faded away, leaving only a close-up of the winged fish-man carving.

Tom hit the cursor pad, but there was still no response: the fish-man remained on the screen, like a logo from some ancient television channel.

He stared at it, puzzled. 'It's frozen again. What's going on?'

'Virus, probably... unplug and try system restore... Can't deal with it now, I'm late...'

3

'Where are you going?'

'A guest lecturer called Professor Jarman is giving a dissertation on "The Delusion of Science".'

'Doesn't make sense,' said Tom. 'How can science be a delusion?'

'It's just a come-on title, I expect. I've read a couple of Jarman's books on the paranormal… and I'd like to meet him.'

'Sounds like a screwball. Where's he come from?'

'Good question. Nobody seems to know anything about him – even his publishers. And there are no biographical details on the book covers.' His father moved to the door, then turned back. 'You'd better start packing, Tommo. We have to be at the airport by eight-thirty. And don't take any jeans with the kneeholes cut out – or Grandpa will think I'm not looking after you properly.'

Tom grinned. 'Okay. As long as you don't take that yucky tweed jacket.'

'What's the matter with it?'

'It looks like you bought it from a charity store. In about 1823.'

'Mum bought it. At Brooks Brothers in Washington, just before we moved up here. And I'm taking it.'

After his father had left, Tom unplugged the compluter and went into the kitchen to make himself a cheese sandwich. But as they were going away, there wasn't any cheese and the bread had gone mouldy. So he took a pizza out of the freezer and shoved it in the microwave.

Through the microwave window, he watched the pizza as it slowly revolved on the turntable. There were never any pizzas while his mother was around: the freezer would have been full of healthy organic stuff, even if they were going away.

He still couldn't work out why she had suddenly walked out: still wondered if it was something he'd done – or hadn't done. His school reports had always been pretty average, and comments like 'Tom hasn't worked hard enough this semester' must have been a big disappointment to her. But that was no reason to take off like that. They'd had a few hassles, but nothing too serious. It just didn't compute.

4

When the pizza was done, he put it on a plate and took it over to the table by the window. As he crunched his way through it, he stared across the river at Beacon Hill, where the rich Bostonians lived. His mother had some friends there – an old senator and his wife she had met in Washington – and soon after his father had started his new job at MIT, they had been invited to dinner. But he didn't know which of the fancy knives and forks to use, and on the way home his mother had been furious. 'Surely you know not to eat meat with a fish-knife, Tom,' she had told him. 'They must think you were brought up in a trailer-park.'

They had never been invited again, and he knew it mattered to her. Was that what had driven her away? Or one of his other faults which she kept nagging him about: his laziness, his untidiness, the fights he kept getting into? But mothers should expect stuff like that: it wasn't as if he'd robbed a bank or murdered someone.

His life had been virtually hassle-free since she left, but that didn't make up for her absence. And even now, a year later, when he came home from school to an empty apartment, it was hard to believe that she hadn't just popped out to the supermarket.

There had been no warning, nothing to suggest she was unhappy. He'd been lying on his bed watching a DVD, when she came in, gave him a big hug and announced that she was leaving. She needed 'me time,' she told him, so she was returning to her old job in Washington. It wasn't that she didn't love him, and she would always be there for him. It was just that she had to get out of Cambridge and do her own thing. *She* had a brain too, and it was going to waste. She had to use it or lose it.

When he woke up the next morning, he was sure it was a bad dream. But it wasn't. All her belongings – her clothes, her books, even the potted plant which stood on her desk – were gone.

His father had tried to explain her sudden departure. 'It's not about you, Tommo,' his father had assured him, 'it's about me. Your mother's a very bright woman, and the academic life must have been very boring for her. I was too wrapped up in my work to pick up the vibes.'

So he felt guilty too, thought Tom. But why should he take the blame? She must have known what she was letting herself in for when she married him. An academic with first-class degrees in mathematics and astronomy at Oxford and a masters at Washington State was bound to be wrapped up in his work. And she must have known that when an American hooks up with a Brit there were bound to be cultural differences. So it couldn't have been that. No, what she'd told him was a load of crap. If you loved someone, how could you leave them? And how could she be there for him if she wasn't there? She had phoned every day for the next few weeks, but he refused to speak to her. And they hadn't had a proper conversation since. If she wanted 'me time,' she could have it: he could get along without her.

He tossed the pizza-crust into the bin, went back to his room and started throwing things into the leather suitcase which his grandfather had given him on his last visit to the States. 'You can use that case when you come to England,' he had told Tom just before he left. 'I can't wait to show you round the West Country. We've got some fantastic Neolithic sites in our neck of the woods, including Stonehenge, the daddy of them all.'

There was something sad about Grandpa Adam. Tom had never met Margaret, his second wife, who had been the curator of the Milbury museum, but he knew all about her. She had died in a car accident three years ago, so when the old man talked about coming to see *us*, he meant his stepdaughter Sandra and her adopted daughter Khonsu.

He was looking forward to meeting Khonsu: judging by her photograph, she looked pretty tasty. And he couldn't wait to see the real Milbury, even if there were no 'wow' moments. But he knew his father wasn't looking forward to the trip, because during his grandfather's last visit he'd heard them talking in the living room after he'd gone to bed. Adam had just bought the Manor House at Milbury, which used to belong to the sinister Hendrick.

'Why Milbury?' his father had asked.

6

'Two reasons,' said Adam. 'Because it's where I met Margaret. And because I'm intrigued by unsolved mysteries.'

'But why the Manor House?'

'Because it was up for sale. And I've always fancied being Lord of the Manor.'

'Suppose it all happens again?'

'It won't,' said Adam. 'I've been back many times, and everything was hunky-dory.'

'How about the natives?'

'They couldn't have been more friendly. And nobody said "Happy Day".'

Then they started talking about his mother. But Tom had never forgotten the nervousness in his father's voice. And professors of astrophysics didn't do nervous without a very good reason.

The next day, he had asked them why some of the Milbury villagers used to say 'Happy Day' to each other instead of 'Hi' or 'Hello'. Adam suggested it was probably some sort of code used by people who had been brainwashed by Hendrick so they could recognise each other. It was the only way you could tell them from normal people like Margaret and Sandra. But he couldn't explain how Hendrick had managed to turn a whole village into zombies, or why he would want to.

Tom stopped packing and glanced at the picture above his bed. His father had spotted it in a junk shop window when he was fifteen, the day before he was due to go to Milbury. It was a primitive oil painting of a prehistoric village surrounded by a circle of rocks. In the middle of the circle was a column of blinding white light stretching up into a dark, starless sky. People were staring at it, mesmerised, or turning away, shielding their eyes. Only two of them seemed to be escaping from the rock-circle: a man and a boy. Were they supposed to be Dad and Grandpa? If so, how had the painter known about their escape before it had happened?

He knelt on the bed and stared again at the Latin inscription at the bottom of the picture, written on an evil-looking snake: *Quod non est simulo, dissimuloque quod est*, which his father had translated for him as 'I deny the existence of that which exists.'

His mother had hated it, and refused to hang it anywhere else in the apartment. Being a practical, down-to-earth woman who didn't believe in anything she couldn't see or touch, she dismissed the inscription as meaningless mumbo-jumbo.

But Tom knew it was an important piece of the Milbury puzzle, so he had offered to hang it in his room. The inscription might be mumbo-jumbo to her, but it obviously meant something to the painter. Maybe to his father too, though he had always denied it. All he would say was that he didn't believe *he* had found the picture: the picture had found *him*. And when Tom asked him how that was possible, he admitted he didn't know. 'We're only at the beginning of knowledge, Tommo,' he had said. 'There are more things in heaven and earth than are dreamt of in our philosophy.'

It was a typical professor's ploy: feigning ignorance to avoid answering a difficult question. But Tom was convinced his father understood the painter's message and was still disturbed by it. He stared at the snake, trying for the umpteenth time to make sense of the Latin conundrum. 'I deny the existence of that which exists,' he whispered to himself. If his father knew what it meant, why was it such a big secret?

The young nurse stood by the window of the guest room on the upper floor of the hotel, watching anxiously as the two paramedics listened to her patient's heart. She didn't know anything about him, except that his name was Professor Jarman, that he was an invalid in a wheelchair and that he was very old. That was all the agency knew, but as the job paid five hundred dollars a day it was all she needed to know.

She hadn't expected him to be quite so frail. The skin was stretched so tightly over his cheekbones that his head looked like a skull, but it was only when she moved up to his chair that she saw the network of tiny lines that covered his face like a spider's web. He had surveyed her with cold, penetrating eyes that were almost translucent, the same colour as the pearl necklace her great-aunt Edith used to wear. They seemed to bore straight through her head.

He had given her his instructions in a thin, rasping voice. 'These are my pills,' he had told her, handing her a small, tortoiseshell box with several compartments in it. 'I must have two blue ones in the morning and evening, two white ones after meals, and if I should lose consciousness, place a red one under my tongue.'

'What are they? Are they prescribed?' she had asked. If they were illegal drugs, she didn't want anything to do with them.

'That needn't concern you. Just do as you're told.' Should she have called the agency and told them to send someone else? Hell no, she couldn't afford to turn down a thousand dollars for two days' work: maybe more, if the old buzzard decided to stay on. So she had kept her mouth shut and prayed that nothing would go wrong.

But something *had* gone wrong. That morning, the day he was due to give some sort of talk, she couldn't wake him, and she couldn't feel any pulse. She had placed one of the red pills under his tongue, but it didn't revive him. So she had dialled 911 in a panic, wondering if her nursing career was over.

Whatever the paramedics were doing to him, it seemed to be working. The patient stirred and opened his eyes. 'You can go now,' he rasped, 'I'm perfectly all right.'

'You need a complete check-up, Professor,' said the grey-haired medic. 'We'll take you to the hospital.'

'No!' The Professor's voice was surprisingly strong for someone who had just emerged from a coma. 'I have to give a lecture this afternoon.'

'You're in no condition to give a lecture, sir,' said the younger medic, 'you'll have to cancel.'

'Out of the question.' The ice-cold eyes flicked in the nurse's direction. 'If I have another attack, the nurse knows what to do.'

The medics glanced at each other helplessly. 'In that case, you'll have to sign this waiver,' said the grey-haired one. 'We don't want any come-backs.'

He produced a form, which the Professor signed with an illegible scrawl. 'You've done your duty, gentlemen,' he said, handing it back to them. 'Now go.'

The medics packed up their equipment and left. The Professor turned to the nurse. 'I'm not paying you to call for help, young woman,' he snapped, 'I'm paying you to follow my instructions.'

'I did follow your instructions, Professor,' she told him, 'but I couldn't feel any pulse. And the red pill didn't seem to work.'

'It always works. But it takes time, so if it happens again don't summon the emergency services. I'm a very private man, and I hate publicity.' He wheeled himself into the bathroom.

She took a few deep breaths to stop herself exploding. She had looked after a few difficult patients in her short nursing career, but none of them were as crabby as this one. She wondered how long it would be before she lost it and walked out on him.

What was he doing in the bathroom? He hadn't used it since she arrived, which was odd for a man of his age. Did he need any help? He hadn't mentioned it, but perhaps she had better make sure.

She knocked on the door. No reply. She opened it a crack and peered inside.

She couldn't see the Professor, but she saw his reflection in the mirror. Suddenly, to her amazement, the reflection started to fade. Then she thought she heard his voice croak something that sounded like 'Not yet!' And as if in obedience to his will, the reflection came slowly back.

She closed the door silently, her heart racing. Had she really seen what she thought she saw? Who was this man? What had she let herself in for?

MIT's McNair Building on Vassar Street housed the Kavli Institute of Astrophysics and Space Research. Matthew had been to several lectures there, and had even given one himself – on dark stars and invisible sources of radiation in the galaxy – which had later been published in *New Scientist*.

As he drove into a parking space, he wondered who had engaged the reclusive Professor Jarman and how they had managed to contact him. Or had the Professor himself hired the room and issued the invitations? In which case he was either very brave or very arrogant, because a lecture on 'The Delusion of Science' wasn't likely to go down too well with a bunch of scientists. Maybe Tom was right: he was an attention-seeking screwball.

But Jarman's published work certainly had to be taken seriously. His knowledge of astrophysics was extraordinary: even Matthew, with a first-class degree in the subject, had found some of his equations difficult to follow. They were an uncomfortable reminder of his first day at Milbury school all those years ago, when the brainwashed pupils at the senior table had all proved to be mathematical geniuses.

He had discussed Jarman's theories with some of his academic colleagues, most of whom dismissed them as the ramblings of a nutcase. Only Matthew's old tutor, Professor Harrison, a distinguished British cosmologist at the University of Massachusetts in Amherst, agreed they were worthy of serious consideration – particularly Jarman's suggestion that life on earth couldn't have arisen by chance.

'I don't believe in chance either,' Harrison had told Matthew one evening, as they sat in a riverside bar working their way through a bottle of Rioja. 'If there had been the slightest variation in the strength of gravity, the speed of light or the electric charge on an electron, the universe would be completely barren. So it's possible that life on earth was created by beings of superior intelligence feeding small amounts of matter at very high energy into a black hole. It's a perfectly reasonable suggestion.'

It brought back another disturbing memory that was indelibly printed on Matthew's mind: the day he and his father Adam had discovered the Milbury circle was aligned to a black hole.

Perhaps Jarman had a theory about how Hendrick had managed to turn this anomaly to his advantage. Perhaps, if he didn't believe in chance, it wasn't chance that had brought this oddball to Boston.

Henry Armitage, Head of the Physics Faculty, was standing outside the McNair building, talking to a group of students. As

Matthew approached, he grabbed his arm and pulled him aside.

'Matt… do me a favour, will you… what d'you know about this Jarman guy?'

'Not much. All I know is he rides the same hobbyhorse as Harrison, my old tutor.'

'Hobbyhorse?' Armitage's bushy black eyebrows shot up towards his receding hairline. 'Well it's never going to win the Kentucky Derby. You've read his books?'

'A couple of them.'

'The man should be sent to a funny-farm. And he's asked me to be his babysitter, God knows why. It's not even my department.'

'You mean, you didn't invite him?'

'No. He just called me up out of the blue.'

'So who did?'

'Nobody seems to know. If he'd told me the title of his lecture, I'd have told him to get lost.'

Matthew wondered why Armitage had agreed to act as Jarman's watchdog. This wasn't the sort of thing a pedantic old plodder would usually lend his name to. He must have been piling into his vintage cognac when he got the phone call.

'What d'you want me to do?'

Armitage patted his arm. 'Just stick around after the lecture. I'm supposed to host a reception for him, and you can keep him off my back.'

'Okay. But why me?'

'You can talk to him in his own gobbledegook. And he mentioned your name.'

Matthew frowned, puzzled. '*My* name?' But Armitage was already disappearing into the building, his gown flapping behind him like bats' wings.

The Marlar Lounge was a conference room, used as a lecture theatre for the Spring Colloquia. On show there were astronomical photographs taken from the Hubble Space Telescope, a map of the United States taken from space, and two plasma experiments constructed by the MIT Center for Space Research for the Voyager and Mariner satellites.

Between them, the satellites had visited all the planets in the solar system except for Pluto, measuring the solar wind as it passed them. Voyager was now on its way out of the solar system towards uncharted space.

The Lounge had only seventy seats, but it wasn't even half-full. This was surprising, because Armitage had promised that alcohol would be served at the reception, and there were plenty of students and members of the faculty who would go anywhere for a free drink. Perhaps most of them had already left for the vacation, thought Matthew, as he took the seat reserved for him in the front row. Or perhaps everyone had gone to Fenway Park, to watch the Red Sox play the Yankees.

There was a smattering of applause as the Professor appeared, wheeled by a young nurse. He surveyed the sparse audience with a hint of a smile. 'I see my fame has not yet spread to Massachusetts,' he said drily. Then he turned to stare straight at Matthew. 'Happy Day, Professor Brake.'

The hair at the back of Matthew's neck bristled. He stared back at Jarman, hypnotised by the pale, mesmeric eyes. How could this old man have known about that? And how did he know his name? They had never met, never even corresponded with each other.

Jarman nodded to the nurse, who retired to a chair by the door. Then he began to speak in a dry, rasping voice, without notes.

'Astronomers in Hawaii, using the world's most powerful telescope to study the gas-clouds at the edge of the universe, have recently found something completely unexpected – carbon, the element contained in all living things. Its presence means that the clouds cannot date from the origin of the universe, but must represent the ashes of a generation of stars that formed and disappeared before the present galaxies came into being. This undermines the Big Bang theory, suggesting there was an earlier universe preceding the one we know, which has left only its carbon behind, like the enigmatic grin on the face of the Cheshire Cat.'

There was a murmur of amusement from his audience, and Henry Armitage snorted derisively. Matthew wondered what Einstein or Stephen Hawking would have made of it. Professor

Harrison would certainly have approved, because it tied in with his theory that super-intelligent beings had lived on earth long before the first amphibian had crawled out of the sea. But why had they left? Had these other beings anticipated some cataclysmic event, like the huge meteorite that was supposed to have killed all the dinosaurs?

'You scientists are narrow-minded children,' Jarman went on. 'You can just about see what is under your noses, but no further.' He pointed a bony finger at the exhibits. 'Look at these toys of yours. I suppose you think you are at the cutting edge of technology at this institute. But I can assure you, ladies and gentlemen, that you haven't even begun to understand the mysteries of the universe. They cannot be reduced to mathematical equations, or explained by orthodox reasoning.'

Armitage stood up, his face flushed with anger. 'What are your qualifications, Professor?'

'I have none that you would recognise.'

'So what are you doing here?'

'I am trying to persuade you to open your eyes. To think the unthinkable. That is why I called this lecture "The Delusion of Science". If you believe that your microscopes and telescopes will tell you all you need to know, you are deluding yourselves. They may give you knowledge, but not enlightenment.'

'Then why don't you enlighten us, Professor?' said Armitage silkily. 'Give us some examples of mysteries that can't be explained by orthodox reasoning.'

'Very well. Extra-sensory perception. The fourth dimension. Out-of-body experiences.'

'Oh please!' By now, Armitage's face had turned bright scarlet. 'Don't tell me you believe in all that twaddle?'

Jarman didn't seem at all offended. 'I believe that as man became more civilised, he lost touch with the ancient wisdom.'

'Well I didn't come here to listen to fairy stories. Out-of-body experiences indeed! Ha!' Armitage stormed out, followed by several other members of the faculty.

Jarman turned to those that remained. 'The trouble is,' he said calmly, 'that innovative thinking is often rejected by scientists simply because the theory was submitted by an outsider. A scientist should always be open to new ideas, wherever they come from.'

The rest of his lecture was concerned with various aspects of the Ancient Wisdom… the legend of Atlantis, the Tibetan shamans who were able to levitate themselves, the story of Noah's Ark… all of which he claimed were supported by physical evidence. He spoke for over an hour, by which time his voice sounded like a creaking door.

'So to sum up my thesis,' he croaked at the end of his lecture, 'I suggest to you that there is a body of lost knowledge which is, at present, scientifically unacceptable. But take my word for it… future science will be based as much on rediscovery as discovery.'

About a dozen members of the audience stayed for the reception, gathering round Jarman and plying him with questions. Matthew stayed in his seat, trying to make sense of what he had heard. He wanted a one-to-one interview, so he decided to wait.

Lost in his own thoughts, he suddenly became conscious that everyone else had left, and that Jarman was sitting by the door next to the nurse, staring at him like a snake contemplating a rabbit. 'Come, Professor Brake,' he rasped.

Matthew crossed over to him and shook his claw-like hand. 'Interesting lecture,' he told him, 'but not what some of my colleagues were expecting.'

'No.' Jarman clasped his hand tightly. 'I believe that only you understood what I was trying to say.'

'How did you recognise me?'

'I read your paper on dark matter in the *New Scientist*. Your photograph was printed alongside it.'

'What did you think of it?'

'I found it extremely perceptive. It's what I would have expected from the son of such an illustrious father.'

'You've read some of Dad's stuff?'

'Of course. Adam Brake's books are required reading for anyone with an interest in astrophysics. He is a world authority in his field.'

Matthew studied the old man in silence for a moment. 'And what exactly is *your* field, Professor? Ancient Wisdom?'

'That is part of it.'

'Part of what?'

'The paranormal.' Jarman produced a wallet and took out a card. 'If you wish to get in touch with me, this is an email address.' Matthew was about to put the card in his pocket when he noticed the symbol above the Professor's name: it was an exact reproduction of the winged fish-man on Tom's computer. He looked up to find the pale eyes scanning him intently.

'You recognise it?'

'Yes.'

'Tell your son to contact me before you leave for England. Goodbye, Professor.' Jarman turned and beckoned to the nurse, who wheeled him away.

Matthew stared after him, his head spinning.

How could this wizened gnome have known that he and Tom were going to England? And what was the connection between him and the fish-man, between the fish-man and Milbury? If Jarman knew about the 'Happy Day' greeting, he must also have known its significance. Was it a demonstration of his psychic power, or had he himself managed to escape from a previous time-anomaly in the village? Perhaps it happened every thirty years, and Jarman was trying to warn him it was about to happen again. The sense of foreboding that had engulfed Matthew ever since he booked the tickets turned to alarm.

On the drive home, he wondered what all this had to do with Tom. Why did Jarman want to contact him? The boy was still hurting from the divorce, and Matthew hoped that the vacation would be part of the healing process. He needed a break, to get away for a while. What he didn't need was some mad old Professor putting pressure on him.

But was Jarman mad? To Matthew, who had good reason to believe in the paranormal, his suggestion that scientific knowledge was in its infancy made sense. It would certainly have made sense to Professor Harrison, who maintained that the more discoveries scientists made, the more they realised how little they knew.

Harrison's theory was that the secrets of the universe were covered by layers of masks, and that though each generation claimed it had discovered its true nature, all that had so far been revealed was another mask. In their books, both Jarman and Harrison had asked their readers the same question: 'Do we now stand on the threshold of knowing everything there is to know, or is our knowledge of the universe still in its infancy?' No, Jarman was perfectly sane. But who was he? Where had he come from? And how did he know so many things he couldn't possibly know?

Tom was still awake when he got home, watching the Red Sox game, so Matthew told him what Jarman had said and gave him his card.

He stared at it, puzzled. 'That logo. It's the fishy-man thing.'

'That's right.'

'So who is this guy? And how does he know about me?'

'No idea,' said Matthew, trying to make light of it. 'Maybe he looked me up on the internet.'

'But I'm not on your website.'

'Then perhaps he's been reading your blogs.'

Tom thought for a moment. 'You think it was this weirdo who put the virus into the Milbury construct?'

'Maybe. It certainly got your attention, didn't it?'

'Why would he want my attention?'

'There's only one way to find out... Did you get rid of that glitch? I'm going to finish packing.'

Tom took the card into his bedroom and booted the computer. The virus seemed to have sorted itself out, so he copied Jarman's email address and sent him a brief message: 'Hi! It's me... whoever you are... what do you want? Tom Brake.'

To his amazement, a face appeared on the screen: the face of a frail old man with cold, piercing eyes. 'Thank you for your message, Tom,' he said. 'I understand that you are interested in virtual reality. So I'm going to show you a construct that will blow your mind.'

The face gradually faded, to be replaced by what looked like an ancient temple, with a marble floor and huge stone columns supporting an arched roof. On each column was a carving of the winged fish-bird creature.

Tom's avatar appeared from behind one of the columns, followed by another avatar, a digital replica of the frail old man. They started to wander round the temple, stopping at each carving as if to emphasise its importance. Finally, they stood side by side, gazing into an enormous mirror hanging between two of the columns.

Suddenly, the old man's avatar vanished and reappeared in the mirror. Then his reflection started to fade, to be replaced by Tom's reflection. A moment later, the mirror exploded into small pieces which scattered across the floor.

The shards of glass lay still for a few seconds: then, as if attracted by an invisible magnet, they began to move together, fitting into each other like the pieces of a jigsaw until the mirror was complete again. Except it was no longer a mirror: it had turned into a silver pool, out of which emerged the silhouette of a winged fish-man. It loomed above Tom's avatar for a moment, then slowly merged with his body...

Matthew, about to pack his tweed jacket, stopped as he heard something crash in Tom's room. He called to him: 'Tommo? You okay?' There was no reply, so he put down the jacket and hurried along the corridor to investigate.

He found Tom lying on the floor, next to his upturned chair. He looked dazed, as if he wasn't quite sure where he was.

Matthew bent down and felt his pulse. 'What happened?'

'I don't know,' said Tom, sitting up and rubbing the back of his head. 'I just blacked out.'

'Did you contact Professor Jarman?'

'I think so. But I don't know what he was trying to tell me...'

Matthew picked up the chair and gently lifted him into it. 'We've got a long flight tomorrow. Maybe you should see a doctor.'

'No, I'm fine.' Tom turned to the computer and clicked the SENT icon. His message was there: 'Hi! It's me... whoever you are... what do you want? Tom Brake.'

He sent it again but the web server bounced it back immediately with a single word attached: 'Undeliverable.'

The next morning, at Logan airport, Matthew discovered how complete the dead end was. He bought an early edition of the *Boston Globe* at the bookstall, to find that the lead story was headlined: 'Mysterious Disappearance of Eminent Professor.'

Jarman's wheelchair had been found in his hotel bathroom, all its mirrors and lights smashed to pieces. But its occupant had vanished without trace.

CHAPTER TWO

MATTHEW, SITTING AT AN airport bar, read the article twice to make sure he'd got the facts right. Then he drained his cup of coffee and went out onto the concourse, hiding the newspaper under his coat. This was supposed to be a vacation, and the sooner Tom forgot about the enigmatic Professor the better.

The sound system cut across the meaningless muzak, and a bored-sounding female voice echoed across the concourse: 'This is the first call for passengers travelling to London by British Airways flight 214, now boarding at Gate 18.'

He stared across at the shopping mall. Tom had been under strict instructions not to stray too far, but there was no sign of him. So he picked up his overnight case and pushed his way through the crowd, stepping over backpacks and dozing travellers, until he caught sight of him emerging from the Food Hall with a brown paper bag.

Risking embarrassment, Matthew yelled at him: 'Tom!!!'

He spun round, as if he was half aware that he had heard his name: then continued on towards the games emporium. Matthew raced after him, murmuring apologies to people he barged into, still yelling.

Finally, Tom heard him and turned. They shouldered their way towards each other through the milling throng. 'Where the hell have you been?' demanded Matthew, conscious that his voice had risen about a hundred octaves.

Tom opened the bag. 'Stocking up at the Wok and Roll,' he said. 'I've got some dim sum, mixed noodle salad, spring rolls, dumplings, samosas…'

'They have food on the plane, you know.'

'Not my sort of food.'

'Since when has that stuff been your sort of food?'

'Since today. Remember what Mom used to say? "Lips that touch liquor shall never touch mine"?'

'That was a joke. To keep you off the booze as long as possible.'

'Well from now on, my lips will never touch anything that ever had a face.'

Matthew frowned at him. 'I'm beginning to worry about you, Tommo.'

'There's no need, Dad,' said Tom, producing a white paper bag from the brown one. 'See how I look after you?'

Matthew opened the bag. Inside were two doughnuts.

He smiled, mollified. 'Peace offering accepted.' He nodded towards the travelator, on which passengers were gliding sedately away towards the departure lounge. 'We've got to get a move on. They've only just called the flight, but the gate's miles away.'

As they entered the aircraft, he realised too late that Jarman's face was staring at them from every newspaper in the rack. Tom had grabbed one before he could stop him. 'Hey,' he said. 'This is…'

'I know.' Matthew glanced at the tickets. 'We're in 13A and 13B. You can have the window seat.'

'Lucky thirteen,' said Tom excitedly, as they buckled themselves in. 'This is going to be a fantastic trip.'

Matthew said nothing. If the boy believed thirteen was lucky, he certainly wasn't going to disabuse him. Or point out that in the Tarot deck, the thirteenth card was supposed to be the symbol of Death. In any case, that had no connection with the paranormal: it was just primitive superstition.

He watched as Tom started to read the *Globe*'s Jarman story, cursing himself for forgetting there would be newspapers on the plane. Now he would have to admit that he had tried to keep the story to himself, which would probably turn it into a big deal.

Tom looked up at him with a troubled frown. 'Have you read this?'

'Yes.'

'Why didn't you tell me?'

'I wanted you to forget all about Jarman and his conjuring tricks.'

Tom stared at him searchingly. 'You think they're just tricks?'

'What else could they be?'

'That doesn't explain why he's trying them out on me.'

This was the sort of conversation Matthew had wanted to avoid. 'He's just using you, Tommo. I'm the one he's trying to impress.'

'Why?'

'Maybe because we both work in the same field, and he thinks of me as a rival.'

Tom stared at him with a troubled frown. 'I'm not a kid any more, Dad. And I know when you're lying.'

One of the stewards bustled up to them. 'We'll be serving dinner as soon as we're airborne, gentlemen. Would sirs like an aperitif?'

Matthew ordered a whisky sour. 'And my son will have…'

'Just water, please,' said Tom. 'Sparkling.'

Matthew glanced at him in surprise, but bit his tongue, realising that to ask him why he didn't order the usual cola might be interpreted as a criticism in his present mood.

Another steward started to go through the safety routine. 'Yada yada yada,' said Tom, loudly enough for the elderly woman across the aisle to hear. She shot him a dark look, her thin lips pursed in disapproval.

'For God's sake, Tom!' said Matthew sharply. 'He's only doing his job. What's the matter with you?'

Tom turned away from him and stared out of the window. Matthew wondered where this sudden tetchiness had come from. So far, their father-son relationship had been entirely without the usual angst: no teenage problems, no accusations of a parental lack of understanding. Even after Sherry had left, when other boys of Tom's age might have blamed their fathers for the break-up, there had been no recriminations.

But Matthew knew he was at least partly to blame. The sense of guilt, the sense of failure as a husband and father, still haunted him. He had an uneasy feeling that life was passing him by, and he might not get a second chance. All he had was Tom, and some day soon he too would be gone.

The silence between them lasted all through the tensions of take-off, and he searched for the right words to break it. Then, as people started moving round the cabin, the steward arrived with the drinks.

'Those seats convert into beds, should the gentlemen wish,' he told them. 'If the young sir has any difficulty, he has only to press that button and I shall fly to his aid.'

To Matthew's relief, this broke the ice. As the steward moved on to the next row, Tom exploded with laughter. 'Do all Brits talk like that?'

'Yes,' said Matthew, as the smooth Scottish firewater slid down his throat. 'Before the soccer players make a tackle, they always say: 'Please may I kick your ankle, young sir?' For the first time since the cab deposited them at the airport, he started to relax.

Tom pointed to Jarman's photograph. 'So what's-his-face... your friend the Professor... What's he want with me?'

This time, Matthew tried to give him an honest answer. 'He's not my friend. He's just another theorist with some interesting ideas.'

'Okay. But why's he trying to climb into my head?'

Matthew stared at him in alarm. 'What d'you mean?'

'That's what it feels like, Dad,' said Tom, taking a long swig from the water-bottle, 'so please don't ask me to contact him again. He's too weird.'

When it was time for the two sirs to convert their seats into beds, Matthew settled down to sleep under a blanket and eye-mask, while Tom brought down his laptop from the overhead locker and plugged it into the power-socket in the armrest. 'Why were you so jumpy about leaving Boston?' he asked as he waited for it to boot up. 'Or was it about going back to Milbury?'

'Goodnight, Tommo,' said Matthew. He lifted the eye-mask a fraction, to see a photograph of the Milbury painting materialising on the laptop screen.

23

'Those two guys escaping from the circle,' said Tom, peering closely at it. 'You reckon they're supposed to be you and Grandpa?'

Matthew pulled back the eye-mask. 'Not now,' he said firmly.

' "Quod non est simulo dissimuloque non est." That's what you're doing, isn't it? Denying the existence of that which exists?'

This time there was no mistaking the signing-off from beneath the blanket. 'Goodnight, Tom!'

From the air, England looked exactly as Tom had imagined it: small, green... and very wet.

At Heathrow, they collected the car Matthew had rented and set off through the same industrial sprawl that seemed to surround every other airport.

Many miles later, as the day awoke, they emerged into open countryside. Through the driving rain, Tom could see forlorn-looking cows sheltering under trees and bedraggled sheep huddled together in the corners of the fields. Then, as they reached the brow of a hill, a watery sun broke through the clouds, revealing a vast green carpet beneath them that stretched away towards the horizon.

Tom's spirits rose. 'Is this the West Country?'

'The start of it.' His father was staring intently at the road ahead, gripping the wheel tightly, knuckles white, his breathing shallow. Tom tried to think of something reassuring to say, but couldn't come up with anything. Maybe coffee would help his father to relax.

'Let's make a pit stop,' he suggested. 'Are the pubs open yet?'

'Yes. Good call, coach.'

They pulled off the motorway and found a rickety-looking black-and-white inn called 'The George' with 1462 carved above the entrance.

'Is that the date this place was built?' Tom asked the bewhiskered barman as they settled onto two stools.

'No sir,' said the barman, 'that's the year it was *re*built. The original house was burned down during the Black Death.'

'Wow!' Tom glanced up at the ancient wooden beams. 'So everything's genuine fifteenth century, right?'

'Except that juke-box over there... that's fourteenth century. What can I get you gentlemen?'

'I'll have a large whisky,' said Matthew.

'No he won't,' said Tom quickly, 'he'll have a large black coffee. And I'll have some fizzy water.'

His father glanced at him with amusement while the landlord poured the coffee from a percolator. 'This is my country, young sir. I'm supposed to be the boss around here.'

'Not when you're driving, Dad. I don't want to end up in intensive care.'

'Anyway, what's with this water thing? You used to say water was a waste of space.'

'That was then,' said Tom.

Matthew pointed to a great conical mound ahead, rising above the low-lying mist. 'That's Milbury Hill.'

Tom stared at it, speechless. So this was the largest man-made mound in Neolithic Europe: still a mystery, still the subject of speculation among the archaeologists. Was it an ancient monument or burial ground? Nobody knew.

The signpost said 'Milbury 2 miles,' and Tom could sense his father's disquiet as they left the main road and headed north along the avenue of stones leading to the village. There it was, nestling serenely inside the circle of giant sarsens.

As they reached the point where the Avenue passed through the circle, his father seemed to find it difficult to breathe. Had something happened here during his first visit, wondered Tom, or were fragments of the past coming back to him?

Suddenly, a woman leaped from behind one of the stones and stood in the middle of the road, waving frantically at them. His father stamped on the brake and the car skidded to a halt a few feet in front of her. He closed his eyes and leant forward, resting his head against the wheel. 'No!' he said softly, 'Not again!'

Tom touched his shoulder. 'It's okay, Dad. It's just some woman. Looks like she knows you.'

The woman wrenched open the driver's door and poked her head inside. She had jet-black hair and dark, intelligent eyes. 'Matthew!' she shouted excitedly. 'Dearest Matt! Get the hell out of the car so I can give you a big hug.'

Tom watched as his father raised his head from the steering wheel, looking confused. Then recognition dawned. 'Sandra,' he whispered. 'Is it you?'

'Of course it's me,' said the woman briskly. 'Who else would risk life and limb to welcome you back?' She pulled him out of the car and they embraced, clinging to each other and shrieking like children.

What's going on? thought Tom. It was hard to believe that this quiet, laid-back, caring man he had known all his life had suddenly turned into a gibbering idiot. His mother's departure had hit them both hard, but that was no excuse for behaving like a spaced-out kid. Had the proprietor of 'The George' slipped some illegal substance into his coffee?

There was further embarrassment when he got out of the car and his father introduced him to the woman as 'my main man'. What was happening in his head? He didn't do homey-speak: he talked the talk and walked the walk of a professor. If this was what Milbury did to people, it wasn't surprising he had stayed away for so long.

Then the woman's name suddenly registered. Sandra! Of course! Grandpa's stepdaughter, adopted after her mother had died in that car accident.

'Hi, good to meet you,' he said, offering his hand.

'Just listen to that sexy American accent!' To his horror, she grabbed him, kissed him on both cheeks, then stood back and stared at him appraisingly. 'Your photograph doesn't do you justice, Tom. You're going to break a few hearts in a year or two. Or maybe you already have?'

This was toe-curling stuff, and he looked round to make sure no one was watching.

But somebody *was* watching. A slim, olive-skinned girl in a red T-shirt and jeans was hanging upside down from a branch of a nearby oak tree, clinging on to it with her knees, her long raven hair cascading from her head. She was smiling and waving.

'My daughter Su,' said Sandra. 'She's been longing to meet you.'

For Tom, the sun came out.

The four of them piled into the car and they drove into the village. Tom covered his eyes, visualising the construct and pointing blindly left and right as they passed familiar landmarks. Each time he was correct, his father hit the car horn…

'There's the shop!' (hoot) … 'pub!' (hoot) … 'church!' (hoot) … 'the school' (hoot) … 'the museum!' (hoot) … 'Hawthorn Cottage' (two hoots) … and finally 'the Manor House!' (three hoots).

As soon as the car had stopped, Su jumped out and opened the passenger door. 'Come on,' she said to Tom, 'Grandpa's been twitchy all week. He kept asking why you weren't here yet.'

It was a shock to hear this awesome stranger call his grandfather 'Grandpa'. But of course, he was *her* grandfather too: they were related, though he wasn't quite sure how.

He followed her into the wood-panelled hall and was immediately conscious of the age-old silence of the house, broken only by the ticking of clocks. On the right-hand wall was a portrait of a beautiful woman he recognised from her photograph: Adam's dead wife, Margaret.

'Grandpa will be in the study,' said Su. 'He's researching the previous Lords of the Manor. And probably swearing at the computer.'

On cue, a roar of rage echoed from the depths of the house. Su giggled. 'That's nothing. You should hear him when he's really cross.'

Tom followed her down a long corridor to a wood-panelled room at the end. Adam was sitting at a desk, peering at a PC monitor over half-moon spectacles. A leather-bound tome was propped up on a bookrest beside it.

He turned as Tom and Su appeared. 'Ah there you are, Thomas,' he said as if he had just come back from school. 'Are you on intimate terms with Dame Electronica?'

Tom stared at him blankly. 'Who?'

Adam tapped the screen. 'This disobedient beast. I believe your generation knows how to tame it.'

'He could have asked me,' whispered Su, 'but he thinks girls and technology come from different planets.'

The old man stood up, motioned Tom to take his place at the computer and picked up the book. 'Take this down,' he said. 'Reginbald the priest... that's capital R-e-g-i-n-b-a-l-d... holds the church of Milberie... that's the old spelling, ending e-r-i-e... to which belong two hides worth forty shillings...'

'Oh for heaven's sake, Adam!' Sandra was standing with Matthew by the door. 'You haven't put the poor boy to work already? He hasn't even got his bearings yet.'

The old man put down the book, looking sheepish. 'Sorry, got carried away. It's just that I wanted to finish the Reginbald section. He sounds such a boring old fart.'

He took off his spectacles and stared at Tom as if he was seeing him for the first time. 'Welcome to England, Thomas. How old are you now? As I shrink, you seem to grow.'

'Lunch,' said Sandra firmly. 'I've asked Mrs C to set it up outside.'

They went out through the back door into the walled garden, where a light lunch had been laid out on a table in the middle of the lawn. Tom turned and stared back at the house. From this angle, it seemed much more forbidding: the mullioned windows high up in the old grey walls looked like dark, unfriendly eyes.

Su must have read his thoughts. 'Aaarh!' she said in a strange accent that sounded like a dog growling. 'The Manor be full of ghosts, young Thomas. That be why we put you in the annexe. So you wouldn't be troubled by ghoulies and ghosties and things that go bump in the night.'

As they sat down at the table, a shambling figure of indeterminate sex appeared, carrying a large flagon. It was clad in a crumpled overall, an old felt hat and carpet slippers. The apparition thumped the flagon down: then, to Tom's astonishment, reached out and ruffled his hair.

'Hello, Master Matthew,' it cackled. 'I'd have known you anywhere. You haven't changed a bit.'

'Who was that?' asked Tom, after the apparition had tottered away.

Adam smiled. 'Your father should know.'

But Matthew looked mystified. He glanced at Sandra, who was also smiling. Then his memory seemed to kick in. 'No,' he said, 'it can't be old Crabface?'

'It is,' Sandra told him.

The name meant nothing to Tom. 'Who's old Crabface?'

'Mrs Crabtree, our housekeeper at Hawthorn Cottage,' said Adam. 'She's a good cook, so when I moved in here I took her on.' He picked up the flagon and poured some light brown liquid into Tom's glass. 'Try some of this. It's pretty strong, so go easy with it.'

Tom stared at it doubtfully. 'What is it?'

'Cider,' said Su. 'It's what we West Country folk drink when we want to get bladdered.'

He picked up the glass and took a sip. 'Ugh!' he said, banging it down again. 'I think I'll pass. Can I have some water?'

Su stood up. 'I'll get it.' She disappeared into the house.

'Have some of this liver pâté, Tom,' said Sandra. 'It's home-made. Mrs C's speciality.'

He sniffed at it suspiciously. 'Thanks, but I'm not that hungry. I'll just have some bread and cheese.'

His grandfather frowned and turned to his father. 'Bread, cheese and water? Is that what you've been feeding the lad? Maybe *you* should hire a housekeeper.'

They finished the meal just in time. A summer shower sent them scurrying indoors, carrying what was left of the food into the kitchen, where Mrs Crabtree was snoring in a rocking chair.

'I'll make coffee,' said Sandra. 'How about you, Tom?'

'No, thanks.'

'Well, why don't you fetch your stuff from the car, and Su will show you to the annexe.'

Su grinned. 'It's a very special annexe for a very special guest. But there's no extra charge.'

He collected his laptop and suitcase and followed her round the house into a small courtyard. Parked in a corner was an elaborately decorated wagon with a narrow chimney sprouting from its roof.

'It's an old gipsy caravan,' said Su. 'You like?'

Tom stared at it, enchanted. 'It's awesome!'

'That's a relief. We were afraid you'd expect an en suite bathroom with a jacuzzi. Come and see.'

He followed her up the steps into the wagon. There was a living space with a stove, gilded panels of bevelled glass, and beyond it, a narrow bed.

'Everything a young man could desire,' said Su, 'except a shower. For that, you have to come into the house.' She switched on a lamp. 'You're hooked up to the Manor's electric supply, and within range of Grandpa's wi-fi. Anything else you need?'

Tom looked round, in love with England and everything else that was happening to him. 'Doesn't look like it. It's brilliant!' He dumped his luggage on the bed and they sat opposite each other in the living area. 'So where did this thing come from?'

Su hugged her knees. 'It belonged to my dad. He bought it from a farmer while he was studying at Oxford. Then he parked it in a friend's garden and lived in it.'

'What was he studying?'

'Archaeology. That's how he met Mum. She was studying medicine.'

'Dad said he was French. So what was he doing at Oxford?'

'No idea. I never knew him.' Su was silent for a moment, staring into the past. 'He died of typhoid. In Iran, while he was researching a book on "The Cradle of Civilisation". Mum was there too, working for the Red Crescent, but there was nothing she could do.'

Tom hesitated, wondering if he should intrude any further into her memories. 'So how come...'

'...Mum adopted me? My blood parents were killed in an earthquake when I was a baby, and I was sent to an orphanage. Mum had just lost her husband, and wanted a child. So we needed each other...' Su glanced round the caravan, misty-eyed. 'That's why this thing is so important to us. It reminds Mum of Dad, and it reminds me how lucky I've been.'

'So what does that make *us*? I mean, how are we related?'

'God knows. Mum couldn't work it out either. Stepcousins, maybe.' Su jumped to her feet. 'You must be dying to explore the village. Come on – I'll show you round.'

Tom followed her out of the caravan, walking on air. His stepcousin or whatever she was had exceeded all his expectations. He wondered if she had a boyfriend.

Matthew watched as Sandra poured him a third cup of coffee. The dark-eyed girl of his youth had grown into an extremely attractive woman. Memories of their struggle against Hendrick and the 'Happy Day' people came flooding back.

'So you're a doctor?' he said as she passed him the cup. 'I should have thought running this house and looking after Dad was a full-time job.'

She glanced at Adam, who was asleep in an armchair with his spectacles perched on top of his head. 'Oh he's no trouble. And I only have a part-time consultancy at the hospital. I also work part-time at the museum.'

'Following in your mother's footsteps?'

'I like to keep busy. It stops me thinking too much about the past.'

'Yes. Work's a great anaesthetic, isn't it?' They smiled at each other, re-establishing a long-ago intimacy. Everything seemed so normal, it was hard to believe the nightmare ever happened.

Matthew drained his cup and put it down on a side-table, next to a photo of a handsome, fair-haired young man. He was standing in a rocky desert, grinning at the camera and holding up some dusty artefact. 'Is that your husband?'

'Yes,' said Sandra quietly. 'We only had a few years together, but they were worth more than a lifetime with anyone else.'

'You were lucky.' The moment the words were out of his mouth, Matthew wished he could take them back. They sounded bitter, full of self-pity. 'How did you meet?' he asked quickly, hoping she hadn't noticed.

'I was in a pub with a bunch of medical students. They were throwing bread rolls at each other, and Jean-Jacques must have seen how bored I was. So he came over, oozing Gallic charm, and offered to take me away from "les enfants".'

'And that was that?'

'Yes.'

'Where was that photo taken?'

'At the Susa site in southern Iran... just before he became ill.' Sandra gazed at the photo for a long moment, then stood up. 'Come on, I'll show you your room.'

As they climbed up to the first floor, the grandfather clock in the hall whirred into life, striking five. Matthew glanced down at it, remembering the fateful night when Hendrick had kept him and his father captive in the house. Link, his manservant, had been adjusting the old timepiece as they followed him up the stairs.

He froze in the doorway of the bedroom, realising where he was. It was the same room where they had altered Hendrick's atomic clock, catching him in his own trap and allowing them just enough time to make their escape. But it was different now, very different. A four-poster bed, a fine oak chest, tapestries on the walls depicting medieval hunting scenes. And on the mantel, instead of the atomic clock with its digital read-out, an ormolu glass-domed timepiece. Time, he thought: it can kill, but it can also save.

'Will this suit the honoured guest?' asked Sandra.

Matthew grinned. 'Don't you have anything better?'

'I'm afraid not.'

'Then I suppose I shall have to slum it in here.'

Adam appeared behind him. 'Sorry I nodded off,' he said, wheezing from his stair-climb. 'You must have given me your jet-lag.'

'Rubbish,' said Sandra. 'He always has a snooze after lunch. Well now he's had his beauty sleep, I'll leave you to talk.' She disappeared down the stairs.

Adam sat on the bed. 'Remember this room, Matt?' he said quietly.

'How could I forget? I still have nightmares about it.'

'You won't have any more after this visit. As you see – everything's tickety-boo now.'

Matthew sat beside him. 'How do you explain it?'

Adam thought for a moment. 'I can't offer a scientific explanation. But I believe that when we escaped, we destroyed Hendrick's power. Released everyone else from his shackles.'

'What happened to this house after we left?'

'According to Mrs Crabtree, Link stayed on as caretaker. Then another strange chap called Sir Joshua Lytton bought it. Some sort of psychiatrist, who hired Link as his personal assistant. Not too popular with the locals, I gather, because he didn't participate in village activities.'

'What happened to him?'

'Apparently, he and Link came to a nasty end while on safari in Africa.'

'Apparently?'

'That's what the locals believe.'

Matthew listened with interest while Adam filled in the details. Lytton and Link never came back from Africa. Their kit and traces of human body parts were discovered, so it was assumed they had been eaten by animals. When the news reached the village, no one shed any tears. Mrs Crabtree seemed to speak for everyone when she told Adam, 'Eaten by wild beasts they was, and good riddance. They probably gave some poor lion indigestion.'

The house had remained empty for almost twenty years, and by the time Adam saw the advertisement in the property section of the *Times* it had fallen into serious disrepair. 'Cost me an arm and several legs to fix it up,' he told Matthew, 'but it was worth it. Got a bit lonely though, till Sandra and Su moved back.'

This was said without reproach, but it only added to Matthew's sense of guilt. He had been unable to come to England for Margaret's funeral because it coincided with his interview for the MIT job. His request for a postponement had been refused, but he knew he should have come anyway. To be by his father's side as he buried his wife was more important than his career.

'Sandra looks just like her mother,' he said. 'That must be some consolation.'

'Yes. Sometimes on a summer evening, when I watch her dead-heading the roses...' Adam remained silent for a moment. 'But what about you, old chap? How are you bearing up?'

'I'm fine. It's Tom I'm worried about.'

'Poor lad. He must be feeling completely discombobulated.'

'Trouble is, he never talks about Sherry. And whenever I try to get him to open up, he just slams out of the room.'

'Why didn't she wait till he was away at college?'

'God knows. I still don't understand it. There were no warning signs, nothing to pick up on.'

'Anyone else involved?'

'I don't think so. I think she just... fell out of love with me.' Matthew wondered, not for the first time, if it would have been less painful if Sherry had found someone else. He could have understood that, and there was nothing he could have done about it. But to be rejected because of his own inadequacy, because he had allowed his work to take precedence over his family, that was hard to take.

He felt his father's arm across his shoulder. 'Life's a rum go, old boy. D'you want her back?'

This was another question that Matthew had often asked himself in the still of the night. Why hadn't he tried harder to persuade Sherry to stay? Why hadn't he fought for her, apologised for his selfishness, promised that he would put her at the centre of his universe? But he had finally realised that the wound was too deep. If her career was more important to her than her family, he no longer wanted her.

They had divorced without acrimony. Sherry wanted nothing but her freedom: no property, no alimony and no legalised contact with their son. He had kept the terms secret from Tom: the boy was suffering enough as it was, though he hid it behind a façade of indifference. If he found out that she hadn't insisted on access to him, his hurt would turn to anger.

His father stood up. 'I want to show you something. Prepare to be boggled.'

Matthew followed him up the narrow staircase leading to the top floor, towards the room which had haunted him for a quarter of a century: the room where, if their plan hadn't worked, they would literally have lost their minds.

He stopped, half-way up. 'I'm sorry, Dad. I don't think I can do this.'

Adam turned. 'Yes, you can, Matt. You have to exorcise the past.'

Matthew forced himself to climb up to the door, remembering how his entrails had turned to jelly as he made the same climb as a boy. Even now, he was shaking like a leaf.

When his father threw open the door and stepped back to allow him to be boggled, he stared at the nightmare room in amazement. Gone were the circular stone table, the stone chairs and the rock-throne on which Hendrick had sat, eyeing them like some hungry bird of prey. In their place was an enormous telescope.

'Good grief!' said Matthew, awestruck. 'That's a pretty expensive toy.'

'It's an apochromatic refractor. Boggled?'

'Totally boggled. How could you afford it?'

'A grant from my old university. And most of your inheritance.' Adam crossed over to the telescope and patted it as if it were a pet dog. 'Twinkle twinkle little star... how I wonder what you are...'

Matthew grinned. '...flames of soda, streaks of tin... sulphuretted hydrogen.'

'You still remember that? I hope you pass it on to your students.' Adam pressed a button by the door and the roof rolled back, just as it had done at Hendrick's command all those years ago. Above them, small fluffy clouds were gliding across an azure sky.

'What happened to Hendrick's throne,' asked Matthew, 'and that great stone dish he used as a table?'

'Sold them to a film company. They needed props for something called *King Arthur and the Seven Dwarfs*. And look what was exposed when they took them away!'

At Matthew's feet, exactly where the table had stood, was a circular legend carved into the stone floor. He walked slowly round it, his heart thumping as he read the strange words that the ring of villagers had chanted outside the Manor while they were at dinner.

He read them aloud. 'Anger of fire... fire of speech... breath of knowledge... render us free from harm... return to us the innocence that once we knew... complete the circle... make us one with nature and the elements...'

'Gibberish!' said Adam dismissively. 'I don't want to be at one with the elements. I want to be at one with central heating.' He moved to a control deck, hit more buttons, and the telescope revolved majestically round to a preset position. 'Su chose these coordinates. Wouldn't be surprised if she became the third astrophysicist in the family.'

Matthew stared up at the sky, in the direction the telescope was pointing. 'What's she so interested in? You haven't told her about our old friend Ursa XB1?' This was Hendrick's Supernova, whose implosion had created the black hole to which the stone circle was aligned.

'No,' said Adam grimly. 'These are the coordinates of an even more intriguing puzzle... Sagittarius A. She won't see it through this thing, of course, but she'll keep trying.'

Matthew could well understand why Su was interested in Sagittarius A. Astronomers all over the world were puzzled by the mysterious celestial object at the heart of the Milky Way. It seemed to anchor everything else in the galaxy, including an estimated hundred billion stars, because it was the only object which remained motionless in relation to everything else around it. It was also a powerful radio transmitter, suggesting that its high-energy signals could be the death-throes of gas whirling around a supermassive black hole. This in turn suggested that Sagittarius A was a binary system, and that the signals came from the black hole's companion star, Sagittarius B.

Adam glanced at his watch. 'Sun's almost over the yardarm. I suggest we stroll down to the Red Lion and investigate their Scottish wine.'

As they walked through the village, the huge sarsens were casting long shadows in the evening sun. A horned ram, a slab of dirty white, lay in the shade of one of the stones. As Matthew watched, a crow landed on the ram's back, walked unchallenged up its spine and perched on its head between its curved horns.

He had seen the same phenomenon on the day they had first arrived in Milbury. Was it some sort of omen? Despite Adam's assurance that everything was now tickety-boo, the old fear lay coiled up like a snake in a corner of his mind. He didn't trust this village: even in the bright sunshine it made him uneasy. As if it had been waiting for him to return, so that it could reveal more of its dark secrets.

'Ever heard of a chap called Jarman?' he asked. 'Calls himself a Professor, but he doesn't seem to have any qualifications.'

'No,' said Adam. 'Why?'

'He writes weird books about the Ancient Wisdom. He seems to know all about Milbury and the time anomaly.'

Adam stopped and frowned at him. 'How *could* he know?'

'Maybe it's happened before, and he was caught in one himself. He's very old.'

'Interesting. What made you bring him up?'

'He gave a lecture at MIT yesterday. His main thesis was that scientists are narrow-minded children.'

'That must have upset a few applecarts.'

'The physicists walked out en masse. But afterwards, he gave me his card and asked Tom to contact him before he left for England.'

Adam's frown deepened. '*Tom?* Did he say why?'

'No. And we never found out, because his email address didn't seem to exist. And according to this morning's *Globe*, he disappeared from his hotel room last night.'

'Extraordinary. I hope it didn't upset the boy?'

'I just want him to forget it, Dad. He said something rather disturbing this morning… that he felt as if Jarman was trying to climb into his head.'

As they walked on, the crow spread its wings and rose into the sun, cawing resentfully.

The pub was full of raucous laughter and West Country accents. 'I'll have a large single malt,' said Adam as he headed for a snug.

Matthew elbowed his way to the bar and called to the burly landlord. 'Large single malt, please. And I'll have a pint of your best...'

'Who d'you think you are, sunshine?' said the landlord. 'Coming in here, flashing your foreign dollars and expecting to be served before my regulars? You Yanks think you own the bloody world!'

To Matthew's astonishment, his face split into a wide grin. He came round the bar, grabbed his hand and pumped it.

'Matty, me old mate... don't you recognise me? I'm Bob... we were at school together, back in the dark ages...'

'And I'm Jimmo,' said a voice behind him. 'Better known as Detective Inspector Jim Browning of the Wiltshire CID... What are you having, Matt? It's my shout.'

And that's how the party started.

By the time Matthew left the pub, he was legless. 'Better take our time,' he said blearily. 'Don't want Tom to see his revered father like this.'

Adam too seemed to be finding it difficult to walk in a straight line. 'Do him good. Teach him to steer clear of alcohol. The road to perdition.'

They set off back towards the Manor, grateful for the cool evening breeze. The stones loomed like sinister black sentinels in the last of the light.

'What puzzles me,' said Matthew, 'is that none of them seem to have any memory of the time Hendrick owned their minds.'

'Thank the gods,' said Adam. 'Sandra has no memory of it either. Age may have wearied them, but they're the same people.'

'Except for Kevin. He used to be a real tearaway, but Jimmo told me he's turned into some sort of hippy... joined a gang of New Age travellers who've settled here. Jimmo's had to arrest him a dozen times.'

Adam pointed towards a distant paddock, some way beyond the Manor. Shadowy figures were sitting around a blazing fire, surrounded by a ring of battered vans and trailers. 'They call themselves the Disciples of Gaia. I made a big mistake, letting them camp in Four Acre Field. Whenever they break the local by-laws, which seems to be increasingly often, the council blames me.'

Someone in the camp started to play a tuneless dirge on a guitar. 'Why don't you give them their marching orders?' asked Matthew.

'It's not that easy. You remember your old chum, that poacher?'

Matthew stopped in his tracks, stunned. 'Dai? Can he still be upright?'

'The Gaians have elected him their leader,' said Adam, 'some sort of shaman. And unfortunately, I'd just given him a life-lease on our old cottage. So I guess his tribe is here to stay.'

Matthew thought for a moment. 'You go on, Dad. Make my apologies to Mrs Crabtree. I won't be long.'

Hawthorn Cottage showed no light. Matthew banged on the door, but there was no response. Then, remembering his first bruising encounter with Dai which had resulted in expensive repairs to his bicycle, he took out his notebook and drew a clumsy outline of the wreck. Tearing off the page, he was about to shove it through the letter box when he had another idea. Dai had lived outside the circle, in the Neolithic sanctuary which was supposed to protect people from harm.

Circling the cottage, tripping over a clattering bucket, he thumped on the back door and called. 'Come out, you old fraud! I need sanctuary! Do you hear me – sanctuary!'

Silence. Then a bolt was drawn back and the door opened the merest crack. 'Who is it?' rumbled a familiar voice with a lilting Welsh accent. 'Who disturbs the Lord of the Leylines at his meditations?'

Matthew slid the bicycle-sketch through the crack. There was more silence – followed by a roar. 'Matthew? Matthew boy – is it you?' The door was flung open, to reveal a white-bearded figure in a shabby overcoat and mittens. He looked a hundred years older, but it was unmistakably Dai.

He peered at Matthew warily, then held out his arms and they hugged each other. 'Never thought I'd see you again, boy,' said Dai, snuffling into Matthew's jacket. 'Never thought I'd have the joy. Come in, come in…'

He led the way into the jumbled living room and collapsed into a chair, wiping his eyes with a filthy snot-rag. 'What libation can I offer you? Cup of my home-made mead, maybe? To warm the old cockles?'

Matthew sat opposite him. 'No thanks. My cockles were warmed at the pub.'

Dai trumpeted into the snot-rag. 'You don't want to drink their piss-water, boy. My mead is dedicated to Gaia, the goddess I serve. It'll blow your socks off.'

'I hear you've come up in the world?'

'True, boy, true. The Truth has raised me to my present eminence.'

'What are you up to, you old reprobate? What's this current scam?'

'Scam!' Dai's feigned indignation was magnificent. 'Scam! I'll have you know, boy, that I am an icon. A high priest. Scam indeed!'

Matthew laughed. 'So poaching and petty theft are no longer your way of life?'

Dai stood up angrily. 'By Gaia, boy, I'll make you eat those words.' Then he sat down again. 'If only I wasn't so glad to see you.'

'Tell me about these disciples of yours.'

The old man explained how he had come to be chosen as their leader. Apparently they had admired his spirit, living off the land: they thought it fitted well with their principles. Kevin, their spokesman, had suggested that he should become their wise man, a teacher of country lore, a sort of Druid. Dai didn't really understand it: perhaps he looked the part, with his white beard and wrinkles. Anyway, it was an offer he couldn't refuse, because the Disciples promised to look after his needs, supply him with food, wood for his fire and a little money. In exchange, he would assume the Robes of Office, pass on wisdom and advice and preside over their ceremonies.

It seemed like a good deal at the time. He was not allowed to bathe in still water, so his followers had plumbed a power-shower into the cottage. If he had the slightest wish, he had only to hint. And he had become a media celebrity: half-naked girls with microphones kept pestering him for interviews.

But recently, he had begun to wonder whether the game was worth the candle. Tonight, for instance, was the full moon before Litha, the Celtic fire festival to be celebrated in two weeks' time on Midsummer Night. And he was supposed to officiate at the ceremony.

Unfortunately, heavy rain was forecast, so he was likely to get cold and wet and miserable. And he'd had plenty of nights like that when he was a poacher. Maybe Matthew would like to take his place at the ceremony as his deputy High Priest?

Matthew stood up. 'Sorry, Dai. I have to get back to the Manor. Why don't you come with me – and bring a flask of mead with you?'

'Can't do that, boy,' said Dai gloomily. 'They'd smell it on my breath.'

Matthew headed for the door. 'I want you to meet my son Tom. He's a year older than I was when you wrecked my bike.'

'Clever lad, is he?' asked Dai. 'Chip off the old block? Maybe he'd like to become a Disciple?'

'Not a chance. He worships the great god cyberspace.'

When Matthew arrived back at the Manor, Mrs Crabtree met him at the door. 'Nobody told me,' she said accusingly. 'Why didn't someone tell me?'

He stared at her, confused. 'Tell you what, Mrs C?'

'That he was a vegeterarian.'

'Who?'

'Your son.'

'Tom isn't a vegetarian.'

'Having me on, is he? Well I don't think it's very funny. I ordered that venison specially.' Mrs Crabtree disappeared through the green baize door at the back of the hall, muttering to herself.

Matthew found Adam, Sandra and Su in the dining room, their plates piled high with meat and vegetables. A half-carved haunch of venison stood on the hotplate near the door.

'Sorry, Matt,' said Adam. 'We couldn't wait. Mrs C insisted.'

'Where's Tom?'

'He felt sick,' said Sandra, 'so he's lying down in the caravan. I've given him some anti-acid tablets.'

'He tried, Mr Brake,' said Su. 'He really tried to eat it. But he just couldn't.'

Matthew went out into the courtyard and climbed into the old wagon. Tom was lying in the bed, staring at the roof. He looked very pale, and even under the heavy blanket he was shivering.

Matthew crouched down beside him. 'What's all this, Tommo?'

'I told you, Dad,' said Tom weakly. 'I can't eat anything that used to have a face.'

'Even burgers?'

'Ugh!'

Matthew stared at him with concern. 'Okay, so now you're a vegetarian. It's no problem.'

But this sudden aversion to meat puzzled him. The fact that it used to have a face had never worried Tom before, and whenever Sherry had asked him what he would like for his birthday dinner he had always chosen steak. Perhaps it was the excitement of seeing Milbury for the first time, thought Matthew, as he walked back to the house. But it was still very odd.

They came for Dai at eleven-thirty that night... six young Disciples, all of them girls. They robed him in his priestly vestments and hung his chain of office round his neck. Then they lit pitch-torches and escorted him up the avenue of stones to Milbury Hill, chanting hymns in praise of Gaia.

On the flattened top of the ancient tumulus, surrounded by a ring of flaming torches, Dai began the incantation to the moon which the Disciples had taught him.

The wind tore at his robes, and a sudden clap of thunder drowned his words. The Disciples, straining to hear, crowded closer around him so that they could give their responses. Then, as a flash of lightning blinded them, they fell to their knees.

Dai's voice rose above the storm. 'Anger of fire... Fire of speech... Breath of knowledge... Render us free from harm... Return to us the innocence that once we knew... Complete the circle... Make us at one with nature and the elements...'

With their brows pressed onto the sodden grass, the Disciples didn't see the sudden flash of electricity that streaked down from the darkness and for a brief moment engulfed the body of the old man in a blinding fireball. Nor did they hear his anguished cry as he collapsed to the ground and lay still.

CHAPTER THREE

'THIS IS THE WHITE Lady's Walk,' said Su, as she led Tom down a narrow garden path flanked by tall hedges. 'It's supposed to be haunted by the ghost of a young woman whose lover was killed in the Civil War. She threw herself out of an upstairs window.'

Tom glanced back at the Manor, picturing the heartbroken girl plunging down the grey walls to her death. 'The Civil War. That was four hundred years ago, right?'

'Yes. She's been wandering round the garden ever since.'

'She must be getting tired.'

Su stopped and stared at him thoughtfully. 'You don't believe in ghosts?'

'No. I take after my mom. She didn't believe in any of that psychic stuff.'

'Didn't?'

'I mean – doesn't.'

'How about your dad?'

'He tells me to keep an open mind.'

'That's good advice, specially in this village. It can get quite spooky sometimes.'

They walked on, into the sunlit orchard. Tom gazed across the adjoining fields, where sheep were peacefully grazing. In the distance, behind the house, someone was playing Bob Dylan's *Brownsville Girl* on a guitar. On this glorious summer morning, the village couldn't have looked less spooky.

And yet... Su didn't seem like the sort of person who was easily spooked. So maybe his father had good reason to be nervous about coming back. The stone circle hadn't moved in the intervening years: it must still be aligned to a black hole, and its powerful magnetic field which had astonished his grandfather couldn't have changed. There was a timelessness about this place, which made four hundred years seem like yesterday. Inside the circle, the idea of a restless spirit like the White Lady haunting the garden didn't seem so far-fetched.

They sat down under a gnarled apple tree. Su leant against the trunk and closed her eyes. In the dappled shade, she looked older and even more beautiful. There was a timelessness about her too, thought Tom. She reminded him of a picture of an Arabian princess in an exhibition his mother had dragged him to at the Boston Museum of Fine Arts. Even if she didn't have a boyfriend, she was way out of his league.

'Has anybody actually seen this White Lady?' he asked her.

'Not lately. But Grandpa's found lots of references to her in the village records. Other ghosts too.'

She told him about an early owner of the Manor, a Royalist who was supposed to haunt the Cavalier Room. About a knight called Sir John Stowell who killed himself when he lost all his possessions in the Civil War, whose appearance was always preceded by a smell of roses. And about an angry spirit called Florrie, dressed in black, who was drowned in a well by her soldier husband for being unfaithful. There were also countless reports of visitors being touched by some unseen hand, appliances being turned on and off apparently of their own accord, and phantoms appearing in mirrors.

Tom wasn't sure what to make of all this. He thought about making a joke about a ghosts' convention, but his first one hadn't gone down too well. If Su took these fairy stories seriously, he didn't want to offend her.

'Don't worry,' she said, mistaking his silence for alarm. 'They don't haunt the wagon. It hasn't been in the village long enough.'

'What was that thing you said? About ghoulies and ghosties…?'

'It's an old Litany which Mum found in a Cornish shop. "From Ghoulies and Ghosties and long-leggity Beasties and things that go bump in the night, may the good Lord deliver us." You'll find it in the downstairs loo.'

'If I have to visit the john in the middle of the night, I'm the one who's likely to go bump.'

This time she laughed. 'Well don't scare the ghosts.'

'Do *you* believe in them?'

Su thought for a moment. 'Not ones you can see. But I believe in *presences*. Invisible ghosts.'

Tom stared at her, puzzled. 'If you can't see them, how d'you know they're there?'

'It's in my blood.'

'What d'you mean?'

She took so long to reply that he thought he hadn't heard him. 'I was born in a city called Tabriz,' she said eventually. 'It's near the Zagros Mountains, on the edge of what some archaeologists think was the Garden of Eden. I don't remember my blood parents, but I'm still their child, still part of the country of my birth. And I feel things that... I suppose your mum would call it psychic stuff.'

'What sort of things?'

'Vibes from the past. If ghosts do exist, this is the sort of place they'd hang around in.'

Back in Boston, Tom would have assumed that the Brits pretended their houses were haunted to boost the tourist trade. But here in Milbury, he wasn't so sure. The Manor's old grey walls were steeped in history, and he could well believe that the 'presences' of people who had died here were still around. As for the village, if it made a scientist like his father nervous, all these stories should be taken seriously.

Su jumped to her feet. 'Come on. Let's go and get an ice-cream at the shop.'

From behind one of the exhibits in the museum, Matthew watched Sandra sitting at the reception desk, patiently answering questions from a group of noisy schoolchildren... Yes, the Milbury Circle was older than Stonehenge, older even than the pyramids of Giza. Radiocarbon dating had proved that it was over five thousand years old, constructed around 3400 B.C., at the beginning of the Bronze Age... No, nobody knew for sure why it was built, but it probably had some religious significance... They were the same answers her mother used to give when she was the curator.

How was it possible that Sandra had no memory of Hendrick and his malign power? What exactly *did* she remember? Miss Clegg, their creepy schoolmistress, who somehow managed to turn their indoctrinated classmates into little Einsteins? Dr Lyle, their friend and ally until he too was caught in Hendrick's web? And how did she explain the gap in her memory? Was she even aware that there *was* a gap?

He moved on to the next exhibit – a model of Milbury Hill in a glass case. Next to it was a placard headed 'The Mysterious Chalk Hill,' listing the various theories that experts had come up with to explain its existence. A recent dig had discovered hundreds of sarsens buried inside it, which suggested that it may have been some kind of tomb, and that the stones represented the spirits of the dead. Another so-called expert had speculated that as it stood on the intersection of ancient leylines, the prehistoric builders may have been trying to harness the earth's energies. Some archaeologists believed the hill was a primitive sundial, and that it used to have a large pole on its summit which cast a long shadow across the fields below.

'Which theory do you go for, Matt?' He turned, to find Sandra standing next to him.

'None of them.'

'So what's yours?'

'I think the locals got bored with Neolithic television. And someone said, "Anything's better than *The Flintstones*. Let's build a hill." '

Sandra laughed and glanced at her watch. 'I'm free for the rest of the day. I'll drive you out there if you like.'

Her bright red two-seater was surprisingly sporty for a doctor. It was a young person's car, the sort of girl-puller that when Matthew was up at Oxford only the rich undergraduates could afford. There was one particular girl – a gorgeous blonde he had invited to his college's graduation ball – who had dumped him and driven off with some chinless wonder who owned a car exactly like this.

'Not really me, is it?' said Sandra, as they sped down the Avenue towards the main road. 'I bought it after Mum died, to cheer myself up.'

'I'm sorry I couldn't come to her funeral.'

'It's okay. I knew you'd have come if you could.'

He leant back in his seat and watched her out of the corner of his eye. She had put the roof down, and her raven hair was streaming in the breeze. It might have been her mother sitting next to him: except for the colour of her hair, the resemblance was uncanny.

She waved her hand at the stones, some of which were large and bulky, some small and insignificant. 'The Druids believe that the big ones represent the male inhabitants, and the little ones the females.'

He smiled. 'They probably believe in the tooth fairy.'

She was silent for a moment, staring at the road ahead. 'When we were kids, there were fifty-three people living in the village. And there are fifty-three stones.'

'Yes, I know. But there must be a lot more people living here now. And there are still fifty-three stones. So it must have been a coincidence.'

'That's what Mum thought.'

'But you don't?'

She glanced at him as they reached the end of the Avenue and turned right. 'This place is an enigma, Matt. The Druids may be weirdos, but who's to say they're wrong?'

She drove into the car park and they walked across the road to the hill, joining a crowd of tourists who were standing by the wire fence, clicking cameras and gazing up at it in awe. This close, it seemed more like a mountain than a hill.

'It's forty metres high,' said Sandra, switching into her curator mode. 'That's a hundred and thirty feet to you and me. Consisting of five hundred thousand tonnes of chalk, covering an area of five acres. According to the latest estimate, our ancestors spent eighteen million man-hours building it.'

Matthew stared at her, impressed. 'How d'you remember all that stuff?'

'It's part of my job. Luckily, I've got a good memory.'

'So you remember Dr Lyle? Miss Clegg? Those "Happy Day" kids?'

'Of course.'

'And Hendrick?'

She shuddered. 'I'll never forget him. He gave me the creeps.'

'Do you remember the night you and your mother had dinner with him at the Manor?'

She frowned at him, puzzled. 'We'd never have done that.'

'Why not?'

'Because he wouldn't have invited us. And if he had, we'd never have accepted. Neither of us could stand him.' But her dark eyes looked troubled, as if she had caught a glimpse of a long-forgotten fragment of the past.

'One more question, Sandra,' he said gently. 'Do you remember where we said goodbye to each other?'

She remained lost in thought for a moment. 'No. I'm sorry. Where was it?'

'I don't remember either.' Matthew watched a group of tourists climb over the fence and set off round the hill. 'How about taking a closer look?'

'We're not supposed to go any nearer,' said Sandra, pointing to a sign warning visitors to stay behind the fence. 'There's already been quite a lot of erosion.'

'Okay, we won't go any nearer. We'll stay the same distance from the hill all the way round.' He climbed over the fence and held out his arms. She hesitated, then climbed up onto the top rail and jumped down into them.

For a brief moment they clung to each other, their faces inches apart. She made no attempt to move away, and Matthew wondered whether she was thinking what he was thinking, feeling what he was feeling. Or was it just that it had been so long since he had held a woman in his arms? He released her, and they started to walk round the hill.

It loomed over them, blotting out the sun. How could something so massive be in danger of erosion? Surely, if it had withstood the elements for five thousand years, there was no need to fence it off?

'There's been a lot of work done on it since you were here,' said Sandra. 'After three centuries of tunnelling by treasure hunters, it began to collapse from the inside. So to stabilise it, they dug another tunnel straight down through the hill and packed it with chalk.'

'Did they find any buried treasure there?'

'No. But they found something much more interesting – fresh grass that didn't come from this area.'

Matthew laughed. 'There aren't many people who'd think grass was more interesting than treasure.'

'It just adds to the mystery. Why would the builders have carried turf from miles away when they could have dug it up here?'

'I suppose the Druids have a theory about that too?'

'Yes. They believe this was a sacred place, and that to damage it would have been sacrilege.'

'Sacred to whom?'

'The water-gods.' Sandra pointed to the ditch that ran round the base of the hill. 'They're convinced that moat was once filled with water, and that the hill stood at the centre of a huge underground lake which flooded in winter. The dowsers agree with them.'

Matthew snorted with derision. 'Dowsers! Another bunch of crackpots!'

'It makes sense, Matt. Neolithic people were very superstitious, and their lives depended on water. It's quite possible they worshipped water-gods.'

'How about the geologists? Have they found any evidence that there's a lake under the hill?'

'Not a lake. But they found the spring that turned out to be the source of a local river. It's over there, just two hundred metres away.'

Matthew stared across the fields, picturing the magical illusion the prehistoric builders must have created – a chalk-white island, standing in the middle of the flooded countryside. It must have seemed like a place where their gods might live.

They walked on, out of the shadow of the hill into the sunlight. A man stood motionless, silhouetted against the sun, barring their way. 'Where's your boy?'

It was Dai, though it hadn't been *his* voice that asked the question. It sounded not only angry and hostile, but slightly metallic.

Matthew shielded his eyes, trying to see his face. 'I don't know. I think he's with Su, Sandra's daughter.'

'That's right, Dai,' said Sandra. 'She's showing him round the village.'

'Tell him it'll soon be time.'

Matthew moved round him, so that Dai had to turn towards the sun. 'Time for what?'

'That's between him and me.'

'Okay, I'll bring him round to the cottage this evening. And you can tell him yourself.'

'No need for that. I'll find him.' Dai was swaying slightly, and his eyes were bloodshot.

Matthew glanced at the stone flagon in his hand. 'You've been at the mead, haven't you?'

'Maybe I have. So what?'

'Why don't you wait till you're sober?'

'Why don't you mind your own business?'

This belligerence was disturbing. The old rogue might be drunk, but it didn't explain the change in him since the previous night. Matthew tried to think of anything he'd said which might have offended him. But that still wouldn't account for his metallic voice or his hostility: they were old friends, and Dai wasn't the sort of man to let some trivial remark come between them. Anyway, for some reason his malevolence seemed to be directed at Tom.

'What's the matter, Dai? Why are you so interested in my son?'

'You wouldn't understand,' said Dai darkly, 'but *he* will.'

Matthew began to lose patience with him. 'Of course he won't. He's never even met you.'

The old man took a long swig from his flagon. 'Keep out of it, Matthew,' he growled, wiping his mouth on his sleeve. 'What will be will be.' He turned and stumbled away.

Matthew glanced at Sandra, who was looking equally nonplussed. 'That mead must be powerful stuff.'

'Extraordinary,' she said, staring after him. 'I've seen Dai drunk many times, but he's never been aggressive.'

Su stood by the barber-stone, watching Tom as he walked round it, inspecting it closely. 'You see?' she said. 'It's not lying on its side, and there's no carving on it.'

'I just had to make sure.'

'Why? Didn't you believe your Dad?'

'Yeah. But there's this weirdo called Professor Jarman...'

They sat down on the grass, and he told her about the Professor: about the strange behaviour of the avatar, the virtual-reality trip round the ancient temple, and about the blinding flash of light at the end of it that had knocked him out. She listened intently, her brown eyes never leaving his face.

'This man,' she said. 'What did he look like?'

'About a million years old. And very scary.'

'You never found out why he wanted to contact you?'

'We got cut off before he could tell me. I sent him another email, but it came back.'

'Interesting.' Su lay down on her back, staring up at the cloudless sky. 'What did your Dad make of it?'

'Dunno. He tried to play it cool, but I think that guy really got to him.'

She remained silent for a moment. 'D'you miss your mum?'

'No. Dad and me get along fine without her.'

'Come on, Tom. Talk to me. Get it off your chest.'

To his dismay, his eyes started to tingle, and there was something in his throat which made it difficult to swallow. 'Okay, I miss her,' he said gruffly, 'but only sometimes.'

'Like I miss my dad and my blood parents. I often look at their photographs, wondering what sort of people they were. At least you knew your mum.'

Tom wasn't sure which was worse – never to have known your parents, or to have them walk out on you. But he didn't want to think about his mother on such a beautiful day. He took a pencil and the airline ticket-cover out of his pocket, drew a rough outline of the winged fish-man and handed it to Su. 'Ever seen anything like this before?'

She sat up and studied it thoughtfully. 'Yes. It's in my father's notes for the book he was researching. Why?'

'That was the carving the avatar was pointing at on the barber-stone. And there were carvings exactly like it in the construct Jarman showed me.'

Su jumped down from the rock. 'Let's go and check it out.'

They hurried back to the house, where Adam was once again swearing at the computer. 'I'm going to throw you out of the window, you insubordinate swine!' he was shouting as they entered the study. He turned and scowled at them. 'You come most carefully upon your hour, young people,' he said grimly. 'You're just in time to prevent an electronic murder.'

Su giggled. 'Sorry to disturb you, Grandpa. We just want to look up something in Dad's notes.'

'No need to apologise. You've saved me from a long prison sentence.' Adam watched as Su moved over to the bookcase and pulled out a battered folder from the top shelf. 'What is it you wanted to look up?'

She opened the folder, leafed through some yellowing pages covered with neat handwriting and laid one of them on his desk. 'This.'

Tom peered over his shoulder as he picked it up. It was a hand-drawn replica of the winged fish-man.

'Your mother showed me this drawing,' said Adam. 'She told me it's the Sumerian symbol for Fate.'

Su glanced at Tom. 'Maybe that's what your mysterious Professor was trying to tell you. You can't escape your destiny.'

'Who were the Sumerians?'

'The original inhabitants of Mesopotamia. The earliest known civilisation, dating from around the twenty-sixth century B.C. They're supposed to have invented the wheel.'

'That's my girl,' said Adam. 'Spot on.'

Tom was impressed. 'How come you know so much about them?'

Su tapped the folder. 'It's all in Dad's notes. Plus a lot of stuff about the Babylonians and the Persians. Some of them could have been my ancient ancestors, so I got hooked.'

'And these Sumerian guys built temples, right? With carvings like this on the pillars?'

'Yes. They were called ziggurats, where they worshipped their gods. Every city had one, designed by their priest-kings. And they *could* have had that symbol carved on the pillars, because the Sumerians believed their fate was ordained by their gods.'

Tom stared at the drawing. It was beginning to make some sort of sense, but there were still a lot of unanswered questions. Why had Jarman shown him the temple construct? What was he trying to tell him? And why had the fish-man carving appeared on the barber-stone in his own Milbury construct when it wasn't there on the real one? He felt like a puppet, whose strings were being manipulated by some all-powerful puppet-master. Maybe Su could come up with some answers.

'Let's go,' he said to her. 'I want to show you something.'

Adam turned back to the computer. 'Don't be long, children. I've asked Mrs C to pack us a picnic lunch, and as soon as your progenitors get back we're going off on a spree.'

As they closed the door behind them, they heard him resume his verbal battle with Dame Electronica. 'If you do that again, you imbecile, I'll drown you in the bath...'

Tom led Su to the gipsy wagon, switched on his laptop and inserted the Milbury disc. Then he fast-forwarded it to the point where his avatar was standing by the barber-stone. As before, it was lying on its side, and the carving was still there.

Su stared at it in amazement. 'You're sure you didn't program that?'

'Positive. Dad checked it with the photographs. It wasn't there when we set it up.'

'Can you go in closer?'

He clicked the magnification icon and the fish-man carving filled the screen. 'These temples,' he said thoughtfully. 'You said they were built around the twenty-sixth century B.C.?'

Su shook her head. 'No, I didn't say that. The Royal Cemetery at Ur dates from around then, but the oldest known temple was built much later – around 5400 B.C.'

'What's the connection with Milbury?'

'I haven't the faintest idea. Except they were probably both sacred places.'

'But they're... what... over a thousand miles apart? So the ancient Brits couldn't have worshipped the same gods.'

'No.'

Yet there had to be a connection, thought Tom. Jarman might be a weirdo, but he must have had some reason for hacking into his laptop and planting the fish-man in the Milbury program. 'Maybe this wasn't just the symbol for Fate,' he said. 'Maybe they thought the god that was in charge of their fate looked like this. I mean, for the Sumerians that would have been the same thing, right?'

He was rewarded by a smile that lit up Su's face. 'Hey, that's pretty good thinking, Tom. Why don't you look up fish-gods on the net?'

He typed in 'fish-gods' and there they were: carved onto an ancient clay tablet were the seven chief Sumerian gods known as the Anunnaki, meaning 'Those who from heaven to earth came,' or 'The Mighty Ones of Eternity.' They had human bodies, covered with fish-skin.

'There you go,' said Tom triumphantly. 'Look at these dudes.'

Su reached over and scrolled down the rest of the article. 'There's pages of this stuff. Why don't we print it out on Grandpa's printer and see what the wrinklies make of it?'

They rushed back to the study, where Adam was slumped in his chair, staring helplessly at the computer screen. 'It's all yours, Thomas,' he said, when Tom asked to use the printer, 'and when you've finished, perhaps you could pour a little poison into one of these sockets.'

Tom attached his laptop to the printer, printed out five copies of the article and handed two of them to Adam and Su. They all sat down and started to read it.

There was a lot more stuff about the seven Anunnaki. The Sumerians believed they were gods and goddesses who came to earth four hundred thousand years ago to create the human race. There was Anshar, the god of the sky, his consort Ki, their son Anu, their grandchildren Enlil, Ea and Inanna, and their great-grandson Ninurta. Anu was killed by Ninurta, for which he was sentenced by the Grand Council of Deities to wander the earth until he had atoned for his crime. He was known as the Lord of the Apsu, the watery deep, which is why he was depicted emerging from the sea. In the carvings, all the other winged fish-gods carried water-buckets...

Tom was just getting into it when Sandra and Matthew returned. Adam climbed slowly to his feet. 'Here endeth the history lesson. It's picnic time.'

'I want to finish this, Grandpa,' said Su. 'It's a great story.'

'Take it with you. And bring the other copies. I think your mother might find it of interest.'

'You will too, Dad,' said Tom. 'It'll blow your mind.'

Matthew groaned. 'I don't want my mind blown. I want a quiet afternoon breathing some good old English ozone.'

'I know just the place,' said Adam. 'We'll take Georgina.'

By the time they had collected the picnic from the kitchen, a sleek black Daimler was standing outside the door. Adam was sitting in the driver's seat, wearing a chauffeur's cap.

He climbed out, opened the back door and saluted. 'Milbury Luxury Cars at your service, ladies and gents. This is Georgina, the pride of our fleet.'

'I'm surprised she hasn't died of shock,' said Sandra, as she climbed into the back seat. 'She hasn't been out of the garage since about 1866.'

They set off down the Avenue at a sedate pace. There wasn't much room in the back seat, which meant that Tom had thigh contact with Su. This wasn't exactly a hardship, and he hoped it would be a long drive.

Matthew, sitting in the passenger seat, glanced at Adam. 'Where are we going?'

'The Sanctuary.'

Despite the heat, he suddenly felt cold. This was where Dai had fled on that last terrible day, because the Sanctuary was outside the Circle. It was on the top of a small hill, at the head

56

of the pagan Solar Serpent that was supposed to protect the Neolithic people from harm. But for some reason the old man had left the Sanctuary and run back towards the circle. Matthew had run after him down the Avenue, shouting at him to stop. But Dai either hadn't heard him or took no notice. He had tumbled into an earthwork that marked the edge of the circle, and by the time Matthew reached the spot where he fell, he had vanished. Instead of the body he had expected to find at the bottom of the ditch, there was a fallen sarsen with a carving of the Solar Serpent on it.

What had happened to Dai that day? How had he survived? It was no use asking him, because, like the rest of the inhabitants, his memory of the 'Happy Day' era seemed to have been wiped clean. But there was another question that needed an urgent answer: why had he suddenly become so hostile?

Adam parked Georgina at the foot of Sanctuary hill, and they carried the picnic and the rugs up to the top. The six concentric circles of wooden posts that had guarded the Sanctuary itself in prehistoric times had long gone, their positions marked by modern concrete blocks.

Matthew put down the hamper he was carrying and stared at the spectacular view. A few miles to the north, Milbury was basking in the midday sun. And beyond it, as far as the eye could see, fields, farms and villages were shrouded in a heat-haze. It was hard to believe that this was the same hill he had last climbed as a desperate teenager, trying to save Dai's life.

Adam unpacked the lunch, which included a special box for Tom which Mrs Crabtree had labelled 'Vegiteriun'. Inside were cheese and pickle sandwiches, custard tarts and a bottle of water.

Sandra spooned some prawns onto a plate. 'Sure you won't have some of these, Tom? The fishmonger came round this morning. They're supposed to be straight out of the sea.'

'No, thanks.'

Su handed out the copies of the article on Sumerian mythology and they read them while they ate. Tom found it hard to sort out the names of the seven fish-gods, and which of them was in charge of what. They seemed to have divided all the plum jobs between them. Anshar, the head honcho, seemed to have got fed up with being lord of the sky and passed the title to his son Anu, whose wife Nintu, the goddess of the Earth, apparently created humans out of clay. Their sons Ea and Enlil ruled the seas and the air respectively, though why they should need separate gods to rule the sky and the air was not explained.

Anu and Nintu also had a daughter called Inanna who sounded as if she was a bit of a tease, because she first attracted men and then rejected them. She also took a great delight in making her brothers Enlil and Ea, who had lived together in harmony till she came along, fight each other. Which was very un-goddess-like.

The youngest of the Anunnaki was Enlil's son Ninurta, who seemed to be the god of just about everything else, including the wind, agriculture and war.

It would make a fantastic movie, thought Tom: great underwater sequences, gods bumping each other off, beautiful goddesses in skimpy dresses acting as cheerleaders – what more could a film producer want?

But in the last paragraph, the writer dropped an intriguing bombshell. There was a tribe in Africa – the Dogon of Mali – who still worshipped fish-gods. They call them Nommos, and believe they were amphibious beings who descended from the sky at the dawn of time in a flying 'Ark', accompanied by fire and thunder. And as soon as they arrived, they created a huge lake in which they could swim and take in water.

This could be dismissed as another myth, the writer went on, if it wasn't for the fact that the Dogons' knowledge of astronomy was astonishing for such primitive people. Long before Galileo invented the telescope, they knew that Jupiter had four moons, that Saturn had rings round it and that the planets orbited the sun. They also knew a great deal about Sirius, the dog star, where they believed the Nommos came from.

'Ha!' said Adam, throwing the article down in disgust. 'Not that Sirius nonsense again! That ridiculous theory was discredited years ago.'

Tom stopped reading. 'What theory?'

'Sirius is a binary system, Thomas. And some nutter came up with the idea that the Nommos were visitors from the smaller of the two stars, Sirius B. He suggested that it was they who taught the Dogon astronomy, but it's much more likely that their priests got the information from the early missionaries.'

Matthew took a corkscrew and a bottle of wine out of the hamper. 'Anyway, both stars have been white dwarfs for millions of years. So they aren't habitable.'

'Jean-Jacques knew that, Matt,' said Sandra, 'but he still couldn't explain why a four-thousand-year-old Dogon tablet had the Sirius star-chart on it. Or why the Sumerians, the Babylonians, the Persians and the Greeks all worshipped fish-gods.'

Adam groaned and held out his hand for the wine bottle. 'This is giving me a headache. I need another drink.'

'And I need some exercise,' said Su, jumping to her feet. She turned to Tom. 'You want to go for a walk?'

'Sure.'

As they set off down the hill, Adam called after them. 'I'll meet you at the river, Thomas. Teach you how to tickle trout.'

Tom frowned at Su. 'What's that?'

'You'll see.'

They walked down the hill in silence. Su seemed suddenly remote, as if she regretted asking him to come with her. Was she thinking about her boyfriend? Some handsome hunk at school who was good at sports? What chance did he have against a guy like that?

The silence continued as they crossed the road at the bottom of the hill and started to walk along the riverbank. Su remained lost in a world of her own, and Tom wondered if she was even aware that he was still there. He tried to come up with some way to get through to her, but he couldn't think of anything to say. He felt like Morgan Flender, a pathetic geek in the ninth grade, who was always hanging round with the older guys but never spoke.

Su sat down under a weeping willow and stared at the river, sparkling in the sunshine. 'The question is,' she said quietly, 'why would that Professor send you the Sumerian symbol for Fate?'

He sat down beside her. 'Yeah. And how could he have disappeared from his hotel room when he was in a wheelchair? It's creepy.'

Another long silence. Then, for the first time since they left the Sanctuary, she turned to look at him. 'I think you're in danger, Tom.'

His heart started to race. 'Who from?'

'I don't know. But I think the Fate symbol was a warning.'

'From this Jarman guy?'

'Yes.'

He forced a smile. 'Is that what your psychic stuff tells you?'

'Call it what you like. But I can feel the Milbury vibes getting darker.'

Tom stared at her with mounting alarm. No wonder his father had been so nervous about coming back. Could his return have triggered whatever it was that had happened before? And was it about to happen to *him*?

Su reached out and clasped his hand. 'I'm sorry, Tom. Maybe I should have kept quiet. I'm probably wrong.'

But he knew she didn't believe that, or she wouldn't have mentioned it. 'Has Grandpa told you what happened to him and Dad when they first came to Milbury?'

'No.'

So she knew nothing about the time-thingy, thought Tom. Which made her psychic stuff all the more impressive. But what could he do about it? Get the hell out of Milbury just because Su thought he was in danger? It was out of the question. Anyway, with Hendrick out of the picture, what danger could he possibly be in?

He wondered if he should tell her about Hendrick and the time-thingy. But as his grandfather hadn't told her, he decided against it. He probably didn't know much about it himself, so what could he say? And she already seemed to know that Milbury was no ordinary village.

He was just about to ask her what she thought the mysterious Professor was trying to warn him about, when a harsh, lilting voice called to him from across the river. 'Is your name Thomas, boy?'

Tom turned, to see a white-bearded old tramp in a tattered coat standing on the opposite bank. He had a stone jar in the hand, and was swaying from side to side.

'It's Dai,' said Su. 'Rat-arsed, as usual.'

'Who's Dai?'

'An old poacher. Used to know your Dad. Just ignore him.'

Dai took a swig from the jar, lost his balance and almost fell into the river. 'Are you prepared, boy? Are you ready?'

'Ready for what?'

'Soon. Very soon now, at Litha. But they won't let you back. I'll make sure of that.'

Tom frowned at Su. 'Why is he speaking like a machine? He's the local fruitcake, right?'

'Only when he hits the bottle. Don't worry, he's quite harmless.' She stood up and called back. 'You're pissed, Dai. Go home and sleep it off.'

The old man tried to take a drink from the jar, but nothing came out, so he threw it into the river.

'I'm not talking to you, girlie. I'm talking to the boy.'

Adam appeared through the trees. 'He won't talk to you till you're sober, Dai. Stop making a nuisance of yourself.'

Dai suddenly became obsequious. 'Sorry, melord,' he whined. 'Won't happen again, melord. Save it for Litha, eh?' He made a deep, mocking bow and staggered away towards the village.

Tom stood up. 'What's Litha, Grandpa?'

'The Celtic fire festival at midsummer. Dai and his loonies celebrate it by lighting a bonfire to strengthen the sun. Absolute rubbish, of course, but the locals love it. It's a good excuse for a booze-up.'

'He expects me to be there,' said Tom uneasily, 'but he said they won't let me back. What was that about?'

'How do I know? Maybe he thinks you're one of his Disciples. Now I'll show you how to tickle trout.' Adam sat down, took off his shoes and socks and rolled his trousers up to his knees. Then he waded slowly into the river, taking care not to disturb the surface.

Tom watched, as he bent down and lowered his hands into the water. He remained motionless for several minutes, then suddenly grabbed at something and brought up a wriggling fish. 'You see, Thomas? If you tickle it, it doesn't swim away. You want to try?'

He turned his head away. 'No thanks.'

'Come on, have a go. If we catch four more, we can have trout for supper.'

Tom glanced at the fish, still flapping and struggling in Adam's hands, and was suddenly overwhelmed by an uncontrollable rage. 'Put it back!' he shouted. 'Now!'

Adam shrugged. 'As you wish. But there's a little word called "please" that wouldn't have gone amiss.' He bent down and put the fish back in the river. But it was too late: it had stopped wriggling and floated lifelessly away.

'You've killed it!' Tom heard himself shouting. 'You're a murderer!' He turned and ran – blindly, instinctively, along the riverbank, over the main road and down the Avenue towards the village.

He stopped at the edge of the Circle, gasping for air, already ashamed of his outburst. He had always managed to keep his cool, even when he first went to High School and had to endure the initiation rituals that the sophomores used as an excuse for bullying the freshmen. So where had this sudden surge of anger come from? As soon as Adam came back, he would have to apologise.

As he approached the Manor, he could hear the whine of a vacuum cleaner in the hall. Mrs Crabtree, who was operating it, switched it off as soon as he opened the door. 'There's been a phone call for you, Matthew. I took down the number.'

'Matthew's my father,' he told her. 'I'm Tom.'

'Whatever.' She crossed to a table and picked up a piece of paper next to the phone. 'It was your mum, all the way from America. She says you're to call her collect, whatever that is.'

'Thanks.'

'You can do it now if you like. I'm finished in here.' Mrs Crabtree unplugged the vacuum cleaner, picked it up and disappeared.

Tom hesitated, wondering if he should call his mother later, or if he should even call her at all. But having behaved like a complete moron, it would be good to hear her voice in case no one else was speaking to him.

When she answered, she sounded unnaturally bright and breezy. 'Hi, honey. How was the trip?'

'Okay.'

'What are you up to? Are the kids in the village teaching you how to play that boring cricket?'

'Haven't met any yet.'

'I expect you will. How's Grandpa?'

'Okay.'

'And Dad?'

'Okay.'

'Give them my love.'

'Sure.'

There was a pause at the other end of the line. 'The weather's great here. Is it raining where you are?'

'No.'

'Well if it does, be sure and change out of your wet clothes, won't you?'

'Okay.'

Another pause. 'Got to go. I'm doing a meeting with the Senate environment and public works committee this afternoon.'

'And you think cricket's boring?' Tom knew he shouldn't have said that, but he couldn't resist it.

'It's very important. My client needs planning permission to build a business park in Virginia. The State legislature's playing hardball, so we've got to go right to the top.'

'Yeah,' he said bitterly. 'That sounds pretty important.'

'Love you, honey. Send me a postcard with a picture of jolly old England, okay?' There was a click and the line went dead.

He switched the phone off. It was a nothing conversation, and he wondered why she'd bothered to call.

He wandered into the study and stared out of the window, trying to remember exactly what Dai had said. 'Are you ready?... very soon, at Litha... save it for Litha...' What was supposed to happen at Midsummer, and what had it got to do with him? It wasn't just the rambling of a drunk, because the old loony had known his name.

He turned and sat down at the desk. His laptop was still connected to the printer, so he disconnected it and transferred the Milbury disc to his grandfather's computer. Then he ran the program to the point where the avatar was standing by the barber-stone, pointing to the fish-man carving.

The stone was still lying on its side, so he wiped it and moved it to a vertical position. 'There,' he told the avatar. 'That's how it should be. Just leave it like that, okay?'

Suddenly, the window flew open and a gust of wind blew the papers off the desk. Tom felt himself being catapulted backwards in his chair by some invisible force until it crashed into the wall behind him. Then the room went dark.

CHAPTER FOUR

FAR AWAY, FROM SOMEWHERE deep in the darkness, he heard a woman's voice that he dimly recognised. 'His pulse is perfectly normal,' it said, 'and there doesn't seem to be any serious injury. I think it's safe to move him.'

Tom felt himself being picked up and laid down on something soft. He opened his eyes, to see Sandra staring down at him with concern. Behind her, Su, his father and his grandfather were hovering anxiously. He was lying on the sofa in the study.

'Hi,' he said weakly. 'What's the problem?'

'The problem is you, young man,' said Adam. 'What were you doing on the floor?'

'Dunno.' Tom sat up and looked round. The Milbury Construct was still on the computer screen, and the barber-stone was once more lying on its side, with the avatar pointing at the fish-man carving.

'How d'you feel?' asked Sandra.

'Got a bit of a headache.'

'I'm not surprised. There's a nasty bump on the back of your head. How did you get it?'

When he touched the back of his head, the bump felt enormous. 'Can't remember.'

His father sat down beside him. 'What *do* you remember, Tommo? We found you by the wall, with the chair on top of you. And the window was open.'

Tom tried to pick his way through the fuzz in his head. 'All I did was… was… put the barber-stone back where it should be in the construct.'

'What happened then?'

'There was a hurricane or something. It blew the window open.'

'That's impossible, Thomas,' said Adam gently. 'All the ground-floor windows are locked.'

Tom suddenly remembered the trout and his hysterical reaction to it. 'I'm sorry for what I said, Grandpa. I didn't mean it.'

'No need to apologise. You're not the only one who thinks fishing is a cruel sport.'

'I want to make sure there's no serious damage, Tom,' said Sandra, 'but I've got all my medical equipment upstairs. D'you think you can make it?'

'Sure.' He struggled to his feet, but the room started swimming and he almost lost his balance.

'I'll help you,' said Su. She put her arm round his waist and they followed Sandra out of the room.

Adam shut the door and moved over to the window to examine the lock. 'Come and look at this, Matt.'

Matthew joined him. 'What?'

'The lock isn't broken. So how could the window have blown open?'

'You think Tom unlocked it for some reason?'

'It's the only explanation.'

'It's not very likely. He doesn't have a key.'

'There's one in the desk.'

'But it doesn't make sense, Dad. If he'd unlocked the window, he'd have admitted it. And it doesn't explain this sudden hurricane or whatever it was. There hasn't been a breath of wind all day.'

'I know.' Adam fetched the key from the desk and locked the window. 'So how do you explain it?'

'I can't. But as we know, not everything in this village has a rational explanation.'

'Oh come on, Matt. I've lived here for over ten years, and it's been completely uneventful.'

'But this is the first time *I've* come back.'

Adam frowned at him. 'What are you suggesting? That you're some sort of catalyst?'

'Or perhaps it's Tom. He's almost the same age as I was when we first came here. I hope to God it's not him.'

'And what scientific principle is that based on? The third law of telekinesis?'

Matthew slumped into a chair. 'Scientific principles don't apply here – we both know that. First he suddenly decides to become a vegetarian… then there's the business with the fish… and now this. I'm worried about him, Dad.'

Adam put the key back in the desk. 'I don't think there's any cause for alarm. It's perfectly natural for young people of Thomas's age to believe that all life is sacred, that we shouldn't eat meat or fish. Think back, Matt. When you were sixteen, you wanted to save the planet.'

'What about the hurricane?'

'There's probably a rational explanation for that too. Why don't we all go on a little excursion tomorrow? Get him out of the village for a while? That should sort him out.'

Matthew was silent for a moment. 'There's something else. Sandra and I ran into Dai this morning. He was looking for Tom.'

'So?'

'When I talked to him last night, he was the same sly old fox. And he seemed delighted to see me. But today he was different.'

'Drunk, you mean?'

'No, it wasn't just that. His voice was different. And there was hate in his eyes – real hate.'

Adam smiled. 'Dai could never hate anyone – least of all you. It's only natural that you should be a bit uptight, Matt. What you need is a large single malt to calm you down.'

Upstairs in her room, Sandra put the blood-pressure gauge back in its case. 'You seem to be in good shape, Tom. Apart from that bump.'

'Things that go bump in the day,' said Su, who had been lying on the bed watching the examination. 'The old Cornish Litany didn't mention those kind of bumps.'

'Not funny, Khonsu,' said Sandra. 'He needs TLC, not jokes.'

Su rolled head first off the bed, did a neat somersault and landed on her feet. 'She always calls me by my full name when I'm in the doghouse. But I don't mind. I rather like it.'

Sandra shone a pencil-thin torch into Tom's eyes. 'Still feeling dizzy?'

'No.'

'Well tell me if you do, and I'll take you to the hospital for a scan.' Sandra disappeared into the bathroom.

Tom stood up, grinning. 'Okay, Khonsu. Let's go.'

'Where?'

'I want to go and see Dai. Will you show me where he hangs out?'

Su looked doubtful. 'Are you sure that's a good idea?'

'I have to talk to him. Find out what that Litha stuff was all about.'

The sun was low in the west by the time they reached Dai's cottage. Su was just about to knock on the door when it opened, to reveal the old man, dressed in a ceremonial white robe. To Tom's surprise, he beamed at him, displaying some sparse brown teeth.

'You're Tom, Matthew's boy?'

'Yeah.'

'I knew it. Got second sight, see? Come in, come in.'

Tom glanced at Su, who seemed equally astonished by this unexpected welcome. Had Dai been so drunk that he didn't remember they had met before? Now he was sober, Mr Hyde seemed to have turned into Dr Jekyll.

They followed Dai into the living room, where he picked up a half-eaten packet of biscuits from a battered armchair covered with crumbs. 'Partial to ginger-nuts, are you?'

'Sure.'

'Finish them off then. My Disciples are bringing me some more tomorrow. I put them on my shopping list, see?' Dai stood back and surveyed Tom with approval. 'So you're Matthew's boy. Well, well. Doesn't time fly when you're having fun, eh?'

Tom handed a biscuit to Su and bit into another. 'But you already knew who I was, Dai. We met by the river.'

'No, never go near the river. Can't swim, see? It's dangerous.'

'You don't remember telling me about Litha? And about something happening very soon?'

'Well of course something will be happening at Litha. We'll be lighting bonfires as usual, having a piss-up. You'll be there, I hope?'

'The thing is, Dai,' said Su, 'it sounded like a threat. And your voice was funny.'

'Funny ha-ha or funny peculiar? Now why would I threaten Matthew's boy? Known his father since he was knee-high to a grasshopper.' The old man moved to the window and rubbed away some of the grime so he could see through it. 'Sun's going down. Got to be on my way. Can't be late for the Feast of Modron.'

'What's that?'

Dai touched his nose and grinned. 'I made it up. There's no feasts between Beltane and Lughnasadh, see – and I was getting peckish. Want to come?'

Tom glanced at Su, who shrugged. 'Okay. But we can't stay long.'

As they walked down the path, Dai stopped and pointed to a green plant by the gate. 'Know what that is?'

Su moved closer to it. 'Cannabis?'

'It's not for my own use, mind. The mead's enough for me. But some of my young Disciples – they say it puts them in touch with Gaia, the earth mother. And who am I to come between a mother and her children?' The old man chuckled to himself, then bent double as he was overcome by a fit of coughing.

'Suppose someone reports you to the cops?' asked Tom.

'I'll say I don't know how it got there. They call it weed, don't they? And weeds seed themselves – everyone knows that.'

As they entered the field behind the Manor, a familiar smell drifted towards them from the Disciples' camp. Tom had smoked dope only once, during his first semester at high school, when Bruce Barnes, the captain of the football team, had offered him a spliff in the changing room. His father had recognised the symptoms as soon as he arrived back at the apartment, and had made him promise not to do it again. He had kept his word, because he had never forgotten the scary moment when he got off the bus and couldn't remember the way home.

A different kind of pot was hanging from a tripod over the fire, which smelt much more wholesome. Young people of both sexes – and a few whose sex was hard to guess – were lying around, listening to a long-haired, middle-aged musician strumming dreamily on a guitar.

He stopped playing when he saw Dai, and raised a languid hand in greeting. 'Hail, Master,' he said in an unconvincing American accent. 'Welcome to the Feast of Modron. We hope the dish we've prepared is worthy of him.'

'What d'you mean – *him*?' said Dai indignantly. 'It's a her.'

'Whatever.'

'Can you tell us something about her, Master?' asked a thin, posh-looking girl covered in beads. 'Is she part of the pantheon?'

Dai looked mystified. 'Pantheon?'

'Of deities. Like, was she Gaia's handmaiden or something?'

'That's right, Brenda. Some say she was the Queen of Gwent. A great healer, who lived on the mystical isle of Avalon.'

The girl frowned. 'But Gwent's in Wales. And Avalon's in Somerset.'

'Well she got about a bit. What's in that pot?'

'Vegetable soup,' said the long-haired musician, 'seasoned with saffron and feverfew.' He nodded towards the Manor. 'We nicked the herbs from that garden.'

'You shouldn't have done that, Kevin,' said Dai, glancing uneasily at Tom and Su. 'That's where these mates of mine live.'

Kevin glanced at Tom. 'Well if they're friends of yours, Master, they won't care. Gaia belongs to everyone, right?'

'Right,' said Tom. 'But I don't actually live at the Manor. I'm just over here on vacation.'

'You're a Yank?'

'Yeah.'

'That's cool, man. Ever been to 'Frisco?'

'No.'

'Wish I'd been there in the Sixties. Haight-Ashbury, the Flower People. I know it's so yesterday, but it must have been a gas.'

Tom caught Su's eye, and they started giggling. Kevin's American accent was so appalling that no one could possibly be taken in by it.

He produced a rusty tin from his shirt pocket and took out a suspicious-looking cigarette. 'D'you use these?'

'No thanks.'

'How about your chick?'

'No,' said Su firmly, 'and I'm not his chick.'

So that's that, thought Tom. He'd been crazy to think he ever stood a chance with her.

'Is that stew ready?' asked Dai, eyeing the pot hungrily. 'Had nothing but ginger-nuts the last couple of days.'

Brenda stood up and started spooning the soup into tin bowls. She handed the first to Dai, and the next two to Tom and Su. 'Guests of honour,' she said, smiling at Tom. 'Hey, you're cute. What's your name?'

'Tom.'

'How long are you staying? Maybe we could…'

'Get lost,' said Su beadily. 'He's not interested.'

Brenda shot her a dark look. 'That's for him to decide, sister. Nobody has exclusive rights to anybody.'

So maybe there was still hope, thought Tom. The way Su had warned Brenda off – surely that meant she thought of her as a rival? Or was she just trying to protect him? He wished he could read her mind.

There were no spoons, so they drank the soup from the bowls. His mother would have approved of it, thought Tom, though it was more highly spiced than her home-made soups. It was definitely worthy of old Modron, whoever she was.

When they had finished, Su glanced at her watch. 'It's dinner time. We ought to be going.'

Tom tried to stand up, but for some reason he couldn't make his legs work. Su seemed to have the same problem, and they stared helplessly at each other. 'The soup,' she whispered. 'They put it in the soup…'

Then, to Tom's dismay, two police cars suddenly screamed into the field and parked by the camp. Several policemen got out, and one of them flashed an ID. 'Detective Inspector Browning,' he said. 'We've received a report that some of you have been smoking an illegal substance. If we have reason to believe this is the case, you will all be under arrest.'

Matthew and Sandra listened with disbelief as Jim Browning stood on the doorstep, explaining why he was letting Tom and Su off with a caution.

'We didn't find anything on them, so I'm giving them the benefit of the doubt. They say they didn't know there was cannabis in the soup.'

Su giggled. 'It was pretty good though. Best soup I've ever had.'

'It's not funny, Khonsu,' said Sandra, trying to keep a straight face. 'How many times have I told you that cannabis can be dangerous?'

Matthew frowned at Tom. 'And as for you, young man – you gave me your word…'

'As far as we're concerned it's a first offence, Matt,' said Jim. 'Let's hope they've learned their lesson.'

It suddenly occurred to Matthew that if anyone had told him thirty years ago that Jim Browning, the podgy farmer's son, would one day arrest his own son, he wouldn't have believed them.

'Well I must be getting back to the station,' said Jim. 'I've got to do the paperwork for the kids we're charging with possession. One of them's an old schoolmate of ours, Matt. You had a punch-up with him on your first day.'

'Kevin?'

'He was always a bit of a wild kid, if you remember. He's never grown out of it.'

Matthew did remember. Kevin had attacked him as soon as he walked through the door, to make sure he wasn't one of the 'Happy Day'ers. After they'd got that out of the way, they had become friends.

'Don't be too hard on him, Jim,' he said. 'For old times' sake.'

Jim shook his head. 'No can do, Matt. He's a persistent offender, so I'll have to charge him.'

Adam, who had been listening in the hall, called to him. 'Won't you stay and have a drink, Inspector?'

'No thanks, Professor. Just keep these two away from that camp. And if I were you, I'd apply for an eviction order.'

As Matthew closed the door, Mrs Crabtree appeared from the kitchen. 'Am I ever going to be able to serve dinner on time?' she snapped. 'The shepherd's pie's burned to a frazzle.'

It was an uncomfortable meal. Tom decided to keep a low profile: anything he said was likely to provoke a lecture, so he ate his specially-prepared vegetarian pie in silence. As Su had obviously come to the same conclusion, it was left to Adam, Matthew and Sandra to keep the conversation going. There was no lecture, but a cloud of disapproval hung over the table.

When they had finished, Su stood up. 'I'll clear everything away. Then I'll bring the coffee.'

'I'll help you,' said Tom, eager to escape.

Adam and Matthew exchanged amused glances. 'Let that be your penance, children,' said Adam. 'Then you can take Thomas up to the observatory, Su. Do a bit of stargazing.'

After they had done their penance, Tom followed Su up the stairs to the top floor. 'Grandpa's telescope's brilliant,' she told him. 'You want to see a black hole?'

'You can't see a black hole through a telescope,' answered Tom. 'When a supernova starts collapsing, even light can't escape from its gravitational field. The only way you can see them is through a spectrometer.'

She turned back, staring down at him in astonishment. Then she smiled. 'Sorry. I'd forgotten your dad's an astrophysicist too.'

When Su opened the door to the observatory to reveal the telescope, Tom gazed at it with awe. From his grandfather's description he had expected it to be pretty big, but this looked like a nuclear missile. 'Wow!' he said softly. 'Mount Palomar, eat your heart out!'

Su crossed over to the control panel. 'I'll just check the coordinates. Make sure Grandpa hasn't moved it.' She switched on the computer and some numbers appeared on the screen. 'No, they're still the same settings. Turn the light off and press that button behind you.'

Tom pressed the button on the wall and the roof rolled back, to reveal the night sky studded with stars. Su sat down on the viewer's chair and peered through the eyepiece. 'Has your dad told you about Sagittarius A?'

'No.'

'It's a supermassive black hole about twenty-six thousand light years away. We know it's there because of the gravitational pull on everything around it. Come and look.'

Su moved out of the chair and Tom took her place. All he could see was a cluster of stars surrounding a black area tinged with red. But to be sitting behind this enormous piece of kit, staring across the galaxy at an exploded supernova twenty-six light years away, was awesome.

'Why are you so interested in this particular black hole?'

'Because it's a real monster,' said Su. 'It keeps flaring up, and nobody knows why. And because all the other stars move round it, which means it's the centre of our galaxy.'

Tom took his eye away from the telescope. 'Can you show me an X-ray image of it on the spectrometer?'

'Coming right up.' Su moved to a small machine with a screen on top of it, standing on a table by the wall. She switched it on, and a patch of white light appeared on the screen, surrounded by wispy red clouds.

Tom bent down and studied it closely. 'The white bit's Sagittarius A, and the red stuff's gas, right?'

'Right. It spreads over dozens of light years on either side of the black hole. Looks like there've been some enormous explosions there during the last ten thousand years.'

'So what was it that blew up?'

'Probably Sagittarius B,' said Su, 'a companion star. Those gas-clouds are all that's left of it. Astronomers think it was once a binary system, like Sirius.'

'You got all this from Grandpa?'

'Some of it. But I've done my own research. *I* want to be an astrophysicist too.'

Tom was suddenly conscious of the age gap between them. It was only a year, but Su was light years ahead of him. He had never even thought about what he wanted to do with his life, whereas she had already chosen her career. And he was sure she would make a success of it: having access to all this brilliant technology would give her a big advantage over all the other wannabe astrophysicists. One day, perhaps, she would discover a new planet and have it named after her. And he would be able to say he knew her when she was just a beautiful girl.

He stared up at the starlit sky above the roof. 'Dad told me the Milbury circle's aligned to another black hole. In Ursa Major.'

'Ursa XB1,' said Su. 'Hendrick's Supernova.'

Tom's antennae were suddenly on the alert. 'What d'you know about Hendrick?'

'Just that he discovered the black hole. But he's a mystery. He doesn't have a website, and he's not listed in any of the professional directories. Don't you think that's rather odd?'

'Yeah.'

Su sat down in the viewer's chair again. 'I mean, if Hendrick had a supernova named after him, you'd have thought he'd be pretty well known. But even Grandpa couldn't give me any information about him.'

'Couldn't or wouldn't?'

She hesitated. 'It's funny you should ask that. I got the impression the subject was out of bounds.'

Her psychic stuff was right on the button, thought Tom. Which meant that her warning that his life might be in danger had to be taken seriously. If only she could tell him where the threat was coming from.

He glanced at the X-ray image of Sagittarius on the spectrometer screen. 'Why would the circle be aligned to a black hole?'

Su shrugged. 'So far, nobody's come up with an answer to that.'

'I mean, how did the ancient Brits know about it? It's like those Dogon guys, who knew about Sirius long before telescopes were invented.'

'They might have seen the supernova explode. It would have lit up the whole galaxy.'

'But that would have happened millions of years before they built the circle, right?'

'Not necessarily. Hendrick's Supernova was only four hundred light years away. It could have turned into a black hole much quicker than that.' Su yawned and stood up. 'I'm knackered. Time to hit the sack.'

She switched off the spectrometer and they went downstairs into the hall. Tom stood facing her, trying to think of some way to keep her talking. 'That was great. You certainly know your stuff.'

She smiled. 'So do you. You're pretty clued up for a Yank.'

He continued to stand there, his heart beating wildly, unable to tear himself away.

'D'you want a torch?' she asked him. 'It's pretty dark out there.'

'No thanks. I'll be okay.'

Come on, he told himself: think of something to say. But nothing came, and there was another awkward silence. This was ridiculous: he'd spent most of the day with her, chatting away with no problem, and now he couldn't come up with a single word.

'Goodnight then,' she said softly. She suddenly leaned forward, kissed him lightly on the lips and moved back towards the staircase. Then she turned and smiled at him.

'There's an old Persian song that goes "Last night I dreamt that the sun and moon kissed each other." Isn't that romantic?' Before he could answer, she had disappeared up the stairs.

Tom had never had a problem getting to sleep: he was usually off to dreamland as soon as his head hit the pillow. But this had been such a momentous day that sleep was impossible. He lay on his bunk in the wagon, gazing out of the window at the stars and thinking about everything that had happened.

First of all, there was Su. So she *did* fancy him, though he had no idea why. She was so different from the pretty airheads at school who idolised rock stars or football players, and who wouldn't have the faintest idea what an astrophysicist was. What did she see in him? She knew so much about so many interesting things that she made him feel like Harvey Putnam, the class dumbbell, who didn't know anything about anything. Yet she treated him like an equal, as if she valued his opinion. He wished he could take her back to the States and introduce her to other kids as his girl.

Then there was Dai. Was it just the mead that had made him forget they had already met by the river? Which was the real Dai – the Mr Hyde who had shouted incomprehensible threats at him earlier that afternoon, or the Dr Jekyll who had seemed so pleased to see him a few hours later? Tom knew from personal experience the effect that alcohol had on some men, because his Uncle Jack, his mother's brother who thankfully lived in Wichita, used to hit his Aunt Josephine when he'd had too many martinis. But Uncle Jack always remembered what he'd done and apologised to her the next morning. Maybe it wasn't mead that Dai had been drinking, but a home-made potion that turned him into a monster.

Was *he* the threat that Su had been so concerned about? It seemed unlikely: even when he was drunk, Dai hadn't threatened physical violence. But what would have happened if the river hadn't been between them? Would the screwball have tried to attack him? If he was his father's friend, he obviously didn't have a history of violence. So why now? And why threaten someone he'd never met before? It didn't make sense.

And that wasn't the only thing about Milbury that didn't make sense. How did the Neolithic builders manage to align their stone circle to a supernova they couldn't even see? Could the danger come from somewhere out in space, four hundred light years away? From what his father had told him, that was what seemed to have happened before. But in that case, everyone in the village would be in danger.

He suddenly felt thirsty. He had drunk his bottle of water before he went to bed, so he put on his sneakers and padded across the courtyard to the house.

The hall was in semi-darkness, lit only by a dim lamp by the phone. He went into what Su had called the 'downstairs loo' and filled the bottle from the cold tap in the handbasin. As he screwed the cap back on, he noticed something hanging on the wall behind him, reflected in the mirror: a piece of wood with an inscription etched on it.

It was the old Cornish Litany: *From ghoulies and ghosties and long-leggity beasties, and things that go bump in the night, may the good Lord deliver us.*

Tom smiled to himself, imagining what his mother would have said if he'd brought it home: 'Oh for heavens' sake, Tom, throw that thing in the garbage. I'm not having it on my walls.'

Then, as he turned to switch off the light, he froze in horror. In the mirror, staring straight at him with pale, unblinking eyes, was Jarman's face. It remained there for a few seconds before slowly fading away.

He collapsed onto the loo, his heart thumping. Had he really seen that face, or was it a hallucination caused by the Disciples' soup? He unscrewed the bottle-cap and took a long drink of water.

No, it definitely wasn't a hallucination. So what was it? A ghost? The house was supposed to be haunted, and Su had sensed 'presences' here. But it couldn't have been a ghost, because his father had actually met Jarman. Anyway, if ghosts did exist, weren't they supposed to appear where the person had died? Surely they didn't cross the Atlantic?

Outside, the courtyard was full of menacing shadows cast by the trees on the other side of the garden wall. He stopped several times on his way to the wagon, glancing behind him to make sure that Jarman hadn't followed him.

When he finally reached the safety of the wagon he locked the door and threw himself on his bunk, his heart still thudding like a steam-engine, trying to make sense of what he had just seen.

If Jarman was an expert on the paranormal, maybe he had found a way of projecting the image of himself, like a hologram. But why was the Professor pursuing him? Was *he* the threat that Su had warned him about?

He wondered what his father and grandfather would make of it. Should he tell them? No: his father might insist on taking him back to the States to be examined by some shrink. Anyway, if Jarman had paranormal powers it wouldn't make any difference: he would follow him wherever he went. So he would just have to tough it out. And the only person he would tell was Su.

At breakfast the next morning, Adam was in a jovial mood. 'Geraldine's thinking of taking us all for a guided tour today, young Thomas. First to Stonehenge, then into the wilds of Somerset. How does that sound?'

Tom glanced at Su, who was ploughing her way through a huge pile of muesli. It didn't look as if he would get a chance to speak to her till the evening. 'It sounds pretty cool,' he said, trying to summon up some enthusiasm.

Adam stood up and helped himself to some bacon and eggs from a silver dish on the hotplate. 'I hear tell them Somersetians across the border have become quite civilised. They still eat Americans, of course, and they still keep dragons as pets, but otherwise they're relatively harmless.'

Sandra poured herself another cup of coffee. 'You've heard of Glastonbury, Tom?'

'The rock festival? Sure.'

'It's supposed to be where King Arthur and Queen Guinevere are buried. We can show you their graves.'

At any other time, Tom would have been eager to visit places he had only seen in pictures, but after a sleepless night he felt exhausted. 'Okay,' was all he could think of to say.

'What's the matter, Tommo?' asked his father, reaching for the marmalade. 'Still feeling a bit groggy?'

'No. I'm fine.'

Adam returned to the table. 'We can make it another day if you like. But Geraldine needs some exercise. And you need to get away from Dai's young potheads for a while.'

'No, it's cool,' said Tom. He had tried to put a bit more oomph into it, but the word still came out like a damp squib.

By now Su also seemed to have picked up his negative vibes, and was staring at him with a puzzled frown.

From a distance, Stonehenge was a disappointment. It didn't look at all like the pictures Tom had seen on its website: it looked more like a collection of grey bricks which a child had got fed up with and couldn't be bothered to put back in their box. But as they approached, the stones became bigger and bigger, until they towered over the horde of tourists surrounding them, making them look like pygmies.

Adam drove Georgina into the car park on the opposite side of the road and squeezed her between two camper vans. 'They were going to build a tunnel under those rocks to take the traffic away,' he said grouchily, 'but after spending twenty million on feasibility studies they decided it was too expensive. Never become politicians, children, or I shall come back and haunt you.'

Tom got out of the car and stared at the circle of massive sarsens. Some of them were joined together by smaller stones, to form primitive arches. Two of the arches were standing outside the circle, as if they were doorways through which Stone Age visitors had to pass. The summer wind was sending dark clouds scudding across the sun, so that the ancient rocks were constantly changing colour.

Adam led the way across the road to the fence, where they joined the ring of tourists consulting guidebooks and taking photographs. 'All right, Sandra,' he commanded. 'Do your tourist guide thing for young Thomas.'

Leaning against the fence, with her back to the stones, Sandra began her well-rehearsed 'thing'. 'The civilisation that built this monument,' she said, 'was older than Egypt or Mesopotamia. The builders couldn't read or write, so knowledge had to be passed on by word of mouth. But *why* they built it is a mystery. Nobody knows whether it was an astronomical observatory, a religious healing site or a supernatural shrine. But whatever made them go to all this trouble, it was an extraordinary achievement. These people were obviously not barbarians.'

'I thought Mesopotamia was supposed to be the cradle of civilisation,' said Su. 'That's what Dad was going to call his book, wasn't it? So how could this civilisation be older?'

'Because radiocarbon dating has proved that this place pre-dates the pyramids, even the Sumerian temples. Archaeologists used to believe that civilisation spread across Europe from east to west, but now there's a new theory – that it spread in the opposite direction. That's why your father was going to add a question mark to the title of his book on the cradle of civilisation. He was convinced the archaeologists had got it wrong.'

Matthew looked sceptical. 'Did he have any proof?'

'Yes. The oldest radiocarbon dates for megalithic sites are here in the north-west of Europe – Carnac in France, Stonehenge and Milbury, the oldest of them all. So it's quite possible the early British astronomer-priests passed their knowledge on to other civilisations.'

'The Ancient Wisdom,' said Matthew thoughtfully. 'But where did *they* get it?'

Sandra smiled. 'That's another mystery. All we know is that some of these sarsens have been dated as early as 4500 B.C.'

'So when was Stonehenge built?'

'I can't give you a definitive answer, Matt. The first stone structure dates back to 2600 B.C. But there's evidence that this was a sacred site long before that. The archaeologists have found bones and post-holes here which date from around 8000 B.C.'

Despite his lack of sleep, Tom had been absorbing all this information with mounting interest. 'But why here? I mean, what's so special about this place?'

'Who knows? Originally it was a burial ground. But because there were very few graves here, it was probably reserved for the tribal chiefs.'

'So the stones could be a monument to them?'

'Not just a monument. The ancient Brits believed their ancestors inhabited them.'

'That's pretty creepy. Is it aligned to a black hole?'

'Definitely not,' said Adam firmly. 'It's aligned to the sun: specifically sunrise at the midsummer solstice, and sunset at the midwinter solstice. The Druids celebrate Midsummer Day here, but our ancestors probably came here in midwinter, to pray that the sun would come back the following year.'

Su pointed to a small rock standing between two sarsens on the far side of the circle. 'See that baby stone, Tom? It's called the heelstone. The sun rises exactly above it on Midsummer Day. Isn't that amazing?'

It was more than amazing, thought Tom: it was mind-blowing. 'So where did all these stones come from?'

'That's a question we *can* answer,' said Sandra. 'The sarsens came from this area. The bluestones that formed the inner circle were brought here from the Preseli hills in Wales, about two hundred miles away, probably by floating them on rafts some of the way. And the archaeologists have demonstrated how they could have transported them across the land – by hauling them on wooden rollers.'

'But that would have taken years.'

'Not just years – centuries. The construction of Stonehenge gradually evolved over three millennia. It shows how important this place was to these people.'

A group of Japanese schoolchildren, babbling excitedly to each other, pushed in front of them and started taking photographs. 'Let's go,' said Adam. 'If there's one thing I can't stand, it's the human race.'

As they walked back to the car park, Tom tried to imagine what these early people looked like. Were they long-haired savages, more like apes than humans? That would explain how they had the strength to pull the huge sarsens into an upright position. But they also had the knowledge, handed down from generation to generation, to align them to sunrises and sunsets on a specific day. How the hell did they do that, if they couldn't read or write? How did the Dogon know about Sirius? And how did the builders of the Milbury circle know about Hendrick's Supernova?

They drove west, over rolling green hills and through sleepy villages. As they came down into a wide, misty valley, they passed a sign saying 'Welcome to Somerset'.

'Bandit country,' said Adam darkly. 'Thomas, you ride shotgun. If them varmints get too close, let 'em have it right between the eyes.'

Ahead of them, a cone-shaped hill loomed through the mist. 'What's that?' asked Tom.

'Glastonbury Tor,' said Su. 'Otherwise known as the Isle of Avalon.'

'Isn't that where King Arthur was supposed to have thrown his sword in a lake? And some babe's arm appeared out of the water and grabbed it?'

Su laughed. 'You can't call the Lady of the Lake a babe. She was a Celtic goddess. And it wasn't Arthur who threw Excalibur into the lake – it was Sir Bedivere.'

'Okay, so where's the lake?'

'There isn't one now. But this is a flood plain, and it's often under water in winter. That's when the Tor looks like an island.'

Tom stared at it through the windscreen. 'What's that thing on the top?'

'It's a church,' said Sandra. 'The Tor was a sacred place for the early Christians – and before that, for the pagans. They cut a spiral path near the summit, to make it easier for the pilgrims to climb. They believed it brought them closer to heaven.'

Su turned to Tom. 'There's a fantastic view from the top. You want to climb it?'

'Sure.'

'It's steeper than it looks, Tommo,' said Matthew. 'Grandpa and I climbed it soon after we first came to Milbury. My legs ached for a week.'

The mist had got thicker by the time Adam dropped them at the foot of the Tor. 'We'll pick you up in a couple of hours, children,' he said as they got out of the car. 'If it gets too foggy, abort the mission. You've got your mobile, Su?' She took a mobile out of the back pocket of her jeans and waved it at him. 'Off you go, then. If you see any angels up there in heaven, tell them to save a place for me.'

Matthew watched them set off up the hill, remembering his own long-ago climb. 'What was that poem you made me learn, Dad? Something about being young was heaven?'

Adam smiled. 'It's Wordsworth. "Bliss was it in that dawn to be alive; but to be young was very heaven." '

'Yes. Except when I was young, it wasn't exactly bliss, was it?'

'Age has its compensations, Matt. One of which is real ale. Let's have lunch at the Goat and Compasses.'

Sandra watched Su and Tom disappear into some woods. 'You know what I think? I think your son and my daughter are getting on rather well.'

Tom followed Su up through the misty woods, wishing he had kept himself in better shape. She leaped up the steep slope like a gazelle, and she had to wait every few minutes for him to catch up with her. He decided that as soon as he got back to the States he would forget about the computer for a while and go to a gym.

As they reached the edge of the woods, the mist began to clear. The valley below them was shrouded by an impenetrable white blanket, but above them the Tor was bathed in bright sunshine. Su pointed up at some deep ridges spiralling round it. 'That's the pilgrims' path. It has seven circuits, which is supposed to be a magic number.'

'Why?' asked Tom, trying to delay her so he could get his breath back.

'No idea. But think about it – there are seven seas, seven deadly sins, seven wonders of the world, seven stars in the Pleiades cluster. And if there were six or eight dwarfs in the Snow White story, it wouldn't have the same zing, would it?'

Su set off up the path and the gap between them widened as Tom struggled after her. By the time he reached the top, she was sitting on the grass by the little church, staring down at the sea of white mist. 'Don't you think it looks like a lake?' she said, as he collapsed beside her. 'You can just imagine the Lady's arm appearing out of this stuff and grabbing Arthur's sword, can't you?'

Tom lay on his back, too exhausted to reply. She waited till he had recovered before speaking again. 'Okay, Tom – now we're alone, what did you want to talk to me about?'

He sat up, astonished. 'How did you know?'

'I could see it in your eyes every time you looked at me. That's why I suggested this climb. Something's really scared you, hasn't it?'

He told her about his visit to the house in the middle of the night, and about seeing Jarman in the mirror. It sounded so incredible that anyone else, even his father, would have assumed it was a bad dream. But he knew Su would believe him.

When he had finished, she remained deep in thought, staring across the white blanket below them. 'This man obviously needs you for something,' she said with a worried frown. 'And so does Dai, when he's drunk. Maybe they're connected in some way.'

'But how did he get into that mirror? He can't be a ghost, because Dad went to his lecture the night before we came here.'

Su stood up and started pacing up and down on the grass. 'I can think of two possibilities, but they're both pretty wacky. He could have followed you to England, set up a laser outside the house and projected his image through the window.'

'Why would he go to all that trouble?'

'Exactly. Which leaves the other possibility. That he has some sort of occult power we know nothing about.'

Tom rubbed the goosebumps on his arms. 'D'you think I should tell Dad?'

'That's up to you.'

'He's jittery enough as it is. He'd probably take me back to the States.'

Su sat down again and put her arm round his shoulders. 'Maybe that's what he should do, Tom. Before it's too late.'

'Too late for what?'

'I don't know. But whatever it is, I think you should get out of Milbury.'

'I couldn't do that,' said Tom miserably. 'I don't want to leave you.'

'And I don't want you to go. I just want you to be safe.'

'I feel safe up here.'

Su smiled. 'That's because of the leylines. The St Michael line passes through Glastonbury. It's supposed to bring good vibes.'

'Yeah, I read some stuff about leys. Invisible psychic cables connecting old sacred places, right? Dad thinks they're a load of garbage.'

'What do scientists know? They can be such stick-in-the-muds.'

'The Delusion of Science,' said Tom thoughtfully. 'That was the title of Jarman's lecture. I'll bet *he* believes in leylines.'

'So does Mum,' said Su. 'She says if the builders of Stonehenge were clever enough to make it an accurate observatory, there's no reason why they couldn't have aligned ancient sites with each other.'

'But why would they want to?'

'The Druids believe it was to draw cosmic energies into the earth, to bring them closer to their gods.'

Tom glanced up at the church. 'What's so special about the St Michael line?'

'It's the longest leyline in the country. It stretches right across England, from St Michael's Mount in Cornwall to Bury St Edmunds in Suffolk, connecting hundreds of sacred places... Cadbury, which was supposed to be King Arthur's Camelot... Glastonbury... at least ten churches dedicated to St Michael, the dragon-slayer... and guess what's at it's midpoint?'

'Milbury?'

'Yes. The Mother Circle of Ancient Britain. And the incredible thing is, the whole thing's aligned to the midsummer sunrise. Mum thinks that couldn't have happened by chance.'

Below them, the cloud-lake was beginning to disintegrate in the sun's heat. Tom's mind began to clear too: if he left Milbury now, he would always wonder what would have happened if he'd stayed.

Then he suddenly remembered something his father had told him – that until Hendrick's spell was broken, it had been impossible to escape from the village. Could Jarman have inherited his mysterious power? If so, maybe *he* wouldn't be able to leave.

Anyway, this was a threat he couldn't run away from. With Su in his corner, he could face a thousand Jarmans.

He stood up, held out his hand and pulled her to her feet. 'I'm not going to tell Dad about the mirror thing,' he said quietly. 'I'm going to stick around and find out what this guy wants.'

Su stared at him with concern. 'All right, Tom. But be careful. Don't go into the Milbury construct again unless I'm there. You mustn't do it alone.'

'Okay.'

'We'll fight Jarman together. And let's not wait for him to appear in any more mirrors. Let's try and contact *him* – show him we're not scared of his stupid tricks.'

'Tell him to put up or shut up?'

'Yes.'

Tom smiled. 'I feel better already. And it's nothing to do with leylines.'

When they arrived back at the Manor, they asked Adam if they could play a video game on his computer and headed straight for the study. Su sat beside Tom as he switched it on and keyed in the name 'JARMAN'.

The moment he had typed the last letter, a mighty wind started howling in his ears and he felt himself being blown into a new construct – a large ballroom full of people sitting in rows of chairs, facing a small stage with a grand piano on it. The wind carried him over their heads and deposited him on a chair in the back row.

The people turned to stare at him, as if they were scandalised by his presence, and the fact that he was wearing a T-shirt and jeans. Everyone else seemed to be in fancy dress: the women wore elegant, low-cut dresses, the men silk coats and powdered grey wigs.

There was a sudden hush as a man appeared on the stage, carrying a violin. He wore a fine-looking blue silk coat and a powdered wig. But there was no mistaking the pale, mesmeric eyes. It was Jarman.

'Welcome to Vienna,' he said in a thin, rasping voice. 'Most of you will no doubt have heard of me. I am the Count of St Germain.'

'But you can't be!' cried a woman in the front row. 'I met the Count sixty years ago, in Venice. He was about the same age as you are now. Forgive me, but you can't possibly be the same man.'

'I assure you that I am, Madame. And today I intend to give you a demonstration of both my prowess as a violinist and my paranormal powers.'

Jarman jumped off the stage and began to walk slowly down the aisle...

Tom, whose mind was in turmoil, knew with a terrible certainty that he was coming for him. What was he doing here? Who were all these people? He should be sitting at his computer, yet by some mysterious hocus-pocus he seemed to have taken his avatar's place in this new construct. And it couldn't be a dream, because he was wide awake...

Back in the study, Su had been so absorbed in what was happening on the screen that she hadn't spoken to Tom since he had keyed in Jarman's name. Now she turned to him. 'Maybe this isn't the right Jarman.'

There was no reply. Tom was staring into space, his hands frozen on the keyboard, as motionless as a statue.

Alarmed, she touched his shoulder. 'Tom?' But he still didn't move. She reached over and pressed the power button on the computer, but it didn't work. On the screen, Jarman and Tom's avatar were standing side by side on the stage. The avatar looked more lifelike than the frozen Tom sitting beside her.

She stared helplessly at him, wondering what to do...

Tom found himself standing on the stage, facing the rows of fancy-dress people, with Jarman's arm round his shoulders. 'Tell me, Thomas,' Jarman was saying in a croaky voice. 'Can you read music?'

'No,' he said.

'Louder, so that the audience can hear.'

'NO.'

'Excellent. Yet you and I are going to play Mozart's Sonata for piano and violin in E flat. Look into my eyes.'

Tom did as he was told. The translucent eyes turned into two pools of water which gradually merged with each other until the water closed over his head. The last thing he heard was Jarman's voice telling him to sit at the piano...

Back in the study, Su watched in bewilderment as the old man and Tom's avatar started to play. At the same time, the frozen Tom beside her unfroze, his hands flying over the computer's keyboard as if it was a piano. Music started to scroll across the screen...

Tom slowly emerged from the pool of water, to find himself sitting at the piano. Below him, the fancy-dress people were applauding enthusiastically.

'Bravo, Tom,' whispered a croaky voice he recognised. 'You must take a bow.'

He turned, to find Jarman standing next to him, holding his violin. He stood up, and Jarman led him to the edge of the stage. He had no idea why he was supposed to take a bow, but as everyone seemed to be clapping he again did as he was told.

Then, as the applause died down, Jarman started to speak. 'What you have just witnessed, ladies and gentlemen, was no trick. A boy who cannot read music has given a performance of which Mozart himself would be proud.'

'If it is not a trick, Monsieur le Comte,' asked the lady in the front row, 'how did you do it? And why did you choose that particular boy?'

'How I did it must remain a secret, Madame,' said Jarman. 'I will only say that I have knowledge beyond your comprehension – an ancient wisdom acquired centuries before any of you were born. And the time has come to pass it on to someone I consider worthy to inherit it.' He turned to Tom. 'Come here, Thomas.'

Tom told his legs to run away through the audience, but they refused to obey him. Instead, they carried him to Jarman's side.

'Though my mind is still strong, my body is weak,' Jarman went on, turning back to the audience, 'and for many years I have been searching for a young pupil to whom I could entrust the secrets of my... let us call it alchemy. The moment I entered this room, I sensed that that there was such a youth among you, and that my search was over. As you have just heard, I was not mistaken.'

Tom looked up, to find the pale eyes fixed on him. 'If you don't mind, sir,' he said hoarsely, 'I think I'll pass.'

Jarman bent down and whispered in his ear. 'You have no choice, Tom. You will share my burden and be my spokesman. And you will learn the ancient wisdom...'

Back in the study, the screen went blank. Su turned to Tom, astonished and terrified by what she had seen. He was still staring at the screen like a dazed boxer after a knockout, trying to remember where he was.

'What was that all about?' she asked him gently.

He didn't reply, continuing to stare at the screen as if the construct was still there.

She touched his arm. 'I think you might be ill, Tom. Why don't you let Mum examine you?'

He swung round to face her, his face contorted with fury. 'Don't interfere!' he rasped in an old man's voice. 'Or I shall destroy the boy!'

CHAPTER FIVE

MATTHEW STOOD AT THE window of Sandra's office, sipping coffee from a plastic cup and staring down at the entrance to the Accident and Emergency department. The ambulance which had brought Tom to the hospital was still there, waiting for the next emergency call.

He glanced at his watch. It had been over an hour since Tom had gone down for a CT scan: luckily, there had been a last-minute cancellation, and Sandra had persuaded Dr Hancock, the neurologist, to let him jump the queue.

What was the matter with the boy? He hadn't said a word since Su had rushed into the garden and told him Tom had started speaking in an old man's voice, which she assumed was Jarman's. Neither Sandra nor Dr Hancock could explain it, and their preliminary examinations could find no reason why he should suddenly have become catatonic.

Matthew could think of a reason: the village was up to some new trick. But this was not something a doctor would understand.

He turned to Adam, who was sitting at Sandra's desk, toying with his empty coffee-cup. 'We should never have come, Dad. It's all starting again.'

Adam threw the paper cup into the waste-paper basket. 'Why is the boy obsessed with this Jarman character?'

'It's the other way round. Jarman seems to be obsessed with Tom.'

'You think he's some kind of magus? Like Hendrick?'

'No, not like Hendrick. His paranormal power doesn't seem to be restricted to Milbury.'

'Well this is obviously not a time anomaly. It's linear, not circular.'

'I still think the village has something to do with it. I ought to take him away.'

'I'm afraid that would be pointless, Matt.' Adam stood up and joined Matthew at the window. 'Let's assume you're right – that Jarman has somehow managed to enter Tom's mind. Some sort of post-hypnotic suggestion. This mental virus or whatever it is will stay with him wherever he goes.'

Matthew turned to him in despair. 'So what's the answer?'

'We have to out-think this new magus, just as we did the old one. Find out what his game is, and get ahead of it.'

'How can we do that? Jarman's not... not *human*!'

'Perhaps a psychiatrist could help. I'll ask Sandra if she knows someone who specialises in young people's mental problems...'

'That won't solve this problem. What Tom needs is an exorcist.'

Adam put a comforting hand on Matthew's shoulder. 'Oh come on, old chap...'

Matthew shrugged the hand off and turned to him. 'You're in denial, Dad,' he said angrily. 'After all we've been through, you still don't believe in the paranormal, do you? You still can't accept that science has its limitations.'

Adam was silent for a long moment. 'You're wrong, Matt,' he said quietly. 'Of course I accept that. But I believe that what we call paranormal powers are based on scientific principles which we don't yet know about. That's why I moved back to Milbury. Not just to be Lord of the Manor, but to be the villagers' guardian.'

Matthew frowned at him. 'Guardian?'

'You and I are the only people who know what went on in the village thirty years ago. Margaret never knew, thank God, and neither does Sandra. So I have a responsibility to protect its inhabitants, in case another Hendrick comes along.'

'And how are you going to protect Tom?'

Before Adam could answer, the door opened and Sandra appeared, followed by Doctor Hancock. 'Good news,' she announced. 'The scan's clear. And Tom's speaking normally.'

'Keep him under observation, Mr Brake,' said Hancock, shaking Matthew's hand. 'I've told Doctor de Courville if it happens again to call me immediately, even if I'm off-duty. And I'll come straight in.'

'What d'you think it was, doctor?'

'Hard to say. Some sort of personality disorder perhaps, but that's not my field. All I can tell you is there's nothing physically wrong with him. He's waiting for you at Reception.'

On the drive back to Milbury, Matthew gently plied Tom with questions. How much did he remember? Did he have any idea why he suddenly spoke in Jarman's voice, or why he warned Su not to interfere? And interfere with what?

His answers weren't much help. He remembered everything about the new construct, and the strange feeling that he himself seemed to have taken his avatar's place inside it. But he had no recollection of speaking in Jarman's voice or warning Su off, and no knowledge of what she was not supposed to interfere with.

When they arrived back at the Manor, he announced that he didn't want any dinner. It had been a long, tiring day, and he needed to get some sleep. He walked off towards the wagon, looking pale but otherwise undamaged.

Su was waiting in the drawing room with a sheaf of papers. She jumped to her feet as Adam, Matthew and Sandra appeared. 'How is he?' she asked anxiously.

Sandra reassured her that Tom seemed to be functioning normally, and the scan had revealed no abnormalities in his brain. 'But we have to keep an eye on him,' she said, 'and keep him away from computers.'

'That's not the problem,' said Su. 'He's being stalked. And I know who's stalking him.'

Matthew frowned at her. 'You mean, Professor Jarman?'

'Yes. Known throughout history as the Count of St Germain.'

'What?'

Su waved her sheaf of papers. 'While we were waiting for the ambulance, Tom wrote that name down and gave it to me.

So I've been doing some research on the net. Did you know the Count of St Germain was a real person?'

'No,' said Adam, heading for the drinks cabinet. 'But if he was known throughout history, it can't be the same man.'

'I think it is,' said Su. 'Jarman's the English version of Germain. And the Count of St Germain was supposed to be a brilliant alchemist who discovered the secret of eternal life.'

Sandra slumped wearily onto the sofa. 'I've never heard such nonsense. Don't go filling Tom's head with fairy stories, Khonsu. What he needs is a strong dose of reality.'

'But it's true, Mum. Lots of real people seem to have met him… Casanova, Madame de Pompadour, Voltaire, Anton Mesmer, someone called Horace Walpole…'

Adam handed a glass of whisky to Matthew. 'Walpole? Are you sure?'

'Yes. Who was he, Grandpa?'

'The Earl of Oxford. Member of Parliament in the eighteenth century. Famous for his letters about politics, foreign affairs and the arts.'

'Well one of his letters mentions a Count St Germain. He was arrested in London because they thought he was a spy. And he must have visited Milbury, because he made a sketch of the village, which is now in the British Museum.'

'When was Walpole's letter written?'

'1745. I printed it out. You want to read it?'

'No, I left my glasses in the car. You read it.'

Su leafed through the papers, selected one and began to read. ' "The other day, they seized an odd man, who goes by the name of Count St Germain. He has been here these two years, and will not tell who he is, or whence, but professes that he does not go by his right name. He sings, plays on the violin wonderfully, composes, is mad, and not very sensible. He is called an Italian, a Spaniard, a Pole; a somebody that married a great fortune in Mexico, and ran away with her jewels to Constantinople; a priest, a fiddler, a vast nobleman. The Prince of Wales has had insatiable curiosity about him, but in vain. However, nothing has been made out against him; he is released; and, what convinces me that he is not a gentleman, stays here, and talks of his being taken up for a spy." '

There was a long silence. 'Well it can't have been Jarman,' said Adam, moving back to the drinks cabinet. 'If they're from the same family, this chap must have been his great great grandfather. Or perhaps they aren't related at all.'

Matthew sipped his whisky thoughtfully. 'What about these other people who are supposed to have met him, Su? Is there any written evidence of that?'

'Yes. Voltaire called him "The man who never dies and knows everything." And there's some stuff in Casanova's memoirs about him. They met several times in Paris in 1757.'

'And what did Casanova have to say?'

'He thought the same as everyone else. That the Count was pretty freaky.'

'I doubt if he would have put it quite like that,' said Adam drily. 'I'd like to hear his exact words.'

'Okay.' Su searched through the papers again and produced another page. 'This is how he described their first meeting at a dinner party… "The famous adventurer, known by the name of the Comte de St Germain, would say in an easy and assured manner that he was hundreds of years old, that he knew the secret of universal medicine, and that he possessed a mastery over nature. A scholar, linguist, musician, chemist – also a ladies' man, who had contrived to gain the favour of Madame de Pompadour. He told me the king had given him a hundred thousand francs for the construction of a laboratory. I thought him quite astonishing." '

Matthew glanced at Adam. 'You've got to admit, Dad. He does sound pretty freaky.'

Adam shrugged. 'It's absurd. Just because he *claimed* to be hundreds of years old, it doesn't mean it was true.'

'We don't have to take his word for it, Grandpa,' said Su. 'Everyone who knew him agreed that he never seemed to get any older. They all said the same things – he could speak just about any language, he was a fantastic violinist, he seemed to be very rich but there's no record of him having any bank account. The rumour was that he could change ordinary metal into gold.'

'Rumour's not evidence, Su,' said Adam irritably. 'He could have kept his money in a vault.'

'I know. But even the King of France believed in him. That's why he helped him set up the laboratory.'

'I don't care how many laboratories he set up. Alchemy's a load of rubbish.'

'That's only partly true, Adam,' said Sandra. 'There's a lot more to it than turning base metal into gold. Alchemy wasn't just concerned with prolonging life – it helped the chemists to develop specialised medicines to fight disease.'

Adam sighed and raised his hands. 'All right, I surrender to superior forces.' He stood up and moved to the door. 'I'll go and tell Mrs C we're ready for dinner.'

He disappeared, leaving Matthew deeply disturbed. As a scientist, he had to agree with Adam: the idea of anyone living hundreds of years was ludicrous. Yet Jarman had entered his life just after he'd booked the flight to England. Was that a coincidence, or could there be some connection? Could this mysterious St Germain be still alive, now calling himself Jarman? And if they really were the same man, what did he want with Tom?

He turned to Su. 'Did the internet tell you when the Count first appeared?'

'No.' She tapped her papers. 'But there's records of him turning up all over Europe. The Germans called him the Wonderman, because he said he knew Pontius Pilate, Cleopatra and the Queen of Sheba.'

Sandra laughed. 'I suppose he told them the Queen of Sheba was one of his conquests?'

'He said he made a play for her. But she was only interested in Solomon.'

'And when was the last sighting?'

'1930. An American mining engineer says he met him on some mountain in California.'

'Sounds as if he'd had some of the Disciples' dodgy soup.'

After dinner, as Mrs Crabtree arrived to clear the table, Matthew asked Sandra if she fancied a drink at the pub. The alacrity with which she accepted the invitation was a pleasant surprise.

'You coming, Dad?'

Adam twinkled at him. 'No, three's a crowd. I want to catch up with some work.'

'I'm not coming either,' said Su cheekily, 'but thanks for asking.'

Even Mrs Crabtree seemed to think a visit to the pub was an excuse for some hanky-panky. 'You'll need a chaperone, doctor. I'll be down directly. Order me a gin and orange.' She disappeared into the kitchen with a pile of plates, cackling to herself.

Matthew and Sandra set off down the road in a companionable silence. The stones, fanning out on either side of them, seemed less sinister on this balmy evening – as if they had finally accepted that Matthew belonged in the village.

He had never felt so completely at ease with a woman. There was no need to make conversation with Sandra, no need to keep talking when he had nothing to say. She was a restful person to be with – unlike Sherry, who had resented his silences and complained that it was like living with a piece of furniture.

'Tell me about your wife,' said Sandra suddenly, 'or don't you want to talk about her?'

'I don't mind. What d'you want to know?'

'Why did you split up? Whose fault was it?'

'Mine.'

'I knew you'd say that. But I don't believe it.'

'It's true. I didn't pay her enough attention. You've got to work at a marriage, and I didn't work hard enough.'

'Do you miss her?'

Matthew thought for a moment. 'I miss the woman I married, not the one I divorced. We just grew apart.'

'It happens.'

She was staring at him, just as the girl she once was had stared when he first arrived in the village, the setting sun tingeing her dark eyes with fire. It brought back bitter-sweet memories of their childhood... her face pressed against the window of the cottage... sitting next to her at school, watching the High Table children solve impossible equations on the blackboard... the terrible evening when he had stolen her scarf, so that he could 'see' what happened to her at Hendrick's terrifying dinner party...

And here she was, all those years later, apparently no worse for her experience. They had both been married, lost their partners, had children the same age as they were then. Having spent most of their lives on opposite sides of the world, they were back where they started. The circle was complete.

But he could never be completely honest with her, he thought sadly. He could never tell her how he had watched helplessly as the scarf transmitted pictures of Sandra and her mother being turned into Happy Day-ers by Hendrick. But perhaps it didn't matter: she had no memory of it, and it didn't seem to have done her any harm. Anyway, if he told her what he had 'seen', she wouldn't believe him.

'Why are you looking at me like that?'

He suddenly realised he too had been staring. 'I was just thinking,' he said. 'I used to be able to tell things about people through an inanimate object that belonged to them.'

'You mean – psychometry?'

'Yes. I wonder if I still can.'

She stopped and turned to him. 'Why don't you try? Take this.' She took a ring off her finger and handed it to him. 'It's my wedding ring.'

Matthew held the ring tightly and closed his eyes. For a long time he could see nothing but a swirling mist, and he began to think his gift had deserted him. Then, dimly, some disjointed images started to materialise: a car driving through a rocky desert... the desert turning into a fertile valley with a river winding through it... sheep grazing in lush fields by a lake... orchards and vineyards full of veiled women, picking fruit... the car stopping and two people, a man and a woman, getting out... gazing happily at the peaceful scene, their arms round each other's waists...

Then the picture faded, like a camera whose battery needed recharging. He handed the ring back to Sandra.

She slipped it on her finger. 'Well? Did you see anything?'

'I saw you and your husband.'

'Where?'

He described what he had seen in as much detail as he could remember. When he had finished, she looked stunned. 'That... is... incredible!'

'So where were you?'

'In what's supposed to be the Garden of Eden. It's in northern Iran, near Lake Urmia. That's what Jean-Jacques was looking for, and he reckoned he'd found it.'

Matthew frowned. 'What made him so sure?'

'Because it fits all the geographical references in the Bible. It's the source of four rivers. It's west of the land of Nod, which according to the Book of Genesis was east of Eden. And every village in the area has a wall with a folk-art painting of Paradise on it.'

'Why d'you think those particular images came to me?'

'Perhaps because it was one of our happiest moments.'

They walked on. Above them, a flight of swallows led the way, twittering excitedly and swooping down on either side of the road. Matthew watched them, disturbed by the image of Sandra and Jean-Jacques with their arms round each other. Her happy marriage made him even more conscious of his own failure.

Had that been why his psychometric 'camera' had shown him that image – to remind him what his own marriage might have been? But finding the right partner was a matter of luck. Maybe somewhere out there, his soulmate was still waiting for him. The trouble was, the odds against him ever meeting her were astronomical.

Then it suddenly occurred to him that perhaps they had already met, and that she was walking beside him. Was it too late? Was it possible for someone like Sandra to have two soulmates in a lifetime? And could the second one ever live up to the memory of the first?

As they turned left towards the pub, he saw someone approaching it from the opposite direction. A white-bearded old man, wearing a cloth cap and a shabby jacket. Dai.

Matthew called to him. 'Evening, Dai. First one's on me.'

The old man stopped. 'You shouldn't have brought him here, Matthew,' he called back, 'and now it's too late.' He turned on his heel and walked away down the road.

Matthew stared after him, the old fear tying a knot in his stomach. What did 'and now it's too late' mean? Dai hadn't been either drunk or stoned, and he had never been known to refuse a free drink. So why this unprovoked hostility?

Sandra took his arm. 'That old man needs help. He's losing his marbles.'

'We all need help,' said Matthew, watching Dai disappear behind one of the stones. 'Specially Tom.'

'I shouldn't worry too much, Matt. He's young and healthy. All he needs is some fresh air and exercise.' She tugged at his arm. 'Come on – if Dai won't drink with you, I will. I'll have a spritzer.'

They had no chance to discuss Dai's curious behaviour, because Bob insisted on sitting down with them in the snug and talking about their schooldays. 'Remember when Kevin thumped you on your first day, Matt?' he said, punching Matthew playfully on the arm, 'and when you thumped him back it turned into the third World War?'

'Yes, I remember,' said Matthew. 'Tell me about Kevin. Why has he joined Dai's Disciples? Does he really believe in that Gaia garbage?'

'Maybe, maybe not. His dad left him quite a lot of money, so he doesn't need to work. He turned into a middle-aged hippy.'

Matthew wondered how much Bob remembered. He had lost touch with his schoolmates during the last terrible days in the village, as Hendrick tightened his grip on the inhabitants. By then, Sandra and her mother were the only people he and Adam could trust. And when they too became his puppets, there seemed to be no normal people left.

So what had happened to Bob and Kevin and Jim Browning after he and Adam escaped? Had they all, like Sandra and her mother, gone through the brainwashing process? Bob certainly had, because he had already been turned into a Happy Day-er before Adam and Matthew arrived in the village – though as a down-to-earth publican's son, he couldn't have been an easy subject for Hendrick's mind-games. Looking at him now – an amiable giant with a jolly red face – it was hard to believe that he was once one of the sinister pupils at the High Table.

But what about the other two, and the rest of the class? Had they and their families also been invited to dinner at the Manor? After Hendrick's power had been broken, what did they remember of their transformation into zombies? Did they just get on with their lives, as if he had never existed? And did they still believe that he was just a harmless astronomer, the discoverer of Ursa XB1?

Matthew realised that, as with Sandra, he would have to tread carefully with Bob. If his memory of that time had been erased, there was no point in probing too deeply.

'Tell me something, Bob,' he said. 'Did Hendrick ever invite you and your family to dinner?'

Bob laughed. 'Course not. He was a famous star-gazer, wasn't he? Why would he invite the likes of us?'

'What about Kevin and Jim? Were they ever invited?'

'Not that I know. And I *would've* known. They'd have been bragging about it for weeks.'

'So what happened after we left?'

'Nothing. Except I was a bit miffed you never said goodbye.'

'So was I,' said Sandra. 'I don't know why I'm still speaking to you.'

Matthew drained his beer-glass. 'Yes, I'm sorry about that. There was an emergency. We had to leave in a hurry.'

'Actually,' said Bob, 'something did happen after you left. Everything changed at school…'

'Including Miss Clegg,' said Sandra suddenly. 'I remember now…'

Before she could elaborate, her mobile rang. She took it out of her pocket and glanced at it. 'It's the hospital,' she said. 'I'll take it outside.'

While she was away, Bob filled in the details about what happened at the school. After Hendrick disappeared, he and the other High Table children lost interest in maths. And so, strangely, did Miss Clegg, their teacher. She no longer gave them complicated equations to resolve – which was just as well, because all the pupils suddenly found them much too difficult.

'What happened to her?' asked Matthew.

Bob pulled a face. 'She went a bit doolally, so they put her in a home. Far as I know, she's still there.'

'Which one?'

'Dunno. Somewhere in Marlborough, I think.' Bob stood up and collected the empty glasses. 'I'll bring another round, on the house.'

'There's something else, Bob. When I first arrived here, some of the kids used to say "Happy Day" to each other. Some of the adults too. D'you remember?'

'Happy Day? Why would anyone say a bloody stupid thing like that?'

'I don't know. You used to say it yourself.'

Bob smiled. 'I think you've been away too long, Matt. Maybe you're confusing Milbury with Maine or Massachusetts.'

As he went back to the bar, Sandra returned, looking indignant. 'They want me to fill in for someone tomorrow morning. I'm supposed to be on leave, but they're short-staffed, as usual.'

'In that case,' said Matthew, 'I'll go and visit Miss Clegg.'

'I doubt if she'll remember you.'

'Maybe not. But she'll remember Hendrick.'

'So do I. What can she tell you that I can't?'

'I think she was working for him. Preparing the kids for…' He suddenly stopped, realising that he was entering forbidden territory.

Sandra frowned. 'What d'you mean – preparing them?'

'For life,' he said lamely. 'Let's talk about Tom. D'you think I should take him to a psychiatrist?'

'No. Don't make a mountain out of a molehill. It might do more harm than good.'

'Suppose it isn't a molehill?'

'You mustn't take Su's story literally, Matt. She's a very intelligent girl, but she does tend to exaggerate. I'm sure there's a much more mundane explanation for what happened to Tom.'

'Such as?'

'Too much time on the internet. It's more common than you think, you know – young computer wonks confusing the fictional world with the real one. There was an article in *The Lancet* last month about some kid who spent so much time jumping in and out of virtual reality that he ended up a basket case.'

Matthew took a long swig of Bob's best bitter. 'Yes, I've probably gone too easy on him since the divorce. Allowed a hobby to become an addiction. Time I did my parental duty.'

Sandra smiled. 'Maybe Su can keep his mind occupied with other things. I'll have a word with her.'

'It's not just too much computer time. There's another problem.'

'You mean – Dai?'

'Yes. All these veiled threats. They're unsettling the boy.'

Sandra covered Matthew's hand with hers. 'Perhaps you should call the police, Matt. Ask Jim Browning to have a word with him.'

The touch of her hand was reassuring. '*Someone* ought to have a word with him. But I'm not going to leave it to Jim.'

The next morning, Tom woke up feeling refreshed and invigorated. It was another beautiful day and all was once more right with the world.

Why had everyone made such a fuss, just because he had stumbled onto that strange new construct? Maybe he had misdialled, but so what? There was no need to take him in to the hospital to have his head examined.

But he was sure he had keyed in the right name. So it wasn't surprising that Jarman's avatar had appeared in the construct. He had obviously programmed it himself, for anyone surfing the net to find. Admittedly, it had seemed more real than the previous one, but there was nothing sinister about it. It was just a bit of fun.

There was a knock on the wagon door and Su appeared. 'Hi,' she said. 'I'm going to be busy this morning, and I just wanted to make sure you're okay. Can I come in?'

Tom sat up. 'Sure.'

She moved to the window seat. 'So where did that construct come from?'

'No idea.'

'What d'you remember about it?'

'Everything.'

'That was Jarman, wasn't it? Playing the violin?'

'Yeah.'

Su frowned at him. 'You into classical music?'

'No.'

'Can you play the piano?'

'Not even chopsticks.'

'So why did you program yourself into the construct as a musician?'

'I didn't. Jarman must have done it. I thought I was going to make a fool of myself in front of all those people, but I just let him take control. The next thing I knew, they were all clapping me.'

Su's frown deepened. 'You mustn't let him take control, Tom. It's dangerous.'

'I know. He said something pretty weird just after we'd finished playing. That I had to share his burden and be his spokesman. Like we were on the same side.'

'You're *not* on the same side,' said Su firmly. 'So stay away from computers and mirrors, okay?'

'Okay. What are you going to be busy at?'

'My holiday project. I'm writing an essay on Sumerian history.'

Tom grinned. 'Need any help?'

'No thanks. I want to get an A, not a Z.'

After she had gone, he dressed and went across to the house for breakfast. Adam was sitting alone in the dining room, reading a newspaper.

'Good morrow, Thomas,' he said, peering at him over his half-moon spectacles, 'and how are we today? All shipshape and Bristol fashion?'

'Yeah. I feel great. Where's Dad?'

'He's driven off somewhere. There's some kedgeree on the hotplate. One of Mrs C's specialities. I recommend it.'

Tom had no idea what kedgeree was, but he helped himself to a large portion of it and carried it back to the table.

'I'm afraid laptops and computers are out of bounds for a while,' said Adam. 'We think you're becoming too obsessed with Dame Electronica. You need a break from each other, so we're confiscating your laptop.'

'Okay. No problem.'

'There are plenty of other things to do. Stargazing, exploring, visits to theme parks. And there's always Su. I take it you're not averse to her company?'

'No. But she's busy this morning, doing her vacation project.'

'In that case, I shall be your director of entertainment. And you can repay me by mowing the lawn. There's a motorised mower in the shed, so it shouldn't be too arduous.'

'Okay, it's a deal.' Tom took a mouthful of kedgeree, and immediately spat it out again, feeling sick.

Adam stood up in alarm. '*Mea culpa*, Thomas. I forgot you were allergic to fish. Quick – have some toast.'

Tom grabbed a piece of toast and shoved it in his mouth. Gradually, the nausea subsided.

'Sorry, Grandpa,' he said weakly. 'I thought I was going to pass out.'

'I'm the one who ought to apologise. Unfortunately, Sandra's on duty at the hospital, but I could call another doctor...?'

'No, I'm fine.' Tom poured himself a glass of orange juice and drank it down. 'So what's on the schedule, Mr Entertainment Director?'

Adam smiled. 'First, I shall show you my favourite toy.'

After breakfast, Tom followed Adam to the garden shed at the back of the house. Most of it was occupied by the large motorised mower, but beside it was an extraordinary-looking cart, with two wheels and five vertical struts attached by wires to a metal box on the handle.

Adam pulled it out of the shed. 'What d'you think this is?'

Tom examined the contraption more closely. The central strut was taller than the others and had an antenna at the top, also connected by a wire to the metal box. 'Dunno,' he said. 'Some kind of magnetometer?'

'It's a little more advanced than that. It's a home-made magnetic gradiometer.'

'What's the difference?'

'A magnetometer measures magnetic fields at a specific point. A gradiometer measures the changes in the magnetic field between two points. And it uses the measurements to detect buried magnetic objects.'

'You mean, like old coins and stuff? But that's what a metal detector does.'

Adam patted the cart as if it were a pet dog. 'This is much more sensitive than a bog-standard metal detector. It can detect geological anomalies of historical interest like rocks, earthworks and barrows. So it's designed for archaeological use.'

Tom pointed to the struts. 'And these are sensors, right? Why d'you need so many?'

'To get accurate readings. One isn't enough, because every time you move a single sensor the readings change. But if you've got several sensors aligned with each other, they all register the same change, so they cancel each other out.' Adam smiled. 'Clear as mud, eh?'

'It's pretty cool, Grandpa,' said Tom. 'Have you found anything interesting with this thing?'

'Nothing of value, if that's what you mean. No buried treasure. Just Iron Age artefacts.'

'Can I have a go?'

'As long as I'm with you. You need a permit to use these machines on historic sites. Have you got any metallic objects in your pocket?'

Tom felt in his pocket and produced a few coins which the steward had given him as change on the plane. 'I've got these.'

'Leave them here. They'll distort the magnetic field.'

Adam wheeled the cart out of the garden, and along the path to the nearest section of the stone circle. Then he stopped. 'Now where shall we start?'

Tom glanced round. In the centre of one of the inner circles was a stubby concrete plinth, dwarfed by the massive sarsens surrounding it. It looked like an upside-down ice-cream cone, but he knew from the construct that it marked the spot where the tallest stone of all used to stand. 'How about over there?'

'Near the obelisk plinth? Good choice. I've never explored that area.' Adam pressed a button on the side of the metal box, and it started to beep. 'It's all yours, Thomas. Wheel it backwards and forwards in parallel lines, keeping a steady pace. And watch the dial – if the needle moves, let me know.'

Tom took the handle and started to wheel the cart up and down past the plinth, taking three steps between every beep. But the needle remained resolutely at zero.

'Try the other side,' suggested Adam.

The moment Tom wheeled the cart round to the other side of the plinth, the needle immediately jumped to a high reading. He stopped and called. 'I think I've found something.'

'Stay where you are,' Adam called back. 'Don't move.' He hurried up to the cart and studied the dial. Then he took the handle and slowly wheeled it away from the plinth. Tom followed him, watching the needle until it dropped back to zero.

'Hmm,' said Adam thoughtfully, staring back at the plinth. 'There's certainly something metallic down there. But it's very deep.' He bent down and examined the fringe of long grass running round the base of the plinth. 'That's odd. There's a fissure in the earth here. Must be the dry hot summer we've been having.'

Tom peered over Adam's shoulder. There was a crack a few inches wide between the base of the plinth and the fringe of grass. 'That metallic thingy down there, Grandpa. How can we tell what it is?'

'We won't be able to tell *what* it is. But we can work out its size and shape from the data in that box. I have to do some work in the observatory this morning, so I'll analyse it later. Meanwhile, you can fulfil your part of our deal.'

It didn't take Tom long to mow the lawn. Racing round on the mower, he timed each circuit like a speedway driver at Indianapolis, and took the chequered flag in twenty minutes ten seconds – a new track record. Then he did a lap of honour, waving to an invisible crowd.

He put the mower back in the shed and went into the house. There was no sound, except for the ticking of the clocks. If it wasn't for the delicious smell coming from the kitchen, a stranger would have assumed it was unoccupied.

He followed the smell, and found Mrs Crabtree bent double, peering through the oven window. 'Hi, Mrs C,' he said, moving up behind her. 'Mind if I...'

She staggered back, clutching her chest. 'Oh you gave me such a start, Master Matthew. You shouldn't creep up on people like that.'

'Sorry, I just wanted a glass of water. And Matthew's my father.'

'Help yourself. The glasses are in that cupboard.' Mrs Crabtree opened the oven door and sniffed at the dish inside. 'Another half-hour, I reckon. You like macaroni cheese?'

'Yeah.'

'I made it specially. Seeing as how you're a veggy.'

'Thanks.' Tom took a glass out of the cupboard and filled it from the tap. 'Maybe I could take a cup of coffee up to Su?'

Mrs Crabtree pointed to a coffee machine by the window. 'I don't know how to work that thing, so you'll have to make it yourself. She likes it with a lot of foam, and bits of chocolate sprinkled on it.'

'That's the way Mum likes... used to like it.'

'The chocolate's in the tin marked 'Coffee'. The coffee's in the pot marked 'Tea'. And the sugar's in the fridge.'

Tom made two cups of coffee, put them on a tray and carried them up to Su's room. As he reached the top of the stairs he heard the soft clattering of a keyboard, which stopped when he knocked on the door. Su opened it, looking harassed. Her bed was covered with piles of books, and papers were scattered all over the floor.

He held out the tray. 'Thought you might like a break.'

'Thanks.' She took one of the cups and picked her way back across the floor to her desk.

'Mind if I hang around for a while?'

'Okay. But don't start yakking. I have to concentrate.' She sat down at her word processor and started clattering again. Tom wandered round the room, sipping his coffee. There were none of the usual girlie things lying around: no teddy-bear mascots, no pictures of rock stars or soccer players. The photographs pinned to the wall were all of ancient ruins, which he assumed had been taken by her father.

One particular group of photographs were closeups of some antiquated pillars. Their tops had crumbled away, but each of them had the same pattern of nine dots carved into the stone at about head height.

'What do these dots mean?' he asked, forgetting that he wasn't supposed to speak.

'Sh!' Su went on clattering for a moment, then turned to him irritably. 'What?'

'These dot-patterns. They're all the same. What are they – some religious thing?'

'That's what Dad thought. Nobody knows for sure. He found them in the remains of every Sumerian temple.'

'Mind if I play around with them?'

'Do what you like. As long as you shut your face.'

Tom unpinned one of the photographs from the wall, snatched a pen from Su's desk and started to draw connecting lines between the dots. He tried to make a winged fish-man out of them, but it didn't work. Joined together, the dots formed an object that looked more like a kite, a half-finished tent or a rather wonky house. His theory didn't stand up.

Then he had another idea. The trouble was, he would need to use the computer up in the observatory to check it out. Was that part of the ban his father had imposed? Surely not, if Adam was with him.

Leaving Su clattering away, he let himself out of the room and ran upstairs to the observatory. Adam was standing by the spectrometer, examining a printout through a magnifying glass.

'I'm helping Su with her essay, Grandpa,' said Tom. 'She wants me to check this out.' He handed him the photograph.

Adam stared at it blankly. 'What is it?'

'Dunno. Her dad found the same logo on all the Sumerian temples. We wondered if it could be a primitive star-chart?'

Adam peered at the dot pattern through his magnifying glass. 'I doubt it. If it's carved on their temples, it's more likely to be a representation of one of their gods.'

'But there's this theory that these guys came down to earth thousands of years ago in a spaceship…'

'That's science fiction, Thomas. A lucrative market, but not to be taken seriously.'

'I'd still like to check it out.'

Adam smiled. 'All right. Let's check it out together.' He sat down at the control panel. 'The problem is we have no coordinates for the computer to look for. So before we feed this pattern in, we'll have to measure the distance between these dots to get their exact positions relative to each other. And hope Dame Electronica recognises it.'

'We'll need a pretty accurate ruler then.'

Adam pointed across the room. 'There's a slide rule and a protractor in that drawer. Bring them over here, while I give each of these dots numbers.'

'Okay.'

'We're probably wasting our time. It's highly unlikely this *is* a primitive star-chart.'

Tom grinned. 'I don't care. I always wanted to be a space detective.'

By the time he'd fetched the slide rule and the protractor, Adam had numbered all the dots in the photograph. 'Right, here we go. You call out two numbers, and I'll measure the distance between them.'

It took them over half an hour to calculate the measurements between each dot and feed them into the computer. Finally, Adam asked it to locate a star group or constellation that fitted the pattern.

The answer came back immediately: 'LIBRA CONSTELLATION'.

'Wow!' said Tom. 'That was quick.'

A picture of it appeared on the screen: a magnified replica of the pattern, with stars instead of dots.

Adam looked astonished. 'It appears you were right, Thomas. A triumph for youth over experience.'

'Could you print it out? I want to show it to Su.'

'I'm sure she'll be impressed.' Adam hit the print button, and Tom grabbed the printout as it emerged from the printer. 'Tell me about the Libra constellation, Grandpa. Could there be any planets there with life on them? I mean intelligent life, not plants and stuff.'

'As a matter of fact, there is one candidate for extraterrestrial life – discovered very recently, in April, 2007. It's called Gliese 581d, aka Wolf 562d, otherwise known as Little Wolf.'

'So there's a big bad wolf?'

Adam smiled. 'Yes. They both orbit a red dwarf star.'

'How far is it?'

'About twenty light years away. That's pretty close, in astronomical terms.'

'What makes them think there could be life there?'

'It's the first planet we know of that has all the qualifications. It's in a habitable zone, with a surface temperature capable of maintaining water. It's about the same size as Earth, and its parent star provides a stable source of light and heat. So yes – it's quite possible there's some sort of life on Little Wolfie.'

Tom glanced at the telescope. 'Can we look at it through that?'

'We can look, but we won't be able to see it. It's a deep sky object, and all you'll see is the dim red glow of its parent star.' Adam hit the LOCATE key, typed in 'Wolf 562d', clicked GOTO – and the telescope slewed noiselessly round to a new position.

'Right,' he said. 'Open the roof and sit in the viewing chair. I'll watch the monitor.'

Tom pressed the button by the door, and the roof rolled back. Then he sat in the viewing chair and stared through the eyepiece. He could see the nine stars of the Libra constellation quite clearly, but nothing in between them.

'I can't see anything. Where should I look?'

'Right in the centre of the constellation,' Adam called back. 'Hang on – I'll magnify the area.'

Tom kept his eye on the centre of the pitch black area between the stars. As Adam magnified it, he could just make out a pinpoint of red light. Then, as the magnification increased, the light began to spread into the darkness around it.

Tom gazed at it in wonder. So that was the red dwarf, Little Wolf's parent star. Somewhere out there was Little Wolf itself – the planet where the Sumerians thought their gods might have come from. Was it possible that it was still inhabited by fish-men?

He couldn't wait to tell Su what he had discovered, so he took the spectrometer's X-ray image of the red dwarf which Adam had printed out for him, ran downstairs and burst excitedly into her room. 'I think I've cracked that dot-pattern,' he told her, 'I was right – it's a star chart...'

'Oh for God's sake, Tom!' She swivelled round in her chair, her face flushed with anger. 'I told you I was busy. Go away!'

He stared at her, deeply hurt. 'Okay. I just thought you'd like to know what me and Grandpa...'

'I don't want to know anything. I want to finish this bloody essay. Now leave me alone!'

He laid the printout on her desk and went out again. Nothing in his life – not even his mother's walkout – had wounded him as much as this curt dismissal. He had thought that he'd finally found someone of his own age he could relate to, a knockout girl who seemed genuinely interested in him. But he'd obviously picked up the wrong signals. Maybe Adam or Sandra had told her to be nice to their guest, and she'd just got bored with him.

He wandered disconsolately into the garden, wondering what he was going to do for the rest of the vacation. It was a dismal prospect: no computers, no baseball to watch, and no Su. Just that mad old Welshman, who couldn't seem to make up his mind whether he was a friend or an enemy.

The sound of a car horn roused him from his gloom. His father drove in through the gates and stopped on the drive. Tom walked over to him.

'Hi, Tommo. How are you feeling?'

'Fine.'

'What have you been doing this morning?'

Tom told him about the dot-pattern, the discovery of Little Wolfie and his expedition with Adam to try out the gradiometer. His father looked amused. 'So what did you do in your spare time, Einstein? Write a history of the universe? Circumnavigate the world? Travel to Mars and back?'

Sandra drove up behind them in her open-roofed sports car. She called to them over the windscreen. 'Get out of the way, Professor. You're standing between me and my lunch.' The two cars drove on towards the house, and Tom walked back through the garden.

Su was standing outside the French windows. As soon as she saw him, she ran across the freshly mown lawn and put her arms round his neck. 'I'm sorry, Tom,' she said. 'I've been a selfish cow. Forgive me?'

He held her close, his heart singing again. 'I shouldn't have come bursting in on you like that.'

'Grandpa told me you think those dots are a star chart.'

'Yeah.'

'Why didn't you tell me?'

He grinned. 'You didn't give me a chance, remember?'

'That's brilliant. I'll put it in my essay.' She kissed his cheek. 'Don't worry, I'll give you the credit.'

Adam appeared through the French windows and called to them. 'When you two lovebirds have stopped canoodling, we can eat.'

Matthew and Sandra were already sitting at the dining table, staring hungrily at a large ham on the sideboard. As Tom sat down, Mrs Crabtree carried the dish of macaroni cheese from the hotplate and plonked it in front of him. 'Yankee Doodle came to town,' she croaked, 'riding on a pony. Stuck a feather in his cap and called it macaroni.' She shuffled out, looking pleased with herself.

Adam started to carve the ham. 'So where have you been, Matt?'

'I went to see Miss Clegg, our old schoolmistress,' said Matthew. 'She's in a care home.'

'I didn't realise she was still breathing. Did she remember you?'

'No. But she didn't seem very pleased to see me, for some reason. She stared at me with those dead eyes of hers as if I was something the cat brought in. I was glad to get away.'

'What did you talk about?'

'Hendrick, mostly.'

'So she remembered *him*?'

'Yes. She seemed to think he was the greatest man who ever lived, but she couldn't remember why. And she blamed you and me for not allowing him to complete his work.'

'That's curious. How did she know it was us? Nobody else does.'

'Sorry, I'm lost,' said Sandra. 'What did you two have to do with Hendrick leaving the village?'

Adam and Matthew glanced at each other, each waiting for the other to answer. 'It's a long story, Sandra,' said Adam. 'But take it from me, he was a dangerous man. And we managed to persuade him he wasn't welcome here.'

He carried a plate of carved ham to the table and sat down. 'I've processed that data from the gradiometer, Thomas. You seem to have made another interesting discovery.'

'What is it?' asked Tom, through a mouthful of macaroni. 'Buried treasure?'

'No, something much more intriguing. There seems to be some sort of cavity beneath the obelisk plinth, with a large metallic object in it.'

Sandra stared at him in surprise. 'The obelisk plinth? But that area's already been thoroughly investigated.'

'Perhaps they weren't thorough enough,' said Adam. 'This thing's at least twenty feet deep.'

'Tom isn't the first to make an interesting discovery there,' said Sandra. 'In 1881 a villager was digging a hole in that area for the maypole, and he found an urn containing bones. They weren't human or animal, and the zoologists couldn't identify them. All we know is they were thousands of years old.'

'What was the obelisk used for, Mum?' asked Su.

'Probably some sort of fertility rite. That's why the May Day celebrations are still held there. The obelisk was at the centre of the south inner circle and much taller than the other stones, so it was obviously very important to the early inhabitants.'

'What happened to it?'

'The Victorian farmers probably broke it up and buried the pieces somewhere else. They were ignorant vandals.'

Matthew poured himself a glass of wine. 'Well if there's a cavity down there and the earth above it is starting to crack, it could be dangerous. You should tell someone, Dad.'

'Yes, I suppose I should,' said Adam. 'But first I want to consult the local expert.'

'Who's that?'

'Percy Deverell. You must remember Percy, Matt. Used to be the village weirdo, now our oldest inhabitant. He's one of my tenants.'

Sandra stared at him, puzzled. 'Percy's not an expert. He's just a dowser.'

'He knows more about this place than anyone else, Sandra. Even you.' Adam turned to Tom. 'You up for a post-prandial walk, Thomas?'

Tom had no idea what a post-prandial walk was, but this was turning out to be an exciting day and he was up for anything.

It was some time after Adam rang the doorbell of Percy Deverell's cottage that he finally appeared: a chubby bald man with two tufts of white hair sticking out on either side of his head, wheezing like a steam engine.

He didn't seem particularly pleased to see Adam. 'Oh it's you, Professor,' he said sourly. 'Nice of you to pay one of your humble serfs a visit. Rent collector sick, is he?'

'It's not about the rent, Percy,' said Adam. 'We've come to consult you about the obelisk plinth. May we come in?'

The old man's rheumy eyes settled on Tom. 'Who's this sprig?'

'My grandson. He was using my gradiometer this morning near the plinth, and the machine detected a large metal object buried there. We wondered if you knew anything about it?'

Percy still didn't invite them in. 'Suppose I do?' he demanded suspiciously. 'What business is it of his? Or yours, come to that?'

'Tom's very interested in archaeology,' said Adam smoothly. 'I told him you knew more about the history of our village than anyone else. So he couldn't wait to meet you.'

This piece of flattery proved to be their entrance card. Percy glanced at Tom, then turned and led them down a narrow passage to a tiny sitting room with faded brown photographs of long-ago Milbury on the walls. He waved them to a couple of chairs, but remained standing.

'I thought you scientists had no time for us crackpots,' he said to Adam. 'You don't believe in dowsing, do you?'

'I believe in your ability to find water. And I certainly don't believe scientists have all the answers. I try to keep an open mind.'

Percy, seemingly mollified, turned to Tom. 'Want some tea, young sprig?' he wheezed.

Tom didn't want any tea, but realised it might be a way of breaking the ice. 'Yes, please.'

After Percy disappeared, Adam put his finger to his lips. Tom took the hint, and they waited in silence till Percy returned with three steaming mugs on a tray. He handed two to Adam and Tom, then sat down himself.

'If I tell you what I know about that piece of ground, Professor, what d'you mean to do with the information?'

'I don't know yet. First, I want to make a few tests.'

For some reason, this seemed to increase Percy's hostility. 'Tests? What sort of tests?'

'Well there's quite a large fissure running round the base of the plinth. It must have opened up quite recently, because no one seems to have noticed it before. So the first thing I'd like to do is try and lower my video camera down it. See if I can get a picture of whatever it is down there.'

Percy slurped his tea noisily. 'You'd need permission to do that.'

'Oh I don't think that would be a problem. I'm President of the local Archaeological Society.'

'I mean, you'd need *my* permission.'

Adam stared at Percy in astonishment. 'Why on earth would I need that?'

'Because I'm the guardian of our heritage, Professor. And I can't allow anyone to mess with our sacred ground.'

'What makes you think it's sacred ground?' asked Tom.

'It just is, that's all. My father knew it, my grandfather knew it, and generations of our family before that. We've always known it.'

There was a long silence, broken only by Percy taking more noisy slurps of his tea.

'I don't mean to be rude, Percy,' said Adam eventually, 'but who appointed your family the guardians of Milbury?'

Percy heaved himself to his feet and wheezed his way to a framed piece of old parchment on the wall. He took it down and handed it wordlessly to Adam. Tom stood up and peered at it over his shoulder.

From the Malmesbury Chronicles, it said, *May 5th 1135*. And underneath, in illuminated writing, *The king hath let it be knowne this day that Thomas Deverille, gentleman, shall henceforth be titled Warden-in-chief of the Milberie stones, and hath proclaimed that the title be passed to his heirs in perpetuitie.*

'So I'm warning you, Professor,' said Percy, 'if you start fiddling around with your fancy equipment down there and disrespecting our heritage, I'll call the police.'

Before he put it back on the wall, Tom took a photograph of it with his mobile.

Back at the Manor, Adam told Matthew, Sandra and Su about Percy's threat, and about his claim to be Milbury's guardian.

Sandra took Tom's mobile over to the light and examined the photograph closely. 'The date's about right,' said Sandra. 'William of Malmesbury who wrote the Malmesbury Chronicles was a well-known historian in the middle ages. He died in 1154.'

'It could still be a fake,' said Matthew. 'These certificates are two a penny in the States. People buy them from internet universities because they look good on the wall.'

'Well I don't want him calling the police,' said Adam. 'I can just see the headlines – "Lord of the Manor arrested for digging up sacred ground." So we'll have to do our detective work at night.'

Matthew frowned. 'You're not still going to investigate that cavity?'

'Certainly. I'm not going to be scared off by that crazy old dowser.'

'But he could be keeping watch out there...'

'It's not very likely. You lose interest in nocturnal adventures when you're our age. But just to be on the safe side, we could station our own lookouts outside his cottage. So we'd have plenty of warning if Percy decides to do some snooping.'

'Who did you have in mind?'

Adam glanced at Tom and Su. 'Perhaps these two trainee detectives might like the job. They can run a lot faster than old Percy. How about it, kiddiwinkies? Will you keep him off my back while I solve the mystery of the metallic object?'

'Sure, Grandpa,' said Tom. 'When were you thinking of playing Sherlock?'

'The sooner the better. "If it were done when 'tis done, then 'twere well it were done quickly." How about tonight?'

Tom glanced at Su. Her eyes were shining with excitement.

There were still practicalities to be sorted out, however. They would need some lamps and torches which would have to be screened from prying eyes – a problem solved by the old tarpaulin covering Georgina in the garage.

To prop it up, Tom was delegated to choose the longest implements in the garden shed – a hoe, a rake, a broom and a branch-lopper – and to sharpen the handles with a hatchet so that they would stick into the ground. Su's task was to put new batteries into the torches and new candles into the garden lamps.

After Tom had put the makeshift tent up in the garden, they lit the lamps and carried them inside to see how much light could be seen through the tarpaulin.

Too much, Adam decided. But after they put the lamps in a couple of saucepans, stolen from the kitchen much to Mrs

Crabtree's displeasure, no light could be seen by someone outside until he or she was standing about six feet away.

As it was almost midsummer, they had to wait until eleven o'clock before it was dark enough to set off on their expedition. Tom and Su, who had been keeping watch on Percy's cottage since supper time, had returned half an hour earlier to report that they had seen the old man in the kitchen making a cup of tea, which he had then carried upstairs. A few minutes later, wearing his pyjamas, he had drawn the curtains. So it was safe to assume he had gone to bed.

Adam had written a list of what each member of the expedition would carry: he himself would be responsible for his video camera and extension cable, Su and Sandra for the garden lamps and saucepans, Matthew for the tarpaulin and Tom for the sharpened garden implements and a croquet mallet to hammer them into the ground.

'We'll go in single file,' announced Adam. 'I'll lead the way with a torch. If we see anyone I'll switch it off and we'll crouch down till they've passed. Right – off we go. No talking.'

Luckily, it was a dark night, with the moon hidden behind a blanket of clouds. They walked in total silence, except for one occasion when Adam suddenly stopped without warning and Tom, bringing up the rear, bumped into Su and knocked her to the ground.

'Ow!' she hissed. 'Why don't you watch where you're going, you clumsy Yank?'

'Sorry.'

'Sh!' said Adam.

They all held their breaths and listened. But no one seemed to have been within earshot, and they reached the obelisk plinth without further incident. They quickly erected the tarpaulin-tent round it and lit the garden lamps. Adam unpacked the video camera, plugged in a long cable and attached the camera head to it. Then he switched on the imager head's light and gently lowered it through the fissure at the edge of the plinth.

'You're in charge of the cable, Thomas,' he whispered to Tom. 'If it gets stuck, try and shake it free. Gently, mind – if you damage the imager head, I'll take the repairs out of your pocket money.'

Tom grinned. 'What pocket money?'

But it didn't get stuck. As he fed more and more cable into the fissure and the light at the end of it gradually disappeared into the darkness below, the others stood behind Adam, watching the pictures the imager head was sending back to the screen on the handheld control.

Adam started recording a whispered running commentary to accompany the images. 'After a few feet of compacted earth, there now seems to be solid rock on both sides of the fissure. Which means that either the camera is passing between two large rocks, or a single even larger rock that has split apart for some reason. Probably the latter, because it would explain why the fissure has only recently reached the surface.'

'This is getting really exciting,' whispered Sandra. 'If you're right, it could mean that whatever's down there was buried deliberately.'

'It could also explain why Percy believes this is a sacred place,' said Matthew, 'and why his family have appointed themselves its guardians.'

'D'you think he knows what's buried down there?' asked Su. 'And why it's sacred?'

'No,' said Adam firmly. 'How can he possibly know? Unless it's where one of his ancestors stashed his ill-gotten gains.'

But Matthew was beginning to feel uneasy. 'I don't like this, Dad. We could be desecrating a grave. Maybe we shouldn't go any further.'

'Nonsense. This isn't desecration, it's legitimate research. It might tell us something about our Neolithic forebears.'

'I just don't think we have the right to…'

'Hang on.' Adam was peering intently at the video screen. 'This could be it. Trouble is, there's a lot of interference.'

He held it up, and the others crowded round it. The image the camera was sending back was now extremely fuzzy. But they could just make out a small subterranean chamber, with a long cigar-shaped object lying in the centre of it on a rectangular pile of earth.

'Looks like a coffin,' whispered Tom.

'Not a coffin,' said Sandra thoughtfully. 'A sarcophagus.'

'Isn't that the same thing?'

'Not quite. Sarcophagi were made of a kind of stone, which the ancient Greeks believed consumed the flesh of dead bodies. There was usually some sort of carving on them.'

'Well this doesn't look as if it's made of stone,' said Adam. 'It must be some kind of metal, otherwise the gradiometer wouldn't have picked it up.'

He pressed the magnification button, which brought the object closer to the camera. But they still couldn't get a clear view of it, because the image became more and more blurred.

Su leaned forward, till her face was a few inches from the screen. 'There's a dark patch there – right in the centre of it. That could be a carving.'

Sandra pulled her back so that they could all see, and they studied the object in silence for a moment. There did seem to be a small dark patch on it, but the picture was so out of focus that it was impossible to tell what it was.

'Let's go back to the house,' said Adam. 'I'll run it through the computer and see if I can enhance it.'

On the way back to the Manor, Sandra seemed so absorbed in her own thoughts that as they walked back up the drive Matthew asked what was troubling her.

'I'm just puzzled, that's all,' she told him. 'The Sumerians were supposed to have buried their tribal chiefs that way – in a sarcophagus under some sacred monument. Jean-Jacques met an old man in Iran who told him they were taught to do that by their gods.'

He stopped and stared at her in astonishment. 'You're not suggesting that Milbury was once a Sumerian settlement?'

'No, of course not. The Sumerians pre-dated this village by thousands of years.'

'Some other lot then. Who came after the Sumerians?'

'I'm more interested in who came before them.'

Matthew stopped. '*Was* there anyone before them?'

'I've no idea. Neolithic Man, perhaps. It's an intriguing thought, isn't it?'

'So if that thing down there does turn out to be a sarcophagus, who d'you think was buried in it?'

'Probably someone important. I don't believe our Neolithic ancestors chose the obelisk by chance.'

Matthew glanced back at the plinth. The clouds had rolled away, and it was bathed in moonlight. 'You say that area has been researched before?'

'Many times.'

'Then how come the archaeologists missed that burial chamber, or whatever it is?'

'Perhaps because it was too deep. Or perhaps they weren't thorough enough.'

'Or perhaps it didn't want to be found,' said Matthew softly, ''till now.'

'*What* did you say?'

He took her arm. 'I said, "What I need is a large single malt."'

In the study, they all watched tensely as Adam transferred the disc to his computer and did several scans of the fuzzy image the video camera had sent back. With each scan the cigar-shaped object became clearer, revealing first that the dark patch on it was indeed a carving, and then, as it gradually came into focus, something that set Tom's heart racing.

He waited, frozen with horror. Surely it couldn't be...

But it was. Su, standing beside him, recognised it too. 'I don't believe it!' she said softly.

They both stared in disbelief at the primitive carving. It was the same symbol that had appeared on Tom's computer back in Boston – a winged fish-creature – except that it was sitting on what looked like a throne, and had a semicircle of wiggly lines surrounding its head. Whoever or whatever the fish-creature was, it was obvious from his halo of wiggly lines that he represented some god or a king who wielded immense power.

Tom didn't care who it represented. He had already seen it in two virtual reality constructs – on the barber-stone, and on the pillars in Jarman's ancient temple. All he knew was he had to get away. He turned and ran out of the house.

Matthew started to run after him, but Sandra called after him before he reached the door. 'No, Matt,' she said sharply. 'Leave it to Su. If anyone can find out what's going on in his head, she can.'

But Su had already rushed past him into the hall. A moment later, they heard a loud bang as the front door slammed shut.

As Tom reached the edge of the circle, Dai appeared from behind one of the sarsens. 'It's no good running, boy,' he said in his mechanical voice. 'There's nothing you can do. He's inside you.'

'Get out of my way,' said Tom angrily.

Dai didn't move. 'You know me now, don't you, boy? And you know why we must meet at Litha?'

Tom stared at him, overcome by a sudden, inexplicable rage. He didn't know why, but he now knew for certain that this was his enemy, and that very soon they would have to do battle. 'Yes,' he heard himself saying. 'I will see you at Litha.'

Su, running up behind him, stopped and listened. She couldn't hear what Tom and Dai were saying, but something told her not to interrupt them. So she hid behind the next sarsen in the circle and took a photograph of them with her smartphone.

She waited till Dai had marched off in the direction of his cottage; then moved up behind Tom, who had remained rooted to the spot.

'Tom...' He whirled round and crouched down like a boxer in a defensive position. 'It's okay. It's only me.'

He seemed to relax a little. 'What are you doing here?' he asked suspiciously, in a strange, much older voice.

'I was worried about you. We all are. Why did you rush off like that?'

'Why don't you mind your own business?'

She moved closer to him. 'Come on – let's go back to the house.'

'No. It's not safe.'

'What d'you mean?'

'You and the others. You're all against me.'

'That's not true. We're your family.' She held out her hand. 'Come on – let's go.'

He backed away from her. 'Not yet. I have to get my head straight. And don't come looking for me.' He ran away into the darkness.

As soon as she got back to the Manor, Su rushed up to her room, plugged her smartphone into her computer and printed out the photograph she had taken of Tom and Dai facing each other at the edge of the circle.

But they weren't there. Instead, in the exact spots where they had been standing, there were two balls of brilliant white light.

Could there be something wrong with the image sensor? She froze the frame, pressed the print button and peered closely at the photograph.

In the centre of each ball of light, she could just make out the faint outlines of two figures, one taller than the other.

Dai and Tom? It had to be, because there was no one else around. And it had been a dark night, with no source of light anywhere near them. So how could they be surrounded by it?

CHAPTER SIX

SU PACED THE ROOM, wondering what to do. She couldn't tell Tom what the printout had revealed, because she didn't want to scare him. Nor could she show it to Matthew, for the same reason. She thought about taking it to her mother, but she wouldn't understand the danger Tom was in. Which left Adam.

She found him at his desk in the study, examining the sarcophagus-carving through a magnifying glass. 'Did you find him?' he asked anxiously.

'Yes. I told Mum and Matt.'

'Thank goodness for that. Where was he?'

'At the edge of the south inner circle. Having a row with Dai.'

'What about?'

'I don't know – I couldn't hear what they were saying. But for some reason they seem to hate each other.'

'Did he come back with you?'

'No. He said it wasn't safe.'

Adam frowned. 'Not safe? What do you suppose he meant by that?'

'No idea. But he told me he was okay, and not to look for him. He just wanted to get his head straight.'

'D'you think we ought to call the police?'

'No, Grandpa, that's the worst thing we could do. He'll come back when he's ready.'

'You'd better be right, young lady,' said Adam grimly, 'or you will incur my extreme displeasure.'

Su put the printout on his desk. 'I took this with my smartphone.'

He stared at it, puzzled. 'What's it supposed to be?'

'It's supposed to be Tom and Dai.'

'Must be something wrong with the camera then. I'll take it back to the shop I bought it from. It should still be under guarantee.'

He tried to hand it back to her, but she refused to take it. 'It's not the camera, Grandpa. Take another look – at the shadows in the middle of those two pillars of light.'

Adam picked up his magnifying glass and peered closely at the photograph. 'They look like filaments inside a couple of giant light-bulbs.'

'No, they've got to be Tom and Dai. It's exactly where they were standing when I filmed them.'

'Why would they be emitting light?'

'I don't know. But the camera never lies.'

'Of course it does. There was a photograph of some fairies in the nineteen-twenties which even Sir Arthur Conan Doyle believed was genuine. Needless, to say, it turned out to be a hoax.'

'This isn't a hoax,' said Su. She perched on the edge of the desk. 'I think Tom's being... I don't know... *inhabited* by something. An evil spirit.'

Adam frowned. 'You mean, this Jarman character?'

'Yes. That's what they used to believe in the old days, wasn't it? That people could be possessed by demons?'

'Those were old wives' tales. The poor women they burned or drowned as witches were probably suffering from mental illness.'

'There's nothing wrong with Tom's mind,' said Su. 'At least, there wasn't before he came to Milbury. I've always known there was something weird about this village. Things happen here that don't happen anywhere else. And you know it too, don't you?'

Adam, who had tried to shield her from the past, was shocked that he hadn't been successful. 'What makes you think that?'

'There are some things you won't talk about. Like Hendrick.'

He stared at her for a moment. Then he picked up the photograph of the two light-balls again and examined it more carefully through the magnifying glass. 'I don't believe in demons and evil spirits, Su. But I believe in evil men who can manipulate people's minds. So I suspect that these are man-made illusions.'

'If Jarman *is* a man.'

'Well he's certainly not a ghost. Matthew told me he contacted young Thomas before he left America.'

'But why would he be interested in Dai? He's lived here all his life.'

'I have no idea. All I'm concerned about is Tom. You know where he is, don't you?'

'I think so.'

'Then I want you to stay close to him and keep me informed.'

After Su had gone, Adam wrestled with his conscience. Had he dismissed her concerns too easily? Old Percy might claim to be the guardian of the Milbury sacred sites, but he considered it *his* duty to be the protector of its inhabitants. Yet when it came to his own grandson, all he could suggest was that they keep him under observation. But what else could they do? If this mysterious Jarman had managed to get inside the boy's head, they were in deep trouble.

Tom sat inside the Long Barrow, staring at the tip of the sun which had just appeared over Milbury Hill and shivering with cold. But at least the Barrow was outside the circle, and the massive stones which guarded the entrance gave him some protection. With his back against solid rock, no ghoulies or ghosties or long-leggity beasties could creep up behind him.

He watched through a gap in the stones as the sun's rays gradually spread across the countryside, trying to decide what to do. He didn't want to spend another night in this freezing tomb, but he would rather freeze to death than go back to the Manor. There was no one he could trust – not even his own family. They were all in it together.

But in what? – that was the question. Why were they all against him? Since his latest confrontation with Dai, he had sensed that the old man wasn't his only enemy: he was surrounded by them. And where had this savage, murderous rage come from? It was subsiding now, but he knew it would come back. And that he wouldn't be able to control it.

So was he trying to protect himself or his family? Was he hiding away because he was scared of the power that was growing inside him, and what it might make him do? How could he prevent it? He couldn't hide for ever. And he couldn't run away, because he had to be in Milbury on Midsummer Night, though he still had no idea why. Perhaps he should throw himself out of one of the Manor's upstairs windows, like the young woman who lost her lover in the Civil War. He buried his head in his hands, overcome by despair.

'Tom?'

It was Su's voice, calling from the track below the barrow. Tom stood up, crept back through the five stone chambers to the rear wall and sat down again.

'Come on, Tom. I know you're in there.' Her voice was closer now, calling from the entrance.

'Go away!' he called back. 'I want to be alone.'

He could hear her stumbling towards him through the outer chambers. Then she appeared, a black shadow in the dim grey light, and sat down beside him.

'Why d'you want to be alone?'

'Because I don't trust you. I don't trust anyone.'

'That's pretty hurtful,' said Su softly. 'I thought we had something going.'

'Well we don't. Keep away from me. I'm bad news.'

'You're ill, that's all. You need help.'

'Nobody can help me. I have to see this thing through.'

'What thing?'

'I don't know.'

She heard the despair, the hopelessness in his voice, and her heart went out to him. 'Talk to me, Tom. What's going on inside your head?'

It was a long time before he replied. 'It's like an old film,' he said eventually. 'I can't see it clearly, because it's too fuzzy. But it's getting clearer.'

'Are you in this film?'

'Yeah. I think I killed somebody.'

'That's ridiculous.'

'I know,' said Tom. 'I deny the existence of that which exists.'

'That doesn't make sense.'

'That's what I thought before I came here. Now it does.' He told her about the painting with the Latin legend that his father had found just before his first visit.

Su hugged her knees, trying to keep warm. 'What was in the picture?'

'People running away from a beam of light. Trying to escape from a stone circle. Looked like prehistoric Milbury.'

She reached out into the darkness and touched his arm. His skin was icy cold. 'Come on, let's get out of here. You *can* trust me, Tom. Whatever it is that's attacking you, I'll help you fight it.'

'How about the others?'

'What others?'

'Dad. Grandpa. Your mom.'

'They'll help you too.'

'No, they won't. I don't trust them.'

She pulled him round to face her. 'You *have* to trust them, Tom. Apart from me, they're all you've got.'

He peered at her, as if he was trying to read her thoughts in the half-light. Then he shrugged. 'Okay.'

He put his hand on the ground to lever himself up, but it closed on something sharp. A knife. And when he dug his fingers into the dust, he found other objects buried there: small bones, and shards of something that felt like broken pottery. He filled his pockets with them.

Outside the barrow, he laid out his finds on the grass. Su picked up the knife and examined it. 'Dai must have left this here when he moved to the cottage. He used to be a knife-grinder when he got too old for the poaching game.'

'What about this other stuff?'

'They're rabbits' bones. In the old days, the locals used them to foretell the future. I wouldn't be surprised if Dai still does. He's very superstitious.' Su picked up the pieces of pottery and filled the pockets of her anorak with them. 'I don't know what these are. Let's show them to Mum.'

They set off down the track towards the river. When they reached the spot where Dai had appeared on the opposite bank, Su stopped. 'This film in your head, Tom. Is Dai in it?'

He searched his mind. Snatches of a strange ceremony, which had been flickering fitfully in a corner of his memory, came back to him. 'You're all in it,' he said quietly. 'Dai, your mom, Grandpa, Dad – and you.'

'What are we doing?'

'Just standing around.'

'Where?'

'In the middle of the village. Surrounded by the stones. And a crowd of people holding flaming torches.'

'Sounds like the midsummer ceremony.'

'Litha?'

'Yes. It's an old pagan festival to celebrate the power of the sun. God knows why, because it usually rains.'

As they walked on, following the river towards the main road, Su produced the photograph of the two balls of brilliant light and handed it to him. 'What d'you make of this?'

He stopped and stared at it blankly. 'What's this?'

'Believe it or not, it's you and Dai.'

'Who took it?'

'I did.'

To her surprise, he flew into a rage. 'Been spying on me, have you?'

'No. I was just following you to make sure you were okay. And I saw you talking to Dai…'

'So you photographed us? I call that spying.'

Su moved up to him. 'Tom, it's *me* – I'm on your side, remember? I think this Jarman character's using you… taking over your mind. And we've got to stop him.'

He backed away from her. 'Going crazy, am I? Well suppose I am? What do you care?'

'I care very much. We all do.'

She tried to embrace him, but to her horror he drew the knife from his belt, his face contorted with fury. 'Stay away from me, or I'll kill you. I mean it.'

Dai suddenly appeared from the trees and snatched it from him. 'Quick, girl,' he snapped in his strange mechanical voice. 'The Sanctuary!'

Su turned and ran. Tom started to run after her, but Dai barred his way. 'Still haven't learned your lesson, have you, boy?' he growled. 'There's still evil in your heart.'

Tom flung himself at the old man and grabbed him by the neck. Dai grasped his wrists, slowly pulled his hands away and forced him down on his knees. 'That was very stupid,' he said softly. 'It will count against you at the reckoning.'

They were the last words Tom heard before he lost consciousness.

Adam and Matthew waited impatiently outside the wagon for Sandra to complete her examination. An ambulance and two paramedics had arrived with commendable speed after a tourist had found Tom sitting by the riverbank, dazed and disorientated, and dialled 999. As the paramedics reported that their preliminary tests didn't reveal any permanent damage, Matthew instructed them to take him to the Manor rather than a hospital, so that Sandra could give him a more thorough examination.

She appeared out of the wagon, carrying her medical bag. 'It's a mystery,' she announced as she walked down the steps. 'He doesn't seem to have any memory of what happened, but he's quite lucid. I suggest we keep him under observation for a few days, and if there's any deterioration in his condition, I'll organise another scan at the hospital.'

'Can I see him?' asked Matthew.

'Not now, Matt, let him sleep. I gave him some pretty powerful sedatives.'

Adam glanced at his watch. 'Time for lunch. Has anyone seen Su?'

'She called me from her mobile this morning,' said Sandra. 'She said she'd be back for lunch.'

'Back from where ?'

'I don't know. But her bed hasn't been slept in, and she didn't appear for breakfast. So I suspect she's been out all night.'

'Oh for heaven's sake – what's the matter with these children?' asked Adam grumpily. 'Why can't they stay put for five minutes? Or at least leave us a note, telling us where they're going?'

'Don't worry, Adam,' said Sandra grimly. 'Su and I are going to have a few words later. Trouble is, I'm supposed to take over at the museum in ten minutes.' She turned to Matthew. 'Matt – I wonder if you'd be an angel…?'

'Yes, of course. I'll track her down for you,' said Matthew. 'Tell Mrs Crabface I won't be in for lunch, Dad.'

Adam looked exasperated. 'Well don't *you* disappear. At this rate, I'll have no one to talk to by the end of the week.'

Matthew didn't have to drive the hired car far before he saw Su meandering down the Avenue towards the village. She didn't seem in any hurry: lost in her own thoughts, she was absent-mindedly flicking the long grass by the side of the road with a stick.

He pulled up beside her and opened the passenger door. 'You're in the doghouse, Su,' he told her. 'You'd better get in.'

She climbed into the car without a word, and Matthew did a U-turn before driving back towards the village. 'Your mum had to take over at the museum, so she asked me to…' He stopped abruptly as he saw that tears were rolling down her cheeks.

He pulled in to the side of the road, parked just inside the main circle and offered her his handkerchief. 'Hey – it's not that serious. We were worried about you, that's all.'

'Is Tom back yet?'

'Yes. He was driven back in an ambulance.'

Her eyes widened in alarm. 'Why? What happened to him?'

'He was found unconscious by the river. You don't know anything about that?'

'No,' she said, avoiding his eye. 'Sorry.'

'So where *were* you last night?'

'I went up to the Sanctuary to do some stargazing, and fell asleep.'

Matthew frowned and glanced at his watch. 'It's one o'clock. You slept all this time?'

To his astonishment, she started sobbing uncontrollably. Not knowing what to do, he switched on the engine. 'You must be hungry. Let's go and have some lunch.'

'No!' She put her hand on the steering wheel to stop him driving away. 'I don't want to go home yet.'

Matthew tried to think of some way to calm her down. 'Tell you what,' he said, opening the glove compartment and taking out the pocket magnetometer Adam had bought him just before their last visit over a quarter of a century ago. 'You want to help me re-measure the residual magnetism of the stones? One of them used to be so full of magnetite that when Dad threw a horseshoe at it, it stuck to the rock.'

Su wiped the tears away on her shirt-sleeve. 'What does that mean?'

'It might mean that some tremendous energy had passed through it.'

'Did you measure the others when you were a kid?'

'Dad did. You want to do that now? Then we could record any changes since then.'

'Okay.'

They got out of the car, and he showed her how to press the test edge of the magnetometer against the nearest stone. The needle immediately jumped to the right as far as it could go.

'Is that what happened last time?' she asked him.

'No,' said Matthew thoughtfully. 'None of the stones ever gave a reading as high as this.'

'So what d'you think caused it?'

'I've no idea. Let's try the next one.'

They moved on to the next stone... and the next... then all the way round the circle, with the same result. It was as if every stone had been struck by a gigantic lightning-bolt.

By the time they had finished, Su seemed to have forgotten whatever it was she was crying about. 'So what now? Are you going to write a letter to *The Times* or something?'

Matthew, who had started to wonder whether the stones were up to their old tricks, tried to hide his unease. 'Probably,' he told her. 'But first, let's see if it's affected the magnetic field.'

He went back to the car, took his pocket compass out of the glove compartment and brought it back with him, watching the dial. The moment he re-entered the circle, the needle swung round from north to south.

He glanced round at the village to make sure he hadn't lost his bearings. No, there was the main road to Swindon, which was certainly due north, yet the needle was still pointing in the opposite direction.

Su peered over his shoulder. 'That thing's gone mad. Did you get it out of a Christmas cracker?'

Matthew was too disturbed to reply. He took the compass out of the circle, and immediately the needle swung round to the correct position. But when he took it back again, it gave the same false reading. After he had repeated this test several times, with Su by his side also watching the dial, there was no longer any doubt: outside the circle, north was north. Inside it, north was south.

Su still wasn't convinced. 'That was really weird,' she said as they walked back to the car. 'There's got to be something wrong with your compass.'

Without much hope, Matthew searched for another explanation. 'Have you had a lightning storm here lately?'

'No. It's been a fantastic summer.'

He already knew that this would be a blind alley. A lightning storm intense enough to have caused a reversal of the circle's magnetic field would have been a worldwide story, and his father would certainly have mentioned it in his emails.

As he drove off, he wondered if the phenomenon might have something to do with Hendrick. Though the villagers were no longer in his thrall, was it possible that the sinister magus had left a terrifying legacy behind him? It might be over a quarter of a century after his death, but the circle's alignment wouldn't have changed. The enormous energy of Ursa XB1 would still be targeted on Milbury, and the rock-dish below the stone circle would still act as a receptor.

There was another disturbing possibility: that Hendrick was still alive. After all, his body had never been found. Suppose he still controlled the village from whatever continuum he inhabited? And suppose he had been reincarnated as Professor Jarman?

As an astrophysicist, Matthew knew that such fears were preposterous, but with his experience of the paranormal he couldn't afford to dismiss them.

Perhaps Jarman was right: perhaps science *was* a delusion.

Adam waited impatiently for the last visitors to leave the museum. When he walked in, Sandra had assumed it was because Su had turned up. Not yet, he had told her: it was about Tom. But it could wait till she was free.

She had tried to hurry the lingering tourists out, telling them several times that the museum was closing for the day and she was about to lock up, but a group of elderly Americans hadn't taken the hint. He waited impatiently as they kept plying her with questions about leylines, which they seemed to believe formed a worldwide grid system carrying psychic energy. Not for the first time, Adam wondered why she had taken such a thankless job.

He hadn't been to the museum since Margaret died, because it was too painful. She had been the curator when he first met her, and had to answer the same idiotic questions. Like her daughter, she had the patience of a saint, and she had even laughed at his feeble joke about schoolchildren having to write out a hundred leylines. The pain was less sharp now, but his heart still ached for her.

After what seemed like an age, the Americans left and Sandra collapsed into the chair at the reception desk, listening gravely as he told her about the conclusion he had come to: that Tom needed psychiatric help. Did she know of a good therapist?

She looked doubtful. 'I'm not sure that's such a good idea, Adam. Have you discussed it with Matt?'

'No. I thought I'd run it past you first.'

'Well I think we have to be careful. Sending a child to a psychotherapist can sometimes do more harm than good. It can be very traumatic.'

'Thomas is not a child,' said Adam. 'He's a young adult.'

'He seems perfectly sane to me.'

'I'm not questioning his sanity. I think he's suffering from some kind of demonic possession.'

Sandra frowned. 'Most psychiatrists don't believe such a condition exists. Diseases of the mind such as multiple personality disorder or schizophrenia, which people used to believe were signs of demonic possession, can be treated by medication these days.'

'I don't think this is a disease,' said Adam. 'I believe Tom's mind is being manipulated by an outside agency.'

'You mean – this Jarman person?'

'If it is a person. I looked up demonic possession on the internet, and Tom's behaviour since he came to England ticks all the boxes. A change in personality, a change in diet, sudden violence and abusiveness, nightmares and night-terrors…'

'But all these are symptoms of mental illness.'

'It still has to be treated.'

Sandra thought for a moment. 'Emily Foster. We were at medical school together, and she has a practice in Bath. I'll call her.'

'Thank you, my dear.'

She stood up, crossed over to the door and unlocked it. 'You'll have to get Matt's permission. And I'm not at all sure he'll go for it.' She stood aside, waiting for Adam to go out, but he stopped by a chart on the wall showing the stone circle and a network of lines radiating from it, each identified by a letter.

'What's this rubbish doing in a museum?' he said contemptuously. 'Leys have nothing to do with history or archaeology.'

'It's interesting rubbish,' said Sandra. 'If you extend these lines across a map of Europe, it's extraordinary how many sacred places they connect. This one, for instance – Line A – passes directly through Milbury, Stonehenge, Mount Olympus and Delphi in Greece, ending at the Giza pyramids in Egypt.'

Adam smiled. 'Yes, your mother showed me that. But what does it prove?'

'Maybe nothing. But our stone circles were constructed at roughly the same time as the Giza pyramids – about four and a half thousand years ago. And Milbury Hill was built to exactly the same specifications as the smallest of the Giza pyramids.'

'You're suggesting they were built by the same people?'

'It's possible. Mum must have shown you these artefacts.'

Adam followed her to a display case. Under the glass was a collection of small, beautifully carved silver and gold objects. 'These are ancient Egyptian charms, supposed to help dead people on their journey to the afterlife. They were found in the Long Barrow a few years ago.'

'Why didn't I hear about this?'

Sandra smiled. 'You're too far-sighted, Professor. You spend so much time looking at the stars, you can't see what's under your nose. Come on – let's check up on your grandchildren.'

There was no one around when Matthew and Su returned to the Manor, so Su announced that she was going to catch up on her sleep before the inevitable interrogation by her mother. Matthew went into the study and searched through Adam's desk for the notebook in which his father had recorded his initial magnetism measurements all those years ago. He was sure he would have kept it, because he never threw anything away. And there it was, gathering dust in a bottom drawer.

He leafed through the yellowing pages and checked the figures with the ones he had just recorded. The difference was astounding: in thirty years, the magnetism in the stones had increased by ten thousand per cent. Or had this happened since his return to Milbury? If so, there could be only one reason for the spectacular increase in such a short time: a burst of electrical energy must have passed through them very recently. The question was – what had caused it?

He rechecked the figures just to be sure, but there was no mistake. And he hadn't been mistaken about the polarity reversal either: his compass might be relatively cheap, but it had always given accurate readings.

The fact that there had been a polarity reversal inside the circle but not outside still made him uneasy. They were a rarity – only fifty or so in the last twelve million years – and none of them had been so localised. It didn't make scientific sense, but that was nothing new in this village. Something very disturbing was happening, not only to Tom, but to the stones.

Matthew poured himself a whisky, took it out into the garden and sat in one of the deckchairs. A polarity reversal anywhere in the world was newsworthy. Yet as far as he knew, none of the scientific journals had mentioned it, and there had been no reports issued by the main geological centres. Which raised a very unscientific question: did the Milbury circle have its own magnetic field, separate from the rest of the planet? Nobody knew much about them, so it wasn't completely off the wall.

Then another unscientific question occurred to him: could the change have affected the circle's alignment? Was it no longer aligned to Ursa XB1, but to something else? For the answer to that, he would have to recheck the angles of the stones: then persuade Adam to do a computer simulation in the observatory.

He sipped his whisky, remembering the day he and Adam had measured the angle of the stones with a home-made theodolite, and discovered that though they were different shapes and sizes their plumb-lines were all at a ninety-degree angle to the ground. This, together with his father's discovery that there was a giant magnetised rock-dish under the circle, had led to their startling conclusion that it was aligned *upwards* – to Hendrick's Supernova.

Now Tom, at the same age as Matthew was back then, had made a momentous discovery of his own: that under the plinth where the most sacred stone once stood was an ancient burial chamber. If it had been anywhere else – the mysterious American Stonehenge at Salem, New Hampshire, for instance, which was constructed at roughly the same time – he would have assumed it was a coincidence. But this was Milbury, where nothing happened by chance.

He glanced at his watch: what was he doing, drinking whisky and thinking about magnetic fields when his first priority should have been Tom? Ashamed of himself, he put down his glass and hurried round the house into the courtyard. Trying to make as little noise as possible in case Tom was asleep, he crept up the wagon steps. But when he opened the door, all he found was an empty bunk.

CHAPTER SEVEN

SOMEONE WAS SHAKING SU'S shoulder. She tried to brush the hand away, but it only shook her harder. 'Wake up, Khonsu,' said a voice she vaguely recognised. 'We have to talk to you.'

She sat up, still half asleep. Her mother was sitting on the bed, Adam and Matthew standing at the foot of it. All three of them looked extremely grim.

'Where's Tom?' asked her mother.

'I don't know. Isn't he asleep in the wagon?'

'No, he's disappeared. When was the last time you saw him?'

Su tried desperately to remember what she'd told Matthew, but for some reason her head was full of cotton wool. 'Last night, I think,' she told them.

'Where?' asked Adam.

'By the river. Then Dai told me to…' She stopped, realising this was leading her into deep water.

Matthew's expression became even grimmer. 'So Dai was there too?'

'Yes. I mean, I think so…'

'And what was it he told you to do?'

Just in time, the cotton wool began to clear. 'He didn't *tell* me to do anything,' she lied. 'He said it was a perfect night for stargazing, and the best view was from the Sanctuary. So that's where I went.'

'And you didn't see Tom after that?'

'No. I told you, Matt – I fell asleep.'

Su felt Adam's shrewd grey eyes boring into her. 'I asked you to keep an eye on him, Su,' he said reproachfully.

'I know, Grandpa. I'm sorry. I just fell asleep.'

Now it was her mother's turn. 'So you've no idea where he might be now?'

'No. But I think he might be hiding somewhere. He's very frightened.'

'Of whom?'

'All of us.'

The three of them glanced at each other. 'You can't have been stargazing all this time,' said Sandra. We've been very worried. Where have you been all day?

'Hanging out with Matt.'

'Well you can hang out at the Manor for a couple of days. You're grounded.'

'I did call you this morning, Mum. To let you know I was okay.'

'That's not why I'm grounding you, Khonsu. It's because I don't believe a word of your stargazing story.'

Adam moved to the door. 'I'll call the police.'

'Hold it, Dad,' said Matthew. 'Let me try something first.' He rushed out ahead of him. Sandra gave Su one of her you-haven't-heard-the-last-of-this looks and followed them.

A few minutes later, when Su joined them in the drawing room, she found Matthew sitting in a chair, his face buried in Tom's sweater. She was just about to ask what was going on when Sandra put her finger to her lips, warning her to keep silent.

Several minutes passed, marked by the ticking of the grandfather clock in the hall. Finally, Matthew spoke, his voice muffled by the sweater. 'I see a stone carving. A man trampling on a winged serpent…'

'The church!' said Adam. 'That's the carving on the pulpit.'

He headed for the door, but Su was there ahead of him. 'Let *me* talk to him, Grandpa. Please – it's important.'

Adam glanced at Matthew, who nodded. 'All right, Su. But bring him straight back.'

The church was close by, on the other side of the garden wall. Su ran out of the house, round the churchyard and through the lychgate. At the entrance, she paused and took a deep breath. Then she pushed the door open and went inside.

The church was in semi-darkness, illuminated only by a light above the stone pulpit. Tom was sitting in the front pew, staring at the carving on the front of it. She walked warily down the aisle and sat beside him.

Neither of them spoke. Su wasn't even sure he had registered her arrival. She waited apprehensively, prepared to run if this was the Tom who had threatened her with the knife.

'That's me treading on that serpent,' he said suddenly, pointing at the pulpit. 'Squashing the life out of it.'

Su breathed a sigh of relief. This was the real Tom, even though she had no idea what he was talking about. 'How did you get in?'

'The side door was open.'

She thought for a moment. 'Am *I* a serpent?'

'Maybe.'

'How about Jarman? Or the Count of St Germain, as he used to call himself. Is *he* a serpent?'

'I don't think so. He's just... fighting for justice.'

'What makes you think that?'

He shrugged. 'I just... know.'

She grasped his hand. 'We have to go back, Tom. Let them know you're safe.'

'Safe? I'm not safe yet. Not till after the reckoning.'

'The what?'

'That's what Dai said it was. The reckoning.'

Su took a moment to digest this information, but decided not to pursue it. 'What did you do with the knife?'

Tom looked mystified. 'What knife?'

She stood up. 'Come on, let's go. They're worried about you.'

Matthew was hovering anxiously outside the church. When Tom appeared, he was so relieved that he did something he had never done before: he hugged him.

'I'm sorry, Tommo,' he whispered. 'Tomorrow, we're going to get the hell out of this place.'

Tom pushed him away. 'No, we're not, Dad,' he said wearily. 'We can't.'

'Of course we can. There's nothing to stop us.'

'There's me.'

Su heard the steel in Tom's voice, but also the misery and despair behind it – as if he knew there was now no escape.

When they returned to the Manor, they found Mrs Crabtree complaining loudly to Adam and Sandra. 'I'll want overtime for this, Professor,' she was saying. 'I'm not hanging around all night, waiting for His Lordship to turn up. If he's late for dinner again, I'm going on strike.'

'You're quite right, Mrs C,' said Adam soothingly. 'I'll have a word with him. And I'll double your wages this week.'

Mrs Crabtree seemed mollified. 'I'll serve dinner now then. But I warn you – it'll taste like Santa's old socks. And I'll need a long lie-in tomorrow, so you'll have to get your own breakfast.' She went out, wagging her finger in Tom's face as she passed him.

During the meal – cheese and broccoli flan for Tom, spare ribs for the others – no one asked Tom where he had been before he visited the church. Su guessed that Adam and Matthew had agreed to let him have a good night's sleep before they interrogated him.

She watched him closely as he toyed with his food. Apart from his loss of appetite, he showed no sign of the sudden mood-changes which had so alarmed her. She noticed that her mother was watching him too, like a doctor assessing a patient.

Back in the drawing room after dinner, Tom produced the clay fragments he had found in the barrow and laid them out on the coffee table. Sandra started to fit them together like the pieces of a jigsaw. There were a few small pieces missing, but the fragments gradually formed a small disc with a winged serpent carved on it.

Matthew stared at it in astonishment. 'That's Dai's amulet,' he said to Sandra. 'But it should be in the museum. I took the pieces there, remember? Twenty-five years ago, after Dai… after he disappeared. They fitted with the pieces your mother already had – the ones they found under the barber-stone in the nineteen-thirties.'

'That's still in the museum,' said Sandra, peering closely at the serpent-carving. 'This one looks much older, possibly

Babylonian or Sumerian. Serpent-gods have been worshipped since the earliest civilisations.'

'I thought snakes were supposed to be the bad guys,' said Tom. 'They've got forked tongues, right? And it was a serpent that got Adam and Eve kicked out of the Garden of Eden.'

'That's true. But in other religions, they were the good guys. The Egyptians worshipped a cobra-goddess. And Ningizzida, the Sumerian fertility god, who was depicted as a serpent with a human head, was supposed to heal the sick.'

Matthew pointed to the broken clay disc. 'Does this have anything to do with Milbury's Solar Serpent?'

Sandra nodded. 'I'd be surprised if there wasn't some connection. There's a serpent carved onto the pulpit in the church. And another on the wall of the Long Barrow.'

'Winged serpents and winged fish-men,' said Su thoughtfully. 'How do you explain it, Mum?'

'I can think of only one explanation. If this amulet's as old as I think it is, it means that people from Mesopotamia were here long before the ancient Brits.'

The others digested this mind-boggling possibility in silence. Then Tom stood up. 'This stuff's doing my head in,' he announced. 'I'm going to bed.'

The silence continued after he had left. It was Adam who broke it, when he was sure he was out of earshot. 'So what are we going to do about the boy?'

Sandra opened a silver cigarette box and put the clay fragments into it. 'Let's see what the psychotherapist has to say.'

Matthew frowned. 'Psychotherapist? What psychotherapist?'

She looked startled. 'I'm sorry, Matt. I thought Adam had discussed it with you…'

'Nobody's discussed anything with me,' said Matthew angrily. 'I'm the one who'll decide what's best for my son.'

'Of course,' said Adam. 'No need to get upset, old boy. It was just an idea.'

'Well I've got a better one. I'll take him home.'

'That won't do any good,' said Su quietly. 'It's too late.'

Matthew frowned at her. 'What d'you mean?'

'Jarman – or whatever his real name is – has got control of Tom's mind. And he won't release him till he's done whatever it is he wants him to do. If you try to take him away before that, he could end up in a mental hospital.'

'You're not a doctor, Khonsu,' said Sandra sharply. 'You don't know what you're talking about.'

'Yes, I do, Mum. When Jarman's in his head, he thinks we're all his enemies.'

'He told you that?'

'Yes.'

'When?'

'Last night, before he passed out. He was hiding in the Long Barrow...'

'Ah!' said Adam. 'I thought that story about stargazing on Milbury Hill was complete baloney. What else did he say?'

'When I talked to him in the church, he said something about a reckoning. And he wouldn't be safe till it was over.'

'A reckoning?' Adam frowned. 'With Dai, perhaps – at Litha? Maybe that's what the old rogue meant when he shouted at Tom by the river. But it's very odd. They both seem to agree on two things – that they hate each other, and that it will all be sorted out on Midsummer Night.'

'If it's all in Tom's mind, I think a psychotherapist might be able to deal with it,' said Sandra. 'And my colleague Emily Foster specialises in young people's mental problems...'

Su jumped to her feet in exasperation. 'But it's *not* a mental problem, Mum – can't you see that? Most of the time, Tom's perfectly okay...'

Adam glanced at his watch. 'It's after midnight. I suggest we sleep on it, and talk again tomorrow.'

Early the next morning, when Matthew drew back the bedroom curtains, he saw Tom standing in the garden, staring up at the house. He opened the window and called down to him. 'Hi, Tommo. Have you had breakfast?'

'No,' he called back. 'Mrs Crabface is having a lie-in, remember? I was just going for a walk.'

'Hang on. I'll come with you.'

Matthew dressed quickly and hurried down to join him. 'What were you staring at?'

Tom shrugged. 'I was just wondering how high that top window was.'

'Why?'

'Some girl threw herself out of it after her boyfriend was killed in the Civil War.'

'I hope you're not thinking of doing the same.'

'I don't have a boyfriend.'

Matthew waited for the grin that usually accompanied Tom's jokes, but worryingly, it didn't come. 'Where were you going to walk to?'

'Dunno. Sandra said I should get some fresh air, so I was just following doctor's orders.'

'Tell you what – why don't we go round to Dai's cottage and ask him about that broken amulet?'

'Okay.'

'Stay here. I'll fetch the pieces.' Matthew ran inside and picked up the cigarette box. When he returned, he found Tom in the same position, still staring up at the house. They set off towards the cottage.

As they walked, he watched Tom out of the corner of his eye. The sun was already hot, but he slouched along with his head down and his hands stuck in his pockets, as if he'd been forced to take some exercise under duress. Was this just surly teenager stuff, or something else?

'Did you sleep well?'

'No.'

'Maybe you should take a pill tonight. I'll ask Sandra…'

'Forget it. It won't work.'

Matthew searched for a way to get through to him. 'Why did you hide in the Long Barrow? Who were you hiding *from*?'

'Myself.'

'What d'you mean?'

Tom stopped. 'Don't go there, Dad,' he said with quiet menace. 'Just don't go there.'

There was no reply when Matthew knocked on the door of Hawthorn Cottage. He walked round to the back and peered through the grimy windows, but there was no sign of him. 'Probably still asleep,' he said, when he rejoined Tom at the gate.

'No. I know where he'll be.'

'Lead on, then.'

Matthew followed Tom across the fields to the Disciples' camp. To his surprise, Dai was standing at the centre of the ring of tents, wearing his ceremonial white robe. The Disciples sat around him, listening intently to what he was saying.

He stopped speaking as they approached, as if he'd been caught doing something illegal. The Disciples turned to stare at them with curiosity, but Matthew noticed that they seemed more interested in Tom.

'What d'you want, Matthew?' asked Dai. The question was put politely, with none of his previous hostility. But there was no trace of their old friendship either. This wasn't Dai, the crafty poacher: it was Dai the Gaian priest.

'We had something to show you. But I can come back some other time...'

'No. I have no secrets from my people. Show me now.'

Embarrassed by the Disciples' silent stares, Matthew opened the cigarette box and handed him one of the clay fragments. 'These are pieces of an amulet which Tom found in your old home. We wondered if you knew where it came from.'

The old man's rheumy eyes flicked to Tom. 'Found it in the barrow, eh?' He produced a pair of wire-rimmed spectacles from under his robe, and examined the fragment. Behind the magnifying lenses, his eyes looked enormous. 'Why don't you ask the boy? He knows where this came from.'

'No, I don't,' said Tom. 'I've never seen it before.'

'Then you're not yet ready.' Dai handed the fragment back to Matthew. 'I'm sorry. I can't help you.'

'I'm sorry too. For interrupting your – er – whatever you were doing.'

'We were just communing with Gaia. Gathering together at sunrise to celebrate the coming of Litha.'

'Hail Gaia!' chorused the Disciples.

Matthew glanced at Tom, who was staring at Dai with undisguised hatred. 'We'll leave you in peace then.' He put the fragment back in the box and they started to walk away from the camp.

One of the Disciples called after him. 'Matt?'

Matthew turned. A thin, long-haired man of about his own age stood up, sauntered over to him and offered a grubby hand. 'Long time, no see, man,' he said with a dodgy American accent. 'How ya doin'?'

Matthew stared at him. Under the matted hair was a face he dimly recognised. 'Kevin?'

'Guilty as charged, your honour.' Kevin assumed a boxer's stance and punched the air. 'Fancy another fight?'

'I'm too old for that. What are you doing with this lot?'

'Following the Master. Dai's a great teacher, a new Maharishi. So this is your kid, right?'

'Yes. I gather you've already met him?'

Kevin avoided Matthew's eye. 'We were just introducing him to the earth mother. You into Gaia?'

'Not really.'

'You should be. She's all around us – in the trees, the rivers, the sky. We'll be communing with her at Litha. Why don't you join us?'

Matthew glanced round at Tom, who had almost reached the gate. 'I'll take a raincheck.'

'Yeah, you'll probably need one,' said Kevin. 'But come if you can, man. It'll be a gas.' He headed back to the camp, and Matthew hurried to catch up with Tom.

'What's going on, Tommo?' he asked as they walked back to the Manor. 'Why did Dai say you weren't ready yet?'

'He's the one who's not ready,' said Tom quietly. 'My uncle wasn't there.'

'What on earth are you talking about? You've only got one uncle, and he's back in the States.'

But no matter how hard Matthew pressed him, Tom refused to elaborate. Alarmed by his son's increasingly erratic behaviour, he decided he couldn't wait any longer: it was time to call in Sandra's psychotherapist friend.

He found Adam in the kitchen, making coffee and toast for breakfast. 'I'm sure you're right, old boy,' he said, when Matthew told him of his decision. 'It'll satisfy Sandra, and it might help Tom to fight this thing. So I took the liberty of asking Sandra to make an appointment with this woman. She can see him tomorrow afternoon.'

'She'll probably be out of her depth,' said Matthew miserably. 'If Jarman's behind it, there'll be nothing she can do.'

'She might be able to provide us with some data. Then there might be something *we* can do.'

'I still think I ought to take him away.'

'It's not the answer. We both know that.'

Two pieces of toast popped out of the toaster, and Matthew put them in the rack. 'I feel so helpless. It's not like before, when we could work things out and get ahead of the game. This time, we don't even know what the game is.'

'We have a few clues,' said Adam. 'That burial chamber, for instance. And that amulet. I don't think Tom discovered them by chance.'

'Neither do I, Dad. But try explaining that to someone who hasn't been through what we've been through. They'd probably have us certified.'

The percolator started to bubble, and Adam began pouring the coffee into the pot. 'There's something else,' said Matthew. 'I measured the magnetism in the stones yesterday, and I made two rather disconcerting discoveries.'

Adam went on pouring. 'Disconcerting? For whom?'

'For everyone in the village. But specially for us, because we know what we know.'

'All right,' said Adam, putting the lid on the coffee pot. 'Disconcert me.'

'There's been a polarity reversal. But only inside the circle.'

Adam started loading the breakfast tray. 'Don't be ridiculous, Matt. There's only one geomagnetic field, and it's worldwide, as you well know.'

'Make your own tests, Dad. You'll find I'm right.'

'I will. What was the other disconcerting thing?'

'When was the last time you measured the residual magnetism in the stones?'

'Six months ago. Why?'

'You didn't notice anything unusual?'

'No. There was no change from my previous readings.'

'Well there is now. The magnetism has increased by ten thousand per cent since I was last here.'

'That's impossible. What magnetometer were you using?'

'The pocket one you gave me when I was a kid.'

Adam smiled. 'Maybe it's time you bought a grown-up one. Or use my gradiometer. There's no way the level of magnetism could have altered that much in six months.'

'Yes, there is,' said Matthew quietly. 'but you're not going to like it.'

'Try me.'

'My guess is it has something to do with this Jarman character.'

'You're right. I don't like it.'

'Think about it, Dad. He knew we were coming back here. For some reason he's fixated about Tom, who's about the same age as I was on our first visit. Then, like Hendrick, he disappears without trace. And we know what happened last time there was an inexplicable increase in the stones' magnetism.'

To Matthew's relief, Adam finally seemed to take his theory seriously. 'As a matter of fact, I've made a few disconcerting discoveries myself lately,' he said, sitting on the edge of the kitchen table. 'A few months ago, my gradiometer found a thin vertical seam of highly conductive minerals in the centre of the main circle.'

Matthew frowned. 'So?'

'It appears to go deep into the earth. Well out of range of my machine.'

'And why is that disconcerting?'

'Suppose it goes down as far as the rock-dish?'

'I still don't... oh I get it. You think these minerals might act as an antenna. And together with the rock-dish, it might be able to receive radio signals.'

'It's a bit of a stretch, I admit. But I'm sure the dish played a part in Hendrick's jiggery-pokery. Think how much more powerful it would be with an antenna.'

They considered the implications of this in silence for a moment. 'This conductive seam,' said Matthew. 'D'you think it was here thirty years ago? If so, how did we miss it?'

'I didn't have a gradiometer then.'

'But how did everyone else miss it? Geologists have been nosing around this village for at least two centuries.'

'Because they wouldn't be looking for it. To find conductive minerals in sediments like chalk is highly unusual. I only discovered it a few weeks ago while I was measuring the stones' radioactivity and picked up an extra reading.'

Matthew put two more slices of bread into the toaster. 'Has the radioactivity in the stones increased?'

'Yes. By quite a lot, as a matter of fact. Not enough to harm anyone – I wouldn't have let you and young Thomas come if that was the case – but the Geiger counter recorded five micrograms of uranium per gram of rock.'

'How do you account for that?'

'I can't. We're back in the land of wild surmise, where heffalumps lurk.'

Matthew laughed. 'The good old heffalumps. They still haunt my blue remembered hills…'

'I'll tell you something else we missed on our first visit, Matt – how important the orientation of each stone was. They discovered a couple of years ago that the south poles of all the stones in the Avenue face the next stone in line as you move towards the circle. And the south poles of all the stones in the circle point to the next stone, in a clockwise direction…'

'Like a primitive grid system?'

'There's nothing primitive about it, Matt,' said Adam grimly. 'It's highly sophisticated. I'm going to do a paper on it.'

'In that case, will you help me do a computer simulation? I want to find out if the main circle is still aligned to Ursa XB1.'

'Of course.' Adam moved back to the breakfast tray. 'Now is that everything? Coffee, toast, butter, marmalade, saucers, plates…'

Matthew smiled. 'How about cups, Professor? Or are we supposed to drink out of flying saucers?'

Tom's stroppy mood hung like a pall over the breakfast table. Adam, Sandra and Su tried to include him in the conversation, but whenever they asked him a question he answered in monosyllables. Matthew, deciding that this was no time to mention the psychiatrist, invited him to watch the computer simulation he and Adam were about to conduct, but he wasn't interested. He didn't feel too well, he told them, so he would just hang out in the garden, reading and getting a tan. Su announced that she would spend the day finishing her essay.

After borrowing a theodolite from Sam Wakefield, the surveyor who gave the Manor a clean bill of health before Adam bought it, Matthew and Adam spent the morning checking the plumb-lines of the stones in the main circle. Then, up in the observatory, they fed the figures into the computer.

It soon became clear that the circle's alignment had changed. The stones' plumb-lines, if projected upwards as before, met at a completely different point in the galaxy. Whatever was causing this new disturbance, it wasn't Ursa XB1.

'Fascinating,' said Adam, when he had completed his calculations. 'The alignment would change a little every day, of course, due to the motion of the Earth round the sun and the rotation of its axis. But not nearly enough to explain this disparity.'

'So how *do* you explain it?' asked Matthew, punching buttons.

'I can't. But perhaps I was wrong to dismiss your theory that this Jarman fellow was responsible.'

'Welcome aboard, Dad.'

Adam moved over to the control desk. 'The question is – has this change of alignment occurred gradually, over a period of years, or was it caused by Tom's arrival?'

'You'd better not let your colleagues hear you talk like that,' said Matthew, his eyes on the monitor.

'It has a certain illogical logic, Matt. While Hendrick held sway here, the circle was aligned to his supernova – Ursa XB1. This new magus appears, and the alignment changes. Ergo, it's reasonable to hypothesise that he had something to do with it.'

'But why would he *want* to change it? Jarman hasn't had an imploding star named after him.'

'We can speculate about that when we know more about this new alignment.'

When Matthew had fed all the new coordinates into the computer, he hit the GOTO button, and the telescope slewed round to the requisite position. A magnified section of the galaxy appeared on the monitor.

'It's the Libra constellation,' said Matthew. Then, as he gradually increased the magnification, they recognised Gliese 581, the red dwarf.

'Well well well,' said Adam quietly. 'I think I know what lies at the end of this search.'

'So do I – a dead end. Because a red dwarf's uninhabitable.'

'Not the parent star... If I was a betting man, I'd put money on one of its orbiting planets. Gliese 581d.'

'Little Wolf?'

'Yes. The one that's capable of sustaining life.'

Sure enough, with maximum magnification, the telescope focused on the darkness beside the red dwarf, where Little Wolf was known to be.

It was some time before either of them spoke. 'Right,' said Adam briskly, leaning back in his chair. 'Let's assume that Jarman was somehow responsible for this change of alignment. And let's assume there's intelligent life on Little Wolf. There has to be some connection.'

Matthew started to pace round the observatory. 'What else do we know? We know there's a connection between Jarman and Tom. And between Tom and Dai. And we know there's to be some sort of reckoning at the midsummer solstice.'

'There could be another connection,' said Adam. 'That burial chamber. I've asked an archaeologist friend of mine to take a soil sample from it.'

Matthew stared at him. 'But that'll take weeks, maybe months...'

'No, it won't. He's on the board of the National Trust, so he can cut through all the red tape.'

'How soon can he do it? There's only a few days till midsummer…'

'I told him it was urgent. He's promised to do it tomorrow.'

'How long before we get his report?'

'He'll phone me with his findings. I told him it was top priority.'

After lunch, Matthew drew Tom aside. 'Get some sleep, Tommo. I'm afraid you've only got a few hours. We have to go to Bath this afternoon.'

Tom frowned. 'Why?'

'I'll tell you when I wake you.'

'Tell me now.'

'You have an appointment with a friend of Sandra's. A psychotherapist. There's nothing to worry about – we just want her to give you a checkup…'

Tom's eyes suddenly blazed with anger. 'So *you* think I'm going crazy too?'

'No, of course not. But we have to decide how to deal with Jarman. We've got to find a defence for you.'

Matthew waited for the explosion, but it never came. Tom turned and walked away towards the wagon. 'Okay, Dad,' he said over his shoulder. 'But you're wasting your money.'

When Matthew woke him a few hours later, he showered and dressed without protest. They climbed into the old banger and set off down the Avenue, lost in their own thoughts.

'Sorry about this, old chap,' said Matthew. 'It was Grandpa's idea.'

Tom shrugged. 'It's no big deal.'

As they approached the main road, he glanced in the nearside wing-mirror and his blood ran cold. A pair of eyes were staring at him – pale, translucent eyes which he immediately recognised.

He waited till the car stopped at the junction, his heart thumping. Then he wrenched the door open and jumped out. Ignoring his father's cry of alarm, he started to run back down the Avenue as if the hounds of hell were after him, feeling the terrible eyes boring into his back. He didn't stop till he reached the Manor, where he rushed up to Su's room, knowing what he had to do.

She wasn't there, so he sat down at her computer, switched it on and keyed in 'The Count of St Germain'...

Another construct. This time, a glittering palace. An elderly queen was sitting on a golden throne, addressing a tall, dignified man with a long grey beard. She was speaking French, but for some reason Tom had no difficulty in understanding what she was saying.

'Welcome to my court, Doctor Nostradamus. I understand you have been suffering from gout. I hope it does not pain you too much?'

'It is a cross I have had to bear for many years, your majesty,' said the old man. 'But soon I will be free of it. I haven't long to live.'

The Queen looked concerned. 'You can see your own death in your scrying glass?'

'Yes. I shall die next year – on the second of July.'

'You can see both the past and the future, Doctor?'

'The terms are meaningless, Madame. The future can sometimes lie in the past, while my own past is yet to come.'

'Quite,' said the Queen, looking bemused. 'Now the reason I have summoned you here is I that I have been reading your almanacs from last year, in which you hinted at threats to my family. I want to know more.'

Nostradamus looked uneasy. 'I regret that I am unable to be more specific. All I can tell you is that the danger is very real. And very close to you.'

'One of my courtiers?'

'Yes. The trouble is, I do not know them well enough. Perhaps one of them also has the gift? If that is the case, we might be able to identify the threat together.'

Then please make your choice, Doctor.'

The old man walked slowly round the ring of courtiers, staring intently into their faces. Then he touched one of them on the arm. 'This man has the gift. I will lend him my scrying glass.'

Back in Su's room, Tom gasped. The pale eyes of the man he had selected were unmistakeable. It was Jarman.

Nostradamus produced a small round mirror from his coat pocket and handed it to him. 'Tell us what you see.'

The court held its breath for several minutes, while Jarman gazed into the mirror. 'I see a man with murder in his heart,' he said suddenly. 'He intends to kill Her Majesty.'

As Jarman handed him the mirror, Tom glimpsed a face frozen in it – the face of a black-bearded man with a pearl earring. Nostradamus climbed up to the throne and showed it to the Queen.

'This is the man, your Majesty.'

'The Duke of Guise!' she cried. 'Seize him!'

The courtiers drew their swords and surrounded the black-bearded man. He backed away from them, producing a dagger from inside his doublet. 'You are a traitor to your religion, you old crone,' he shouted at the Queen. 'Marrying your daughter to a Protestant – you deserve to die!' He stabbed himself in the chest and fell to the floor.

The Queen came down from the throne, glanced contemptuously at his body and turned to Nostradamus.

'I owe you my life, Doctor. You shall have a title.'

'No, Madame,' said Nostradamus, pointing at Jarman. 'Here is the man who deserves a reward.'

'What title do you suggest?'

Nostradamus smiled. 'Well, as your Majesty's court is residing at St Germain-en-laye for the summer…'

'An excellent idea.' The Queen turned to one of the courtiers. 'Give me your sword.'

The courtier handed her his sword and she moved to Jarman. 'Kneel, Henri.'

Jarman knelt, and the Queen touched him on each shoulder with the sword. 'In future, you shall be known as the Count of St Germain.'

Su opened the door, to find Tom sitting at her computer, staring at a blank screen. Thinking her watch had stopped, she glanced at the bedside clock. No, it was the middle of the afternoon, when he should have been keeping his appointment with the therapist.

Remembering Tom's violent reaction when she tried to wake him from his previous catatonic state, she called to him softly. 'Tom? What are you doing here? Shouldn't you be in Bath?' He turned to her, his face as blank as the screen.

Then, as he recognised her, he seemed to relax. 'He didn't want me to go to the therapist.'

'Who didn't want you to go?'

'Jarman. The Count of St Germain.' He told her about the hypnotic eyes in the car's wing-mirror, the sudden compulsion to get to a computer.

Su sat on the edge of the bed. 'So he wanted you to know how he got his title,' she said thoughtfully. 'I wonder why.'

Before he could reply, heavy footsteps thundered up the stairs and Matthew burst in. 'What's going on, Tom?' he demanded angrily. 'I've been looking for you everywhere.' He glanced at his watch. 'Come on – if there's not too much traffic, we can still make the appointment.'

Tom avoided his eye. 'No, Dad – I'm staying here. I can't leave the circle.'

'What d'you mean – can't? Who's stopping you?'

'Jarman.'

Matthew stared at him in horror. So it was all happening again: another magus blocking their escape from this benighted village. 'Why does he want you to stay here?' he asked gently, his anger subsiding.

'Because it's ordained.'

'By whom?'

'I don't know.'

Matthew glanced helplessly at Su, who was looking equally horrified. 'If you can't leave the circle, perhaps we can persuade the therapist to come here. How about that?'

Tom shrugged. 'Do what you like, Dad. It won't change anything.'

Su caught Matthew's eye and nodded towards the door, indicating that she wanted him to go. So he left them alone and walked slowly down the stairs in despair, with Tom's last chilling words reverberating in his head.

Sandra was waiting anxiously in the hall. He told her about Tom's reaction to his suggestion that the therapist might be able to come to Milbury. 'She won't be able to save him,' he said, tormented by guilt. 'I know that now. There's no defence against this... this monster!'

She put her arms round him. 'Have you got a better idea, Matt?'

'No.'

'Then let's see what Emily can do. I'll call her and explain the situation. I'm sure it's not the first time one of her patients has missed an appointment.' Sandra crossed to the phone, picked up the handset and started to dial.

Upstairs in her bedroom, Su was sitting crosslegged on the floor. Tom was staring moodily out of the window. 'Okay, let's go through this again, Tom,' she was saying. 'Jarman doesn't want you to leave the circle. And he doesn't want you to see a psychiatrist. So what d'you think he's scared of?'

It took him some time to reply, and when he finally spoke his voice had changed. 'He is not scared,' he rasped. 'He just doesn't want anything to go wrong.'

'At the reckoning?'

'Yes.'

Su hesitated, knowing she was no longer talking to Tom and wondering if she should address Jarman directly. She decided to pretend she hadn't noticed the change of voice. 'This last construct, showing how he got his title. D'you think it was to prove that he's not an evil man?'

Tom turned away from the window. 'He's not a man.'

'So what is he?'

'He was known as a god.'

'*What!*'

'He committed a crime, but he has paid for it. It is time he was released.'

Su stood up, moved close to him and gazed into his eyes. 'Am I talking to Tom – or Jarman?'

He smiled an un-Tom-like smile. 'You cannot tell the difference?'

'Well... you do have a different voice.'

'That is disappointing. It means I have not yet achieved a complete symbiosis.'

Downstairs, Sandra joined Matthew in the drawing room. 'I've told Emily it's an emergency,' she said, flopping onto the sofa beside him. 'She's coming tomorrow morning.'

'It'll be a wasted journey,' said Matthew, 'and it's forty-eight hours to midsummer. What are we going to do?'

Hearing the desperation in his voice, she tried to reassure him. 'I'm sure Emily will be able to help him. She's very experienced.'

'You don't understand what we're up against, Sandra. It's not a psychiatric problem.'

'What else could it be? Whatever this mindbender has done to Tom can be undone.'

The intercom by the door buzzed. Matthew turned, to see the observatory button flashing. He crossed over to it and picked up the handset. 'Yes, Dad?'

Adam's voice sounded worried. 'Can you come up here, Matt? I've been doing some calculations, and something rather disturbing has turned up.'

'On my way.' Matthew turned to Sandra. 'You might as well hear this.'

They hurried into the hall, where they were confronted by Mrs Crabtree. 'There's not much left in the larder,' she said grumpily. 'Is somebody going to do some shopping any time soon?'

'Not today, Mrs C,' said Sandra. 'We haven't got time. Call the supermarket and ask them to deliver whatever you need.'

'They'll charge extra for that. It's twenty quid to come all the way out here.'

'I know. Just do it.'

'All right, there's no need to bite my head off.' She shuffled away, and Matthew and Sandra hurried up the stairs.

Su walked slowly down the road towards the outer circle with a heavy heart. Tom was losing his battle to keep Jarman out of his mind. Soon there would be nothing left of him, and the handsome young face would be a mask behind which a centuries-old man was hiding. It was unbearable.

But Jarman – if that's who she had been talking to – had lowered his guard during their last conversation, and seemed to have dropped an important clue. This had given her an idea about what might be going on, but it was something so weird that she couldn't share it with anyone till she had assembled all the pieces of information and tried to fit them together. She had learned from Adam that every theory had to be rigorously tested before it was offered to the public.

The first stop in the testing process had to be Dai. As far as she knew, he was the only other person in the village who had changed since Tom's arrival, and he had intervened to save her when Tom/Jarman had threatened her with the knife. Jarman and whoever was controlling Dai's mind seemed to be enemies – and as someone once said, the enemy of my enemy is my friend.

She was about to turn off into the narrow road leading to Hawthorn Cottage when she saw Dai in the distance, standing by the obelisk plinth in his white robe. He was gazing up at the sky, with both hands on the plinth, oblivious of the passing tourists who had stopped to stare at him.

As she walked towards him, she saw that he was muttering some sort of incantation. She joined the group of tourists and listened.

It wasn't easy to hear what he was saying, because he had lowered his mechanical voice to little more than a whisper. But she could just make out a few key words…

'Wise Ones… Apsu… all prepared… circle sanctified… judgment may be passed…'

There was more of this disjointed mumbo-jumbo, and the tourists started to giggle. '*Il est druide*,' explained a Frenchman to his wife, tapping his head meaningfully. '*Totalement fou.*'

Dai rounded on him with sudden fury. 'I'm not a druid, you ignorant barbarian! Go about your business! Go on, all of you – leave me in peace!'

The tourists scattered, and he turned to Su. 'What d'you want, girl?'

'This reckoning at Litha. I want to know what it's all about.'

The fire in his eyes slowly died, to be replaced by something that startled her. There was wisdom there – an ancient, primordial wisdom which she'd never seen in him before. Had something happened to him since she and Tom visited him in his cottage – something that made him take his priestly duties seriously?

When he spoke again, his voice had become more human. The Welsh lilt had returned, and it no longer sounded as if it had been filtered through a machine. 'You will know soon enough,' he said quietly. 'You will be part of it.'

Su stared at him, overcome by a sense of dread. '*Me?*'

'You, me, the boy, your mother, your grandfather, and Matthew. You will all be involved.'

'Why?'

'Because the boy needs you.'

'You mean, Jarman needs us?'

'No,' said Dai coldly. 'It's the boy who needs you.'

'Suppose we don't want to be involved?'

He put his hands on her shoulders. 'You want to save him, don't you?'

'Of course.'

'Then you will be there.'

He walked away, but she called after him. 'You know who's buried under the obelisk, don't you?'

He stopped and turned back. 'Yes. But that is none of your concern.'

'Was he murdered?'

The question hung in the summer air like an invisible cloud. Dai remained perfectly still for a moment, seeming to commune with a higher authority. Then he moved back to the plinth. 'Come here, girl. Put your hands on this stone and close your eyes. Whatever happens, keep your hands on the stone.'

Su hesitated. Was the old man as benign as he appeared, or was this another mind game? But as it seemed to be the only way of finding out what she wanted to know, she did as she was told.

At first, she felt nothing. Then the stone began to grow warm. It became warmer and warmer – until it was so hot she thought the heat would burn right through them. But she forced herself to keep them there until she no longer felt the heat.

All she could see through her closed eyes was a swirling mist. Then, through the mist, glimpses of a dark, barren land. There were no trees, no fields, no houses – just a circle of massive stones. And on the spot where she was standing, another stone, taller and thinner than the rest, dominated the bleak countryside.

The obelisk. This, she knew, was what the circle must have looked like at the dawn of time.

A few metres away, strange-looking creatures with human arms and legs but fish's heads were digging a deep pit – not with spades or drills, but with huge metal scoops that cut through the earth as if it was butter. When the scoops were full, they were passed up through a chain of fish-creatures to the surface.

Then the casket which she had seen in Adam's photograph was lowered into the pit, and two more fish-creatures arrived with a prisoner bound in chains. He was led to the edge of the pit and his captors lifted him up, about to throw him into the pit. But another of the creatures appeared and seemed to intercede for him. The prisoner was led away again and the diggers started to rain scoops of earth down onto the casket.

The images faded, and the stone grew cold. Su took her hands off it and turned, to find Dai scrutinising her face.

'I have shown you all you need to know for the moment,' he said in his answering-machine voice. 'Now you must prepare yourself for what is to come. And you must use this knowledge wisely.'

She stared up at the old man. No, she had not been mistaken. He had changed into a genuine shaman since she last saw him – just as Tom was changing into Jarman. But what did it mean? And why did they hate each other so much?

'Just one more question, Dai. Will Tom be in danger at the reckoning?'

'It depends on what is decided.' Dai started to walk away again, and again she called after him.

'Who are the Wise Ones of Apsu?'

'That is two questions.' This time, he kept walking.

Sandra watched tensely as Matthew stared through the telescope's eyepiece. 'What am I supposed to be looking at?' he asked Adam, who was sitting at the control panel. 'I can't see anything particularly disturbing.'

'Those are the coordinates of Gliese 581d. Little Wolf.'

'So?'

'I've been in touch with the Ames Research Laboratory in California. They've just done a detailed spectroscopy of it with their infrared detectors, and they tell me it's started to emit radio signals.'

Matthew took his eye away from the telescope. 'Since when?'

'A couple of days ago.'

'Where is it now?'

'Behind Gliese 581, its parent star. And guess when it's due to re-emerge?'

'Midsummer?'

Adam nodded grimly. 'At midnight.'

Sandra looked mystified. 'Okay, so Little Wolf has started to emit signals. What's that got to do with anything?'

'We have no idea,' said Matthew. 'But knowing what we know, we don't think it's a coincidence.'

'What is it that you know?' But they were both too preoccupied to answer.

'The problem is,' said Matthew thoughtfully, 'we haven't got much data to go on. So it's not like before. We knew a lot about black holes, but Little Wolf's still a mystery.'

Adam stood up. 'That's not quite true, Matt. We know it's a watery planet, capable of supporting life. And what species lives in water?'

Matthew's throat suddenly felt dry. 'Oh come on, Dad. That's not science – it's science fiction.'

Before Adam could reply, Su burst in. 'What have you done with Tom's laptop?' she demanded breathlessly.

'It's in my bedroom,' said Matthew. 'Why?'

'I just want to check something. What are you doing up here?'

Adam told her about the report from NASA's infrared laboratory, leaving her to draw her own conclusions.

'Yes,' she said thoughtfully. 'It fits.' She rushed out again.

Sandra was becoming fed up with being ignored.

'Would one of you please tell me what on earth you're talking about?'

'Later, Sandra,' said Adam, still preoccupied. 'First, we have to find the answer to this conundrum.'

Su carried Tom's laptop into her room, sat down at her desk and switched it on. She waited impatiently for it to boot up – 'Come on, come on, you stupid thing,' she told it – and scanned the icons on the desktop. When she clicked on 'Milbury Construct', the file opened to reveal the original program which Tom had shown her.

She pressed the START button, and watched as Tom's avatar began to plod round the circle. 'You must use this knowledge wisely,' Dai had told her. But she needed to know more – much more – and quickly. At the moment, she only had two pieces of the puzzle, and she was sure this construct would provide another. The virtual reality temple which Tom had described had to be a clue.

But strangely, the end of the program didn't match his description. When the avatar reached the barber-stone and froze, the picture then dissolved, not into an ancient temple, but into the Milbury circle as it must have looked when it was first built, thousands of years ago: sinister black shapes dominating a bleak, barren land.

In the centre of the circle were seven stone thrones, six of which were occupied by black-robed fish-creatures. At their feet, a prisoner was kneeling, his hands and legs in chains, flanked by two guards. They seemed to be passing judgment on the prisoner, because one by one they stood up and silently addressed him. He bowed his head, seeming to accept his fate. Then the guards pulled him to his feet and dragged him away.

The picture then dissolved back to the frozen avatar, and Su tried to make sense of what she had seen. Had this been part of the construct Tom had told her about? If so, why hadn't he mentioned the trial, or whatever it was? And why wasn't Jarman there?

But perhaps he *was* there? Could he have been the prisoner or one of the judges? There was definitely a connection between the trial and the images she had seen when she touched the stone. The prisoner who had been dragged away by the guards had apparently been sentenced to be buried alive in the pit. And just as the sentence was about to be carried out, he had been reprieved.

Su shut down the laptop and switched on her own computer. Another piece of the puzzle had slotted into place, and, dimly, she began to see the whole picture. Was that what Dai had intended her to see? Perhaps her theory wasn't so weird after all. It was time to do some in-depth research on the internet to see if it stood up.

Sandra stood by the drawing-room window, wondering what was going on up in the laboratory. Why were Adam and Matthew talking about some distant planet when they should be concentrating on Tom? And what was it they weren't telling her?

Even Su seemed to be in on the secret. 'It fits,' she had said, when Adam told her about NASA's report. Fits with what? It was as if they were all talking in code.

Outside, Tom appeared with the little paddling pool which Su had splashed around in as a child. Sandra watched as he put it down in the middle of the lawn and started to fill it with water from the garden hose.

She wondered why he'd taken the trouble to take it out of the shed and blow it up. If he'd wanted to cool his feet, he could have gone down to the stream at the bottom of the garden. But it seemed he wanted more than a paddle, because when the pool was full he took off all his clothes and lay down in it, turning his face towards the sun.

Was now the time to break the news of Emily's visit? It was going to be tricky enough, but Tom's nakedness made it even trickier. Should she wait till he'd got dressed again? No, better to get it over.

She had no idea how Tom would react. If he was suffering from some sort of possession syndrome, it was quite possible he would become violent, in which case the fact that he was naked might be an advantage. People were more vulnerable without their clothes.

She fetched a deck chair from the shed and set it up by the pool. Tom watched her warily, but made no effort to cover himself.

'It's going to be hot today,' she said pleasantly. 'I wish we had a proper pool.'

He splashed water over himself. 'So do I.'

She suddenly noticed that he had a patchwork of tiny semi-circular white lines all over his body. She stared at it, puzzled. 'How long have you had that rash?'

'Since this morning.'

'Does it itch?'

'No.'

She reached out to touch his shoulder, but he shrank away from her. 'Don't. I don't like being touched.'

'Sorry.' Sandra stared at the pattern of interweaving lines, wondering what it was. Some kind of acne, caused by hypertension? 'I think we ought to keep an eye on it, Tom. If it hasn't gone by tomorrow, perhaps you should see a dermatologist.'

'No, forget it. I'll be okay.'

'How d'you feel?'

'Fine.' He hesitated. 'Except…'

'Except what?'

He splashed water over himself again. 'It's not important.'

'It could be. Tell me.'

'I feel… different, that's all.'

'What d'you mean?'

'I can't explain. Just… different.'

'And when did this feeling start?'

'Yesterday.'

'Does it worry you?'

'Not particularly.'

But it obviously did worry him, thought Sandra. And if he'd been bottling it up, this strange skin-rash could be a psychosomatic reaction. But that was Emily's department, and it was time to prepare him for her visit.

'I've arranged another appointment for you with the therapist,' she said. 'She's coming here tomorrow.'

Tom stared at her suspiciously. '*Here?*'

'She's just going to make an assessment. See if you need medication.'

'Medication? What for?'

'I think you may be suffering from some kind of mental disturbance. I'm afraid it's quite common in young people these days. They spend too much time at their computers…'

Tom's voice suddenly sounded like a creaking door. 'You don't know what you're talking about, woman,' he snapped. 'Don't interfere!'

Sandra stared at him, shocked. 'Why are you speaking like that?'

'Like what?' he asked in his normal voice.

She decided not to probe any deeper. She had read somewhere that short-term amnesia was a symptom of multiple personality disorder, but that was beyond her competence. Emily could make her own diagnosis.

'Please don't think of this therapist as your enemy, Tom,' she told him. 'She only wants to help you.'

His eyes seemed to be bulging slightly as they stared at her. 'How d'you know?'

'Because she's a friend of mine. And she's cancelled all her appointments to come and see you.'

Tom slid down into the pool and submerged his head in the water. Sandra waited for him to come up for air, but he stayed underwater for about three minutes, until bubbles started to float up to the surface.

As Su climbed up to the observatory, she could hear Matthew and Adam's muffled voices discussing something with great urgency. Expecting a frosty reaction to what she had to tell them, she took a deep breath and opened the door.

They were sitting at the telescope's control panel, studying the printout of a star chart. 'What is it, Su?' asked Adam impatiently. 'We're busy.'

'I've got an idea about what's going on,' she said, sitting sideways on the viewing chair. 'But it's pretty wacky.'

The two men glanced at each other. 'We're not averse to wackiness,' said Matthew. 'Let's have it.'

'Remember that stuff I got from the net about the Sumerian gods – the Anunnaki? Anu being killed by his grandson, and being condemned to wander the earth till he'd atoned for his crime? I've been checking out the other early mythologies – Babylonian, Egyptian, Persian and Greek – and they all have variations on the same legend.'

'That's all very interesting,' said Adam impatiently, 'but what's its relevance?'

'Suppose it really happened?'

'*What!*'

'The Dogon believed that superbeings from another planet landed on earth at the dawn of time. Suppose they were right? For primitive tribes, fish-people must have seemed like gods. That could be why all those Sumerian carvings of them have wings.'

The silence was deafening. Su knew what they were thinking – that she'd been watching too many fantasy DVDs – but it didn't matter what they thought. Her theory fitted all the data, and for Tom's sake she couldn't keep it to herself.

At least Matthew seemed prepared to give her a hearing. 'So your theory is that one of these extraterrestrials killed his leader? And when they went home, they left him behind as a punishment?'

'Yes. If I'm right, he's been around for thousands of years, calling himself the Count of St Germain. Now he calls himself Jarman.'

The men glanced at each other. 'What's all this got to do with Milbury?' asked Adam.

'I have a theory about that too. It's where their leader's buried. I think his body's in that casket.'

'But why would they bury him *here*? Why not in Mesopotamia or Africa?'

'Because this place was sacred to them. Mum says it could be the oldest sacred place in the world – even earlier than the Sumerian temples.'

'We should be able to confirm that,' said Adam, 'when we get the report on the soil-sample.'

Matthew stood up and moved over to Su. 'Let me get this straight. Your theory is that five thousand years ago, Jarman, or whatever his real name is, committed a murder at Milbury, and he's been wandering round the world ever since. So why doesn't he look like a fish-man?'

'I've been wondering about that,' said Su. 'He obviously has the ability to inhabit human bodies. Maybe they all do. His own must be falling apart by now, which is why he needs Tom.'

Matthew stared at her, wondering how much of all this he should take seriously. 'You mean, Tom might be stuck with him for the rest of his life?'

'No, I don't think so. It's only for the reckoning.'

'And what's that all about?'

'My guess is it's a meeting of Jarman's judges to decide whether to let him come home.'

'Time off for good behaviour,' said Adam drily, 'after thousands of years. Maybe we should send *our* murderers to *their* planet.'

Matthew sat down again. 'Okay, suppose you're right, Su. Whose bodies d'you think the judges are going to inhabit?'

'Ours.'

'*Ours?*'

'Dai told me we all had to be involved. All six of us.'

Matthew shuddered. 'You mean, we're going to be inhabited by fish-people? Ugh!'

'I think one of them's already inhabiting Dai. It would explain why he's changed since you've been here. This morning, he was looking up at the sky and talking to the Wise Ones of Apsu – that's a Sumerian word meaning "the House of the Watery Deep". According to Babylonian mythology, there were seven Wise Ones – believed to be gods because of their long life-spans.'

'Seven Wise Ones,' said Matthew, 'but only six of *us*. It doesn't compute.'

'Yes, it does. Because if I'm right, the seventh Wise One is dead.'

'But where's your evidence for all this, Su?' demanded Adam. 'At the moment, it's all smoke and mirrors.'

'There's circumstantial evidence, Dad,' said Matthew. 'The radio signals from Little Wolf – and the timing of its reappearance.'

'When's that going to happen?' asked Su.

Adam glanced up at the open roof. 'At midnight, the day after tomorrow. The summer equinox.'

She thought for a moment. 'The question is – if they decide not to let Jarman go home, what will happen to Tom?'

'My God yes!' said Matthew in sudden alarm.

'Suppose that maniac tries to carry out his threat to destroy him? We can't risk that.'

Sandra appeared. 'Sorry to interrupt,' she said, 'but there's something you should know.'

She told them about Tom's mysterious rash. 'I've never seen anything like it before. It could be nerves – the prospect of being psychoanalysed obviously frightens him – but I think it should be looked at by a dermatologist.'

'Oh no!' said Su softly. 'Please – no!'

Sandra frowned at her. 'What d'you mean – no? It could be infectious.'

'Jarman told me something this morning, through Tom. He said he hadn't yet achieved a complete symbiosis. So it might not be a rash. It could be Tom's skin turning into Jarman's.'

Matthew banged his fist on the control panel. 'This can't be happening! It just can't!'

'Of course it can't, Matt,' said Sandra soothingly. 'Demonic possession – if there is such a thing – affects the mind, not the body.'

'But Jarman isn't a demon. He's some sort of magus with paranormal powers.'

'I don't believe in all that nonsense. I believe in the power of medicine. Anyway, who is Jarman? Another Hendrick? And who was Hendrick, come to that? Why has the subject always been off limits?'

Matthew glanced at Adam. 'I think it's time we told her, Dad. And it ought to come from you.'

Adam sighed. 'I suppose so,' he said reluctantly. He paused for a moment, searching for the right words. 'This won't be easy for you, Sandra. I've hidden it from you all these years, because I wanted you to lead a normal, happy life. I know that what I am about to tell you contravenes every scientific principle, but I assure you it's the truth, the whole truth and nothing but the truth…'

He told her what Matthew had 'seen' the night Sandra and her mother had gone to dinner with Hendrick, which had been erased from her memory. Holding her scarf, he had used his gift for psychometry to see what Sandra was seeing – the view from the window of this very room as she watched the chanting villagers form a chain round the Manor to celebrate the imminent conversion of two more 'Happy Day'ers. He had even felt what Sandra was feeling – her terror as the observatory roof had rolled back to allow the power of Ursa XB1 to do its work. Finally, he told her how he and Matthew had managed to escape the same fate by altering Hendrick's atomic clock.

When he had finished, it was some time before Sandra spoke. 'If this had come from anyone else, I'd have had them sectioned,' she said softly. She turned to Matthew. 'So this is why you haven't been back since, Matt?'

'Yes.'

'And you think Jarman's another Hendrick?'

'No. He has different powers and a different agenda.'

'Which is?'

'We're not sure,' said Adam. 'But Su has a theory, and it's the only one that makes any kind of sense. As Sherlock Holmes said, "When you have eliminated the impossible, whatever remains, however improbable, must be the truth."'

Emily Foster arrived early the next morning, just as they were finishing breakfast. Sandra hadn't cancelled the appointment, because they had messed her about too much already. And what had they got to lose by allowing Tom to be examined by a specialist?

Emily hadn't changed much, she thought, as she let her in. A few more lines round the eyes, but her long blonde hair didn't look as if it had needed any help from a bottle. She was still the honeypot around whom the male medical students had swarmed.

'I wanted to talk to you before I get started,' said Emily briskly. 'Get up to speed with – Tom, is it?'

'Yes. Let's go into the study. Coffee?'

'Thanks. Black, no sugar.'

After Sandra had asked Mrs Crabtree to bring the coffee, she led Emily down the corridor to the study and closed the door. 'I've never believed in demonic possession,' she said, as they sat in the window seat. 'but someone has really got into Tom's mind. He seems haunted by an old man called Jarman.'

'Do we know who he is?'

'Yes. Apparently, he was a real person who used many different names. And when Tom's under stress, he speaks in his voice.'

'*Was* a real person? So he's dead?'

'We're not sure,' said Sandra evasively.

'What sort of things does he say?'

'He warns people not to interfere. And there's something else. Tom has a strange rash all over his body which I can't identify. I'd like a second opinion.'

'Tell me about his background.'

'He's an American. English father and an American mother. They're divorced.'

'That might be something to do with his mental state,' said Emily. 'Does he become violent?'

'Not so far. But there's violence inside him. I can see it in his eyes.'

'I'll need a panic button then.'

'The bell's by the door. And we'll stay within earshot.'

Mrs Crabtree appeared with two cups of coffee on a tray. 'There you are, ducky,' she said, as she handed one to Emily with a shaking hand. 'Nice hair.'

Emily looked surprised. 'Thank you.'

'You should've met my husband. He liked blondes. So on second thoughts, maybe you shouldn't have.'

After Sandra had spent another ten minutes answering Emily's questions about Tom's erratic behaviour, she went to fetch him. He was lying on his bunk in the wagon, curled up in a foetal position.

'Emily's here, Tom,' she said gently. 'She's waiting for you in the study.'

He got up without a word and followed her across the courtyard to the house. 'I'll leave you to it,' she told Emily. 'If you need anything,' she added meaningfully, 'ring the bell.'

Emily waited till Sandra had closed the door behind her, then pushed one of the armchairs round so it was facing away from the window. 'Why don't you sit over here, Tom? I'll sit at the desk and make notes. Is that okay?' He shrugged and sat in the chair.

'Now I want you to close your eyes and relax,' she told him. 'What I'm going to do is take you back to your earliest memories. There might be something in your childhood – something you've been subconsciously suppressing – which we can explore together. So just empty your mind while I count backwards from ten.'

She began to count, slowly and quietly. 'Ten... nine... eight... seven... six... five... four... three... two... one...'

Tom began to feel drowsy. He could hear her voice but it seemed to come from far away.

'How do you feel?'

'Sleepy.'

'Tell me about your primary school. I believe you call it first grade. What do you remember about that?'

'Alan, my best friend. Used to draw pictures of Miss Staniforth, the headmistress. She had bad teeth.'

'How about high school?'

'It was tough. The kids called me a limey, said England was crap. Couldn't let 'em get away with that.'

'Because your father's English?'

'Yeah.'

'So what did you do about these kids?'

'Lot of fights. Left me alone after that.'

'And when you came home from school, who did you tell about it?'

'Nobody.'

'Why not?'

'There was nobody there.'

'What about your mother?'

'In Washington, she was usually working. Then, after we moved to Boston, she suddenly took off.'

Emily made a note. 'How did you feel about that?'

'I hated her.'

'And now?'

Tom hesitated. 'I don't think about her much. She's out of my life.'

'What did you do in the holidays?'

'Sometimes we went to the Cape. If Dad had a conference, we went to the west coast.'

'How do you get on with your dad?'

'We get on fine. But he's got a lot on his plate – research, lectures, faculty meetings. We only really get together during the vacations.'

'What does he do?'

'He's an astrophysicist. Pretty smart guy.'

'Is that what you want to be?'

'Maybe.'

'How about hobbies? What sort of music do you like?'

'Soul. Garage rock. Hip-hop.'

Emily smiled. 'I haven't a clue what you're talking about, Tom. Let's try a little experiment. I don't know if it'll work, but perhaps it'll tell us what *doesn't* work. Why d'you think people are worried about you?'

'Dunno.'

'Can you think of anything you might do to stop them worrying?'

'No.'

'Tell me about Jarman.'

Tom suddenly became agitated and spoke in a voice like a creaking door. 'That's none of your business, bitch.'

Emily made another note. 'I'm told you sometimes speak in his voice. Is that it?'

'I said it was none of your business. Keep out of it!'

'Why are you talking in that voice?'

'What voice?'

'Am I speaking to Jarman?'

Tom suddenly sprang out of his chair. 'Yes!' he shouted angrily. 'And if you get in my way, I'll kill you, bitch...'

Emily leaped to her feet and ran towards the bell. But before she could reach it, Tom caught her and threw her to the floor. She cried out for help, but he knelt astride her, put his hands round her neck and started to throttle her.

Adam, Matthew and Sandra rushed in. The two men pulled Tom away and held him down while Emily picked herself up. 'Where's your medical bag, Sandra?' she asked, gasping for breath.

Sandra rushed out again. While she was away, Tom thrashed and flailed around on the floor, swearing at Adam and Matthew and threatening to kill them if they didn't let him go. It took all their strength to hold him.

Sandra reappeared with her medical bag, took out a syringe and filled it with a sedative, which she injected into Tom's arm. His struggles slowly subsided, until he lay unconscious on the floor.

Adam and Matthew stood up, breathing heavily. 'I'm too old for this,' said Adam, collapsing into an armchair. 'I think I've strained my shoulder.'

Matthew turned to Emily. 'What now?'

'He ought to go into hospital for a CT scan.'

'I'll call an ambulance,' said Sandra. She moved to the desk and picked up the phone...

They were sitting in the hospital atrium drinking their fourth cups of coffee, when Doctor Hancock arrived with the X-rays of Tom's head. 'I don't know what's going on,' he said to Matthew as he sat down, 'but he's got a nodule on the left frontal lobe of his brain.'

'What's a nodule?'

'Well anatomically, it's a small knot or tumour.'

Matthew stared at him, devastated. 'A tumour? Is it serious?'

'That has yet to be determined. All I can tell you is that it's a very odd shape. I've never come across anything like it before.'

'What does the left frontal lobe do?' asked Adam.

'It's the essence of one's personality, the centre of emotion and judgment. It also controls one's ability to understand what makes other people tick.'

'So what d'you recommend?'

'Well the first thing we have to do is establish whether the nodule is benign or cancerous.'

Matthew glanced helplessly at Adam. 'But he had a thorough check-up just before we left the States…'

'It won't do any harm to double-check. Luckily, we have a magnificent new state-of-the-art MRI scanner, which should provide the answer.'

Adam stood up. 'When? Today?'

'No, I'm afraid it's fully booked today. I've scheduled his scan for the first thing tomorrow. Take him home and bring him back at eight-thirty.'

Matthew put his head in his hands. 'It's all my fault! Why the hell did I bring him here?'

Sandra squeezed his arm. 'Don't blame yourself, Matt. You couldn't possibly have foreseen all this.'

Tom appeared, slouching across the atrium with his hands in his pockets. 'Well, doctor?' he said listlessly. 'Will I live?'

'I see no reason why not, Tom. Just take it easy: get plenty of rest and fresh air. I'll give you a mild sedative to help you get a good night's sleep.'

Tom stared at him with contempt. 'A mild sedative, eh?' he rasped. 'You just don't have a clue, do you?'

Hancock stared at him, startled by his sudden change of voice. Matthew, pretending not to notice, glanced round the atrium. Patients and their relatives were chatting animatedly at other tables, while their children ran around squealing. Everything was just as it was when they entered the hospital, and yet everything had changed.

They drove back to Milbury in silence. Then, after Adam had brought Georgina to a halt outside the Manor's front door, he suddenly came to life. 'Tell you what we'll do, young Thomas,' he said to Tom's reflection in the rear-view mirror. 'Let's test your father's theory that there's been a polarity reversal of the magnetic field inside the circle. I'm sure you'd like to help me prove him wrong?'

'It's not a theory,' said Tom. 'It's a fact.'

'How d'you know?'

'Dunno. I just do.'

'Well let's see if you're both right, shall we?'

'Do what you like. I'm going to bed.' Tom got out of the car and disappeared round the side of the house towards the courtyard.

Adam and Matthew turned to Sandra for guidance. 'It's probably the best thing he could do,' she said. 'He needs a good night's sleep.'

They got out of the car and went into the house, just as Mrs Crabtree appeared in the hall to greet them. 'Dunno what the world's coming to,' she grumped. 'You can't depend on no one these days.'

'Why, what's the problem?' asked Adam.

'I phoned the order in this morning like you said, but they never came. So there's not enough food for all of you.'

'That's all right, Mrs C. I don't think any of us are very hungry.'

'I could stop by Mrs Warner's farm on my way in tomorrow and buy a few eggs?'

'Yes, do that,' said Sandra. 'I'll phone the supermarket in the morning to find out what happened to our order.'

'What about 'is Lordship's breakfast? We've run out of muesli, and he don't seem to eat nothing else.'

'Don't worry. He's got to go back to the hospital tomorrow for another scan. He can have his breakfast in the canteen.'

'Poor little mite. He's thin as a rake as it is. Makes you wonder, doesn't it?'

'Wonder what?'

'Whether they've got any food in America. Well as there's nothing for me to cook, I might as well go home. Toodle-oo.'

Mrs Crabtree put on a shapeless brown felt hat that completely covered the top half of her face and disappeared out of the front door.

Matthew turned to Adam. 'You want to recheck the magnetivity inside the circle, Dad?'

'Certainly. If you're so confident you're right, how about a small wager on the result?'

'Okay. I'll bet you five quid the readings of your gradiometer will be the same as mine.'

'You're on.'

Matthew won his bet, but not in the way either of them had expected. Both instruments gave the same reading: a massive increase in magnetivity. And Matthew's compass showed that the magnetic field had reversed again: north and south were back where they should be.

'Fascinating,' said Adam as he pocketed Matthew's five-pound note. He glanced round at the stones.'What are you playing at, you old devils? Are you working for a new master now? Have you no loyalty to your friends?'

Matthew patted the sarsen next to him as if it were a horse. 'No, we've never been friends, have we, you stupid bits of sandstone? Because friends have to be able to trust each other… Ow!' He took his hand away from the stone and stared at it, puzzled. 'That's odd.'

'What?' asked Adam.

'Feel it, Dad. It's like an iceberg.'

Adam pressed his palm against the stone and quickly snatched it away. 'Yes. Pretty weird, as young Thomas would say.'

'I mean, its temperature must be well below zero. How d'you account for that?'

'It's not up to me to account for it. Ask Percy Deverill. He's the keeper of the stones.'

'No, seriously, Dad. According to the UK weather reports, you've had an exceptionally hot spring and early summer. It should have retained some residual warmth by now.'

'Let's check the others.'

They set off in opposite directions, feeling each stone in the circle. All of them felt like gigantic blocks of ice.

When they met again at the same place, they stared round the circle, mystified.

'What d'you make of it?' asked Matthew.

Adam remained lost in thought for a moment. 'Ice-cold stones and a massive increase in magnetivity. It's as if something or someone has sucked all the energy out of them and turned them into a superconductor.'

'Which couldn't have happened naturally?'

'It's highly unlikely.'

'But why would anyone need that much energy?'

Adam didn't reply. He walked over to the nearest sarsen: then turned to face the next one.

'Suppose someone wanted to create an electromagnet inside the circle with its own magnetic field? They'd need an electrical circuit, wouldn't they?'

Matthew joined him. 'And you think they could be using the stones to create one?'

As if in answer to his question, they both felt a sudden magnetic pull which almost knocked them off their feet.

'What was that?' he asked, looking round. 'Wind?'

'No. Look at the trees.' Adam pointed to the trees in the Manor's garden. The leaves were completely still.

'So what was it?'

'Magnetism. The question is – who or what has been messing around with these stones?'

They sat down in the shade of the sarsen. Like the others, its shadow was lengthening across the grass. They looked so placid, thought Matthew: just harmless relics of Britain's heritage. But they both knew these stones were far from harmless, and this new phenomenon made him uneasy.

'You think some new magus has harnessed all this energy?'

'It's possible, I suppose,' said Adam. 'But this is a completely different kettle of fish. Hendrick was drawing energy from the black hole. Whoever or whatever's responsible for this is draining energy from the circle.'

They were both silent for a moment. 'It's midsummer tomorrow,' said Matthew. 'Could it have anything to do with the reckoning?'

'That's the most ludicrous idea I ever heard,' said Adam sharply. Then he paused. 'Though I have to admit it also occurred to me.'

Su and Tom appeared and flopped down beside them. 'I found him skulking in the wagon,' Su told them cheerfully. 'I told him I don't like skulkers, and if he didn't stop skulking and come out of the wagon he wouldn't get any dinner. So he came out. But when he found out there wasn't any food in the house, he went into a strop.'

'Not to worry,' said Adam. 'I'll book us a table at the pub.'

'It's okay, Grandpa. Mum's already done it.'

'Are you sure about this, Tommo?' asked Matthew, shielding his eyes from the sun. 'Don't you think you ought to take it easy this evening? We can bring some food back for you.'

'No, I'm fine.'

But he looked far from fine, thought Matthew. He looked pale and indifferent, as if he'd lost all interest – not only in food, but in everything else.

Matthew watched the trees in the Manor's garden, deep green against the azure sky. It was a perfect summer evening, with not a breath of wind and England in all her finery. If only tomorrow would never come.

Adam held out his hand to Tom. 'If you would be so good as to pull me upright, Thomas, I would be forever in your debt.' Tom pulled him to his feet. 'Thank you. Who was it said: "Age shall not weary them, nor the years condemn"? Well it shall and they do.' He stared at his hand, looking puzzled. 'Let me see your hand, Thomas.'

Tom put both hands in his pockets. 'No.'

Adam took out a handkerchief and wiped his own hand. 'Very well. Let's collect Sandra and go pubwards.'

They set off towards the other side of the circle. But they hadn't gone more than a few steps before another magnetic wave hit them, much stronger than the first. Adam, Matthew and Su just managed to withstand it, but to their amazement Tom was lifted off his feet, carried for a few yards by some unseen force, then flung back onto the grass.

Matthew and Su rushed to help him up. 'Are you okay, Tommo?' asked Matthew anxiously.

Tom sat up, looking dazed. 'Yeah, I'm good. Where did that wind come from?'

Matthew and Adam glanced at their magnetometer dials. Both needles were pointing to the top of the scale.

Dinner at the pub was a depressing affair. The gales of raucous laughter that came wafting into the dining room from the bar made their silence seem funereal.

Su tried to make conversation, but soon gave up. Everyone's mind seemed to be elsewhere. Tom toyed with his pasta, pushing it round his plate till it congealed. Matthew kept a close watch on him, while Adam drew something in his notebook.

It was Sandra who finally broke the silence. 'You feeling okay, Tom?'

'No,' he said. 'Got a splitting headache.'

'I've got some painkillers in my...'

Adam looked up from his notebook and interrupted her. 'When did this headache start?'

'About half an hour ago.'

'You didn't have it before you came out to the circle?'

'No. It was just the air out there. It felt like there was going to be a thunderstorm.'

'Interesting.' Adam closed his notebook. 'We're going to need a continuity tester.'

Sandra frowned. 'I suppose it's no use asking why?'

'In order to check this.' He handed her his notebook. Su peered over her mother's shoulder at the drawing. It was a rough sketch of the main circle with arrows and twirls passing through the stones and wavy lines connecting the top of one stone to the bottom of the next, surrounded by complicated equations.

'I suppose it's no use asking what it is or why you want to check it?' said Sandra. She passed the notebook on to Matthew. 'Does this make any sense to you, Matt?'

At first, the equations took him back to his first day at Milbury school, when he was confronted by a sea of indecipherable numbers on the blackboard. But now it was a language he understood, and the more he studied Adam's arrows and twirls the more sense they made.

He looked up, to find his father watching him. 'Intriguing, eh?'

Matthew handed back the notebook. 'So you think the circle could be a giant solenoid?'

'I think it's possible.'

'How?'

'*Pas devant les enfants*, Matt. We can discuss it when we get home. Now who's for cheese and biscuits?'

On their return to the Manor, Adam and Matthew closeted themselves in the study. 'Well?' asked Adam, pouring two large brandies. 'What do you think?'

Matthew threw the notebook on the table. 'It's certainly intriguing. But even if you're right, I don't see how it helps us.'

'The stones might be able to help us, if we handle them properly. It could be the beginning of our fightback.'

'Against Jarman?'

'And his kith and kin. If they prove to be as troublesome as he is.'

'How are we going to fight back against someone we can't see?'

'Because thanks to Su, we can make some educated guesses about what's going on. And forewarned is forearmed.'

'Go on then. Guess away.'

Adam handed Matthew a brandy and carried his own to the chair behind his desk. 'Why d'you think Tom was affected by the circle's magnetic field more than us?'

'Because he's not carrying so much weight?'

'He also had a headache.'

'So? Everyone has headaches.'

'The question is – what gave him the headache? He said it felt as if there was going to be a thunderstorm. I felt it too.'

'So did I. Where are you going with this, Dad?'

'I think the air might have been ionised. And it's possible – only possible, mind – that Tom has iron particles in him.'

Matthew stared at Adam incredulously. 'You mean…the nodule in his brain…?'

'I know this is hard for you to take, Matt, but I think Tom's turning into another species. The hand he used to pull me up this afternoon felt cold and scaly, like a fish…'

'Okay, you've forewarned me,' said Matthew impatiently. 'What about the forearmed bit?'

'I'm coming to that.' Adam stood up and began to pace round the study. 'We can't just sit back and do nothing. We did that thirty years ago, and it nearly cost us our lives. This time, we have to be proactive.'

'And what d'you propose we do?'

'Well the first thing *I'm* going to do is investigate that new magnetic field. We now know beyond doubt that the designers of the Milbury circles were brilliant scientists. They had an understanding of physics that we can only wonder at, and I believe that's what this Jarman creature meant by calling his lecture "The Delusion of Science". So suppose these extraterrestrials are an iron-based species? And suppose they needed the energy in the stones to travel here for this reckoning? It would explain quite a lot of things, including the extraordinary fluctuations in their temperature.'

Matthew sipped his brandy thoughtfully. 'So that's why you need the continuity tester? To see if there's an electric circuit running round the circle?'

'It would explain Tom's headache. And why he was suddenly blown about like that.'

'I don't see where that gets us, Dad,' said Matthew. 'It's not going to get Jarman out of Tom's head, is it?'

'It might.'

'How?'

'I'd prefer to keep that to myself for the moment. It will require split-second timing and a great deal of luck. But the boy's life will be at risk, so I'd need your permission.'

Matthew stared at Adam in alarm. 'What are the chances?'

'I won't lie to you, Matt. Less than fifty-fifty.'

'Well his life is obviously at risk already. And we haven't got a Plan B.'

Adam glanced at his watch. 'It's a bit late for that. As you pointed out, it's only a few hours till Litha.'

At 4.49 am on midsummer morning, the first rays of the rising sun touched the top of the Milbury stones. By 5.05, they were casting long shadows across the dewy grass.

At Hawthorn Cottage, Dai, having washed his ceremonial robe, was hanging it out to dry.

Ten minutes later, in the Disciples' camp, Kevin woke up and nudged Brenda, who was sleeping next to him in his tent. They went outside, knelt down, facing the rising sun, and made obeisance to Gaia.

Two hours after that, at the Manor, Sandra was woken by the sound of a car engine. She jumped out of bed and watched from her bedroom window as Adam drove Georgina out of the gates. She decided to go back to sleep.

Matthew, who had spent a sleepless night, was in the kitchen, making himself an umpteenth cup of coffee.

Su was in bed, watching the sun climb into a cloudless sky and thinking about Tom. She decided to go out to the wagon to see if he was awake. There was no reply to her knock, so she opened the door a crack.

He wasn't there.

CHAPTER EIGHT

SU RUSHED BACK ACROSS the courtyard to tell Matthew, and together they made a quick search of the house. Then Matthew woke Sandra. 'Tom's disappeared again,' he told her. 'Can you call the police?'

He dashed back to the wagon. Finding Tom's sweater hanging on a hook behind the door, he sat down on the bunk and buried his face in it, praying that his gift hadn't deserted him.

But no images came. It was as if some webmaster had put up a 'This page cannot be displayed' notice on his private screen.

Panic-stricken, he ran all the way to Hawthorn Cottage and banged on the door. Dai opened it immediately, wearing his ceremonial robe and chain of office.

'Need your help,' he said, panting for breath. 'Tom's disappeared. He was supposed to have a scan and maybe an operation at the hospital today.'

'Surgery is not the answer, Matthew,' said Dai in a strange metallic voice. 'What must be must be.'

Matthew lost his temper. 'Why are you speaking like that?' he roared. 'What *must* be is this operation. My son's life is at stake.'

'It is not necessary. If he cooperates, no harm will come to him. You have my word.'

'Why should I take your word? You're not a surgeon. And what d'you mean – if he cooperates?'

'If he is in the circle at midnight. After that, he might be your son again. What is about to happen is both an end and a beginning.'

'I haven't got time for riddles. Are you and your Disciples going to help me or not?'

'Yes, we will help you. But if the boy does not want to be found, our search will not be successful.'

Matthew was on his way back to the Manor when his mobile rang. It was Sandra, in a panic. 'The police say they can't organise a search till Tom's been missing for forty-eight hours.'

'Okay, leave it with me,' he told her.

He called the local CID and asked to speak to Jim Browning. Luckily, he was on duty and listened sympathetically as Matthew explained the problem.

'Bloody red tape,' said Jim. 'Don't worry, Matt. I'll put every man at my disposal onto it.'

Dai went down to Four Acre field, roused the other Disciples from their sleep and told them to look for Tom in Milbury's most sacred places – the Hill and the church, the Cove Stones and the Sanctuary. Meanwhile the police set up road-blocks on all the surrounding roads, in case he had hitched a ride.

Su didn't join in the search, because she knew instinctively where Tom would be hiding and she wanted to talk to him alone. So she waited till everyone had spread out across the countryside, then ran up to the Long Barrow. After looking round to make sure no one was watching, she went into the barrow and felt her way along the cold stone walls to the inner chamber, her heart thumping not only from her run, but from nervousness about who or what she would find.

She couldn't see him at first, but she knew he was there because she could hear a strange rattling sound of someone breathing. And because of the disgusting fishy smell.

Then she saw him, huddled in the darkest corner of the chamber. She wanted to run out again, to get back into the fresh air, but she forced herself to sit beside him.

'Go away!' he rasped in Jarman's voice. 'I have no wish to harm you.'

'And I don't want to harm *you*,' she told him. 'I'm just trying to save Tom's life.'

'The boy is not important.'

'He is to me.'

His head turned towards her. All she could see in the semi-darkness were two bulging eyes.

'You love him?'

'I think so.'

'Human love is a strange concept. It is not necessary for procreation.'

To get away from the smell, Su edged away from him. This was no longer Tom: it was an alien creature with Tom's face, and even that was different.

'Who did you kill?'

The creature's throat rattled as it took in more air. 'Someone who deserved to die.'

'Why? What had he done?'

'That is no concern of yours.'

'Please tell me. I want to understand.'

For what seemed an age, there was no sound except for the rattling in the creature's throat as he breathed in and out. 'He stole the Seal of Destiny from my father,' he rasped eventually, 'and gave it to my uncle.'

'What's the Seal of Destiny?'

'It is the symbol of power, passed down from generation to generation of our family.'

Su wondered if she had missed something. 'But surely, if the thief gave it to your uncle, it would still be in your family's possession?'

'But not in mine,' said the creature bitterly. 'As my father's firstborn, I should be the Keeper of the Seal.'

'So you found out who the thief was, and killed him?'

'Yes.'

'And he deserved to die because he stole the Seal from your father?'

'Not only that. He was a weakling.'

'Who was it?'

'My grandfather.'

This was getting complicated, thought Su. Surely all this couldn't just be a family squabble that had ended in murder?

But as it seemed to be what the reckoning was all about, she had to find out as much as she could.

'Why d'you think he stole it from your father?'

'He said I was not worthy to inherit it from him. But I am far more worthy than my uncle.'

'It doesn't sound like it. I thought you were supposed to have brought civilisation to Earth, yet you settle your family quarrels by killing each other. How could the Sumerians have treated you as gods?'

'Because they were a primitive people. And they needed superior beings to worship.'

Su tried to think of a way to get through to the creature. 'Won't the Wise Ones want you to show some remorse at the reckoning?'

'Remorse is not required. They will have to release me.'

'Suppose they don't?'

'That is inconceivable. They cannot deny me justice. I am a Wise One myself.'

So that was why there were only five judges in the virtual reality temple: one of them was dead, and the seventh was the prisoner, on trial for his murder.

But how could a member of the Anunnaki have committed such a terrible crime, even if his victim deserved to die? If he'd been a Wise One himself, he must have been respected by his people. And he'd been dubbed the Count of St Germain for saving the French queen's life. So perhaps there was still some good in him: some residual compassion she could appeal to.

'What about justice for Tom?' she asked him. 'He has nothing to do with this. Aren't they more likely to release you if *you* release *him*?'

'Perhaps. But he is not my concern. Humans are expendable.'

'*Expendable!*' Su jumped to her feet, blazing with anger. 'So you believe our lives are worth less than yours, do you? You don't care if he lives or dies?'

The creature's throat rattled again. 'Why should the boy die?' it rasped. 'He is young and strong. That is why I chose him.'

'Not strong enough. You've damaged his brain, and he probably needs an operation.'

'The damage will be repaired when I have no further use for him. I am merely using him as a mouthpiece.'

'So why don't you let him have the operation? I'm sure that would count in your favour at the reckoning.'

'I cannot take that risk. He might die on the operating table, before he has served his purpose.'

'He could die anyway,' said Su desperately. 'You want to go home to your own planet, don't you? Isn't that what this reckoning will decide? And if you don't have Tom to speak through, how are you going to plead your case?'

It seemed an eternity before the creature spoke again. 'Perhaps there is a way. But without a host, it is dangerous.'

'For you, or for Tom?'

'For both of us. But I will allow him to have the operation on one condition. Make sure all the members of your family are inside the circle at midnight.'

Adam returned to Milbury from his shopping trip to find the village heaving with villagers, the police and Dai's Disciples. Matthew and Sandra were standing outside the Manor surrounded by police cars, white-faced with anxiety.

'What's going on?' he asked them as he climbed out of the car.

'Tom's disappeared again,' said Matthew. 'I've phoned the hospital. They say they'll reschedule the operation as soon as we find him.'

His mobile rang. 'Yes?' he said tensely.

Adam watched as his whole body seemed to relax.

'That's great, Su. Thanks.'

'She's found him?'

'Yes. She's bringing him in.'

'Give me your phone,' said Sandra. 'I'll call an ambulance.'

By the time Su and Tom appeared, the ambulance was waiting. Adam, Matthew and Sandra were standing by it, talking to Jim Browning.

Matthew rushed up to Tom. 'Are you okay, Tommo? Jim's promised to give you a police escort. They're waiting for you at the…'

'He's very tired, Matt,' said Su quickly. 'Please – no more questions.'

Tom climbed into the ambulance unaided by the paramedics, while Matthew and Sandra ran to the old banger. One of the police cars sped off with a wailing siren, leading the ambulance out of the gate. Matthew followed it, past Dai and the silent Disciples who had formed two lines on either side of the drive.

As the procession sped away down the Avenue and the crowd began to disperse, Adam turned to Su. 'Well done, young lady. Now you and I have some work to do. Are you up for it?'

'Yes.'

'Good.' He opened Georgina's rear door and took out a small box.

'What's that?' asked Su.

'It's a continuity tester.'

'What does it test?'

'Continuities, of course. Oh, by the way,' he said, as they set off towards the circle, 'my archaeologist friend called me on my car phone this morning. He's received the lab report on those clay fragments you found. They're definitely Sumerian. And they found a bone-chip in the soil sample, which is at least fifty thousand years old. The DNA isn't human, and it doesn't belong to any known animal.'

'We've got a bigger problem, Grandpa,' said Su, who was finding it hard to keep up with him. 'Tom isn't Tom any more.'

Adam stopped and stared at her. 'You mean, this creature's carried out his threat? It's completed the symbiosis?'

'I think so.'

'Let's hope you're wrong,' he said grimly.

'Take off your watch, Tom,' the jolly radiographer was saying, 'and empty your pockets with malice aforethought. I take it you don't have a pacemaker?'

Tom glowered balefully at her, but said nothing. He produced several coins and a penknife from his trouser pockets and dropped them into the bowl by the huge scanner.

'In you go, then. Battle stations.' The radiographer turned to Matthew and Sandra. 'There's a waiting room at the end of the corridor, Mr Brake. Doctor Hancock will be down as soon as the lad's finished his scan. It'll take about twenty minutes.'

They went out into the corridor, and the radiographer closed the scanning room door behind them. Sandra took Matthew's arm as they walked towards the waiting room. 'I know it's not much comfort, Matt, but Hancock's an excellent surgeon. He couldn't be in better…' She stopped and turned to him, panic-stricken. 'NO!'

He stared at her. 'What d'you mean – no?'

'Didn't Adam tell you he thought Tom might have iron in his brain?'

'Yes, but it was only one of several …'

'If he's right, the scanner will kill him.' Sandra raced back to the scanning room and rang the bell.

Adam pressed one of the continuity tester's probes into a sarsen and turned to Su. 'Hold it there,' he told her. 'Make sure it doesn't come out.'

'I won't get an electric shock, will I?'

'I hope so. It would be rather exciting, wouldn't it?'

'Grandpa!'

He smiled. 'No, you won't get a shock. Just don't touch the metal parts of the two probes at the same time.'

She watched as he plugged the other end of the lead into the tester. Then he plugged another lead into it and carried the second probe to the next stone. 'Ready?'

Su shut her eyes and turned her head away. 'Yes.'

Nothing happened, except that a buzzing sound came from the tester. She cautiously opened her eyes, to see an arc of light fizzing and spluttering between the two stones.

'Wow!' she said. 'That's really weird.'

'Weirder than you know, my dear.'

'Why? What's it mean?'

'If the other stones behave in the same way, it means that our forebears constructed a superconducting electromagnet here.'

'What would they have needed it for?'

'Power beyond our understanding. Come on – let's see if the current runs all the way round the circle.'

Doctor Hancock stood in the middle of the atrium, staring at Matthew and Sandra in disbelief. 'Are you seriously telling me that the nodule in the boy's brain might have been put there by a ferrous-based alien?'

'Yes,' said Matthew. 'I don't pretend to understand it, but he seems to have paranormal powers.'

'Paranormal powers, eh? Then what's he doing in a hospital? He needs an exorcist, not a surgeon.'

'What he needs is a biopsy, Jack,' said Sandra. 'How soon can it be done?'

'Well I suppose we should be grateful you warned us in time,' said Hancock drily. 'He could have blown up our expensive new scanner.' He glanced at his watch. 'I'll call the lab and tell them it's an emergency. They should be able to do it before lunch.'

Su watched Adam as he slowly circled one of the stones, his eyes glued to the magnetometer's dial. 'Curiouser and curiouser,' he muttered to himself.

'What?'

He switched off the machine. 'D'you know what a solenoid is?'

'It's a helix, isn't it? A spiral?'

'Exactly. And that's what the magnetic minerals in each stone form – a spiral. The whole circle is a giant solenoid.'

'So Matt was right,' said Su. 'The magnetic field *has* changed.'

'Yes. But maybe we can use it to our advantage.'

'How?'

'At the moment, the field is horizontal. But what would happen if we can get an electric current to flow round it?'

Su thought for a moment. 'It would create a vertical field.'

Adam smiled. 'Go to the top of the form and jump off.' He put the magnetometer back in its box. 'Did you know that "magnetic" comes from the same root as "magus"?'

'Can we use that too?'

'No, it's completely useless.' He took her arm. 'I'm feeling rather peckish. Let's see if the supermarket's delivered our food.'

It felt strange sitting at either end of the long dining table, with nobody in between them. Adam suggested to Mrs Crabtree that they sat together, so she wouldn't have to shuttle backwards and forwards with the vegetable dishes, but she wouldn't hear of it. 'It'll do me good,' she explained. 'It's the only exercise I get since my old man popped his clogs.'

As soon as she disappeared into the kitchen, Su told Adam about her conversation with Jarman in the barrow, and about his condition for allowing Tom to have his operation. She knew it was hard for him to accept: even twenty-four hours ago, he wouldn't have believed her. But now there was archaeological evidence of a pre-human civilisation in Milbury to support her theory, he would have to take it seriously.

When she had finished, he remained lost in thought for a moment. 'So you think we're supposed to act as hosts for – what was it you called them?'

'The Anunnaki. The seven Wise Ones. I think it's a kind of supreme court.'

'And you say this creature who calls himself Jarman used to be a member of it?'

'That's what he told me.'

'Did he tell you who he killed? And why?'

'Yes. He killed his grandfather Anu, because he stole something called the Seal of Destiny from his father, and gave it to his father's brother.'

Adam groaned. 'I'm a bear of very little brain, Su. Could you repeat that very slowly?'

'I can do better than that, Grandpa. I've drawn up a family tree of the chief gods worshipped by the Sumerians.' From the back pocket of her jeans, she produced a crude diagram she had drawn...

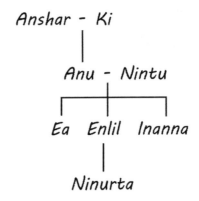

Anshar - Ki
|
Anu - Nintu
|
Ea   Enlil   Inanna
|
Ninurta

'This was the original pantheon,' she told him. 'All these gods had temples dedicated to them.'

'But what have they got to do with Jarman?' asked Adam.

'Are you ready for this, Grandpa? It's rather complicated.'

'I can do complicated. As long as I haven't had too many Scottish bevvies.'

'Okay. According to the legend, Anu stole the Seal of Destiny from his elder son Enlil and gave it to his younger son Ea. It was supposed to be the symbol of power, and whoever possessed it became the greatest of the gods. But the legend also has Anu being killed by Enlil. And that doesn't make sense, because Enlil was known as the father of mankind, renowned for helping those in need.'

Adam studied the diagram. 'So if Enlil didn't kill Anu, who did?'

'I think it was his grandson Ninurta. He was supposed to be an evil god with a terrible temper. The Sumerians called him the god of war, and believed he was responsible for the great flood. He'd never have let Anu get away with stealing the Seal from his father, because it was his birthright. He'd have wanted to get his revenge.'

'Come to think of it,' said Adam, 'I believe your father devoted a whole chapter of his book to Ninurta. Not the sort of chap you'd want in your golf club.'

'No. He was known as a judge who perverted justice. Mum says there's a lot of stuff in the early Sumerian texts about his abominations.'

Adam tried to keep the sceptical scientist in him at bay. 'So your theory is that all these deities were extraterrestrials, worshipped by the Sumerians when they arrived on Earth at the dawn of time? And their leader was killed by his grandson Ninurta?'

'Yes. He sounds like a nasty piece of work.'

'All right, let's assume Jarman is Ninurta, a corrupt judge accused of murder. What about the other members of this supreme court?'

'I think one of them's already here, speaking through Dai. It would explain why he and Jarman seem to hate each other. And why he's talking like a Dalek.'

Adam poured himself another glass of wine. 'But if these creatures really are extraterrestrials, why don't they hold this reckoning on their own planet?'

'Maybe because it's hundreds of light years away,' said Su, 'and if they have the ability to project themselves through space, maybe there's no need for them to be here physically.'

Adam sipped his wine thoughtfully 'You think that's all they need us for? To act as conduits?'

'That's what Jarman said.'

'Can we trust the word of a self-confessed murderer?'

'Do we have a choice?'

'Of course we have a choice,' said Adam angrily. 'We can refuse to act as these creatures' puppets.'

'But we have to be at the ceremony tonight, Grandpa,' said Su desperately. 'It's Tom's only chance!'

'Well Tom's not going to be there, is he? He'll be in intensive care. Which leaves Jarman with no one to act as his conduit.'

'I don't know how it works. He said there was a way – but it was very dangerous.'

'In that case, none of us must go.'

'I meant dangerous for Tom. Suppose Jarman's been waiting five thousand years for this reckoning, and he loses his appeal? He won't care what happens to his host. He'll let Tom die.'

'But we know nothing about these extraterrestrials, if that's what they are. It's too big a risk.'

'It would be a bigger risk if we didn't follow Jarman's instructions. Please, Grandpa. We have to do this. We just *have* to! It might be the only way Tom can come out of this nightmare alive.'

Adam stood up and moved to the window. It was another scorching day, and the garden was full of butterflies.

'So you'd trust this... this creature, who was known for his abominations, rather than Doctor Hancock?'

Su joined him at the window. 'Hancock's out of his depth. He doesn't understand what's going on.'

'I'm not sure any of us do, my dear,' said Adam. 'We're in the same predicament as King Lear. "As flies to wanton boys are we to the gods." '

Matthew watched through the window of the private ward as a nurse shaved Tom's head. Another nurse was checking his pulse and taking his blood pressure. He was quiet and docile, accepting the procedures without protest, but his eyes were glazed, as if his mind was elsewhere. Which it probably was, thought Matthew bitterly.

Doctor Hancock appeared by his side with a clipboard. 'Sorry to bother you with red tape at a time like this, Mr Brake,' he said apologetically, 'but you'll have to sign this consent form.'

'Just for a biopsy?'

'Once I've opened him up, I may have to operate immediately. So I want to get all the formalities out of the way.'

Matthew signed. 'Are you certain you can get this nodule out of his head without damaging his brain?'

'Nothing's certain about brain surgery,' said Hancock. 'It's a very delicate organism. All I can tell you is it's not as hazardous as it used to be. Nowadays, we have a pretty high success rate.'

'Can I talk to him before you give him an anaesthetic?'

'Of course. First, the nurse will give him a sedative. He'll be drowsy, but perfectly lucid.'

Hancock walked away, and Matthew stared through the glass at his half-bald son, his eyes full of tears. This was all his doing, and whatever happened in the operating theatre he would never forgive himself.

Sandra appeared by his side, holding two paper cups. 'Sorry about the receptacles,' she said, handing him one, 'but the coffee's good.'

Her arrival opened the floodgates, and he leant against the wall, sobbing.

He felt her hand on his back. 'Let it out, Matt,' she whispered. 'Let it all out.'

He turned to her in agony. 'I can't bear it, Sandra. To see him like that... I don't recognise him any more. And the terrible thing... the really terrible thing is...'

'What?'

'He disgusts me.'

'I know. But we'll get the real Tom back, you'll see. Once that nodule's removed...'

Matthew tossed his paper cup into a rubbish bin. 'Will you wait here for me? I want to talk to him before they put him under.'

'Of course.'

Matthew opened the door, and the creature that was inside his son stared at him malevolently as he moved to his bedside. Matthew hardly recognised him: his head was now completely bald and his bulging eyes had become old.

When he spoke, it was in a hoarse whisper. 'Go back to Milbury, Matthew. You are needed there.'

'No. I'm staying here.'

'Then the operation will not be successful.'

'Why? What difference will it make?'

'If you are not at the reckoning, you will lose the boy.'

It was a calm, unemotional statement of fact, made with a chilling certainty that sent shivers down Matthew's spine. 'And if I do as you ask?'

'Then perhaps he will be returned to you unharmed.'

'*Perhaps?*'

197

'I can give you no guarantees. It depends on the outcome.'

'Doesn't it depend on you?'

'No. I promised the girl I would allow him to have the operation, and I will keep my word. But only if all the members of your family are inside the circle at midnight. Now go!'

The bald-headed stranger turned his head away. Matthew stared at the son who was not his son in despair. Where was the real Tom? Would he ever see him again, or was Jarman's occupation of his mind irreversible?

Sandra offered to stay at the hospital, but though it would have been a comfort to know that she was keeping an eye on him, he had to refuse. 'He said *all* the members of my family had to be at the reckoning,' he told her, 'and we have to do as he says.'

As they drove back to Milbury, Matthew was haunted by memories of family holidays while Tom was growing up: the cabin on Moosehead Lake in Maine, where he had learned to swim... deep-sea fishing off Cape Cod, when he caught a massive tuna and nearly fell overboard... hiking across New Hampshire, following the Appalachian Trail... canoeing down the Connecticut River through the autumn mist... Tom and Sherry's laughing, sunburned faces. It seemed like another life.

His mobile rang, and he pulled in to the side of the road to answer it. It was Adam, trying to sound calm and collected, but Matthew could hear the urgency in his voice.

'Sorry, old chap, but can you come back?'

'Yes. I'm on my way.'

'Something's come up. I'll explain when you get here.'

'There's no need. Jarman's told me what we have to do.'

'No, it's not about Jarman. It's something else.'

He found his father in the observatory, staring at the computer screen and listening to a strange burbling noise coming through the microphone. He switched it off as Matthew appeared, stood up and gave him a hug.

'Sorry about all this, old boy. You must be going through hell.'

'It's nothing compared with what Tom must be going through,' said Matthew bitterly. 'Hancock's promised to call me if there are any... developments.'

'When's he having the operation?'

'Tonight sometime. They're doing a lot of tests, and they won't go ahead till they get the results.'

'Chin up, Matt. He'll come through all this.'

'It depends on Jarman,' said Matthew bitterly. 'If only we knew what he was up to.'

'I think we might have an inkling, thanks to Su.' Adam told him about her conversation with Jarman, and about her theory that the reckoning was a meeting of extraterrestrial judges to decide whether he should be allowed to return home. 'I know it strains one's credulity,' he said apologetically, 'but it's the only explanation that fits all the data.'

'Why is it so important for us to be at this reckoning?'

'Su has a theory about that. She thinks the judges need humans to act as their hosts.'

'What crime is Jarman supposed to have committed?'

'Murder.'

'*What!*'

'It was a long time ago,' said Adam. 'And Jarman has assured Su that if we all followed his instructions, Tom would come to no harm. So that's what we must do.'

'What about Sandra and Su?'

'They're up for it. Though Sandra needed quite a lot of persuasion.'

Matthew glanced at his watch. 'It's five to twelve. Another twelve hours to go. I must keep busy, or I shall go mad.'

'All right, come and look at this.' Adam sat down at the computer again, and Matthew peered over his shoulder. There were two square pictures on the screen – one black, the other green. The lower half of the black one was covered with a multi-coloured pattern of dots, lines and squiggles, as if someone had scattered miniature confetti over it. The green one looked less interesting, but when Matthew peered closer, he could just make out two parallel lines of faint indentations running across it.

'Radio signals?'

'Yes. You've heard of the SETI project?'

'The Search for Extraterrestrial Intelligence? I know the principle. Thousands of searchers volunteering to have their computers hooked up together via the internet, so they can all listen for narrowband signals from space.'

Adam swivelled round in his chair. 'I signed up for it a few months ago. The increased computer power enables us to cover greater frequency ranges. We process the signals and send them back to California for analysis.'

'And what have you come up with?'

'About a hundred and fifty candidates for intelligent life. Including this.' Adam switched on the microphone again, and the burbling noise filled the observatory. Under the burble were other barely-audible noises – hisses, whistles, and what sounded like a mumbling electronic voice.

'Where's it coming from?' asked Matthew.

'A beacon, half-way between the centre and outer edge of the galaxy. Somewhere in the Libra constellation.'

'And when did the transmission start?'

'Just over an hour ago.'

'So these are live signals coming from Gliese 581d?'

'Looks like it.'

Matthew listened to the galactic chatter for a moment, then slumped into a chair. 'It's started,' he said helplessly, 'and there's nothing we can do to stop it.'

For the rest of the day, time dragged by agonisingly slowly. Matthew didn't know what to do with himself: it was impossible to read, because he couldn't concentrate. And he couldn't walk far from the house, in case Doctor Hancock had lost his mobile number and called Adam. So he mooched around the garden, watching the sun crawl across the sky towards the western horizon and wondering what was going on at the hospital.

Mrs Crabtree appeared at regular intervals with cups of tea and words of comfort. 'Don't you worry, Mr Matthew,' she kept saying. 'I'm sure young Master Tom will be right as rain. I'll make a nice sponge cake for him when he comes home.' At least their correct names seemed finally to have sunk in.

After several hours alone in the garden, it suddenly occurred to him that he was being extremely selfish. What must Su and Sandra be feeling? He himself didn't care what happened to him that night: he would have taken any risk to save Tom's life. But the others must be terrified by the prospect of aliens entering their minds. They were risking their sanity, perhaps even their own lives, and they needed whatever reassurance he could give them.

He found them in the drawing room, sitting silently side by side on the sofa. Despite the old cardigan draped across her shoulders, Sandra was shivering.

'Sorry I've been so unsociable,' he said, sitting opposite them. 'I should have thanked you for agreeing to do this.'

'There's no need, Matt,' said Sandra, 'but I still don't understand what's going on.'

'I don't understand it myself. I'd like to keep you out of it, but we have to try and keep this monster happy.'

'What will it be like when these... these *things* are inhabiting us?' asked Su. 'Will we feel what they're feeling?'

'I've no idea. I don't know how it works.'

'It won't damage our minds, will it?'

'No,' said Matthew, who had been asking himself the same question. 'I think they'll just be using us as transmitters, that's all. We may not even be conscious while they're doing it.'

'I hope we are,' said Su, making a brave effort to hide her nervousness. 'I'd hate to miss it.'

Sandra drew her cardigan tighter around her shoulders. 'Why do we all have to go?'

'I told you, Mum. Because there are seven Wise Ones.'

'But there are only five of us. Six, counting Dai.'

'I know. Jarman admits he killed the other one.'

Adam appeared, looking tense and preoccupied. 'Can I have a word, Matt?'

Matthew followed him into the hall, to find an icebox lying at the foot of the stairs.

'Remember what I said about being proactive?' said Adam, picking it up. 'Well I've come up with a Plan B. But to make it work, you're going to have to go back to the hospital. And take this icebox with you.'

Matthew stared at him, aghast. 'I can't do that, Dad. Jarman said if we wanted to save Tom, we all had to be in the circle at midnight.'

'Are you going to listen to Jarman or to me? It's your choice.'

'I'm just worried about what will happen to Tom if things go badly for Jarman at the reckoning.'

'So am I, Matt,' said Adam gently. 'That's why I need you to go back to the hospital.'

'Okay, what's this Plan B?'

'It's quite simple really,' said Adam, sitting on the bottom stair. 'I've established that there's a continuous electric circuit running in a spiral round the perimeter of the circle. We can use this to create a vertical magnetic field inside it. My guess is that Jarman is full of iron particles, so the field should hold him in place until we break the circuit. And... well, you know what will happen then.'

For the first time since he arrived back in England, Matthew began to hope. 'Yes,' he said thoughtfully. 'That's clever, Dad... really clever. You think it'll work?'

'I don't see why not. And we haven't got anything else up our sleeve.'

'But how are we going to get Jarman into the circle?'

'All we need is that nodule. I phoned the hospital, and Tom's operation is scheduled for eleven-thirty. So you'd better get a move on.'

'Who's going to break the circuit?' asked Matthew.

'You are.' Adam picked up the icebox and handed it to him. 'When you bring that nodule back with you.'

'But I won't know where you've buried the battery.'

'We'll text the information to you. Or rather, Su will. It's much too difficult for me.'

Matthew rushed out of the house, and Adam went back to the drawing room.

'Come on, people,' he said to Sandra and Su. 'Mrs C's left us some soup and sandwiches in the kitchen. Let's eat.'

They sat round the kitchen table in silence, each of them thinking about their forthcoming ordeal and wondering if they would come through it unscathed. Adam noticed that Sandra's hand was trembling so much that most of the soup had fallen out of her spoon by the time it reached her mouth. His heart went out to her: she was obviously terrified, but now he had convinced her that Tom's life depended on her she hadn't hesitated to put her own on the line.

Su kept glancing at the kitchen clock. The time, which had crawled like a snail all day, was now racing past as midnight approached. If only she could stop it: if only she could wind the clock back to Tom and Matthew's arrival in Milbury, before this nightmare began. But the hands moved inexorably on.

At eleven o clock, Adam stood up and peered through the window. 'It's dark enough now,' he said turning to Su. 'I've got a job for you, my dear.'

She followed him to the garage and watched, mystified, as he took out Georgina's battery and handed it to her. 'You take this. I'll bring the cables.'

'Where are we going?'

'On a magical mystery tour.' He took several cables off a hook. 'These should be long enough.' He picked up a trowel. 'Off we go.'

She followed him, staggering under the weight of the battery, across the road to the edge of the main circle. Groups of villagers had already gathered, waiting for the ceremony to begin, but it was too dark to recognise anyone.

Adam stopped at the nearest perimeter stone and stuck the metal crocodile clip at the end of one of the cables to the top of it. Then he moved on to the next stone in the circle, and stuck the other cable to the bottom of it. Both clips were held in place by the stones' magnetism.

'Now,' he said, picking up the trowel. 'Where shall we hide the battery? It has to be outside the circle.'

'Somewhere not too far away,' groaned Su. 'My arms are killing me.'

'How about under that tree over there? D'you think you can describe its position to Matthew?'

'Yes, I think so. It's the one nearest to the Manor. What's all this about, Grandpa?'

'It's midsummer, my dear,' said Adam mysteriously. 'A time for fireworks.'

In Four Acre field, Dai was addressing his white-robed Disciples in his metallic voice. 'On this, the most sacred night of the year,' he told them, 'we dedicate ourselves to Gaia, the earth mother. But this Litha, the power of our prayers must be stronger than ever. They must reach up into space, far beyond the confines of the Earth, so that they are heard by the other gods and goddesses of the Pantheon.'

The Disciples knelt and stretched out their arms up towards the stars. Dai surveyed them with approval. 'The gods are listening, my children. Now we will lead the ceremonial procession to the sacred place. Light your torches...'

The procession, led by Dai and the Disciples, moved slowly and silently along the Avenue towards the main circle. Villagers of all ages joined it along the way, and by the time it reached the Manor, where Adam, Sandra and Su were waiting, it was about a quarter of a mile long. On either side of the road, the stones, illuminated by the Disciples' pitch-torches, looked as if they were on fire.

When they reached the circle, the procession started to fan out, filling the spaces between the stones. The hair at the back of Adam's neck bristled: it was just like the human chain around the Manor the night Hendrick had invited him and Matthew to dinner.

He watched Dai, standing in the centre of the circle next to an enormous pile of wood, directing his Disciples to the few gaps in the crowd that were still left. Dressed in his ceremonial robe, with his white beard and coronet of laurel leaves, he looked like an Old Testament prophet.

The arrangement of the Disciples seemed to take an age. Su, overcome by exhaustion, leaned against the huge sarsen next to her – then gasped and jumped away as an electric shock ran through her body. The stone didn't just *look* as if it *was* on fire: it *was* on fire.

Sandra, hearing her muffled cry of pain, turned to her. 'What's the matter?'

Su rubbed her arm and glanced resentfully up at the stone, looming menacingly over her. 'Don't touch the stones, Mum. They're full of electricity.'

Dai walked over to them. 'Welcome to the Litha celebrations,' he said. 'Where is Matthew?'

'He's at the hospital,' said Adam. 'His son's having an operation.'

'That is extremely inconvenient.'

'It's pretty inconvenient for Tom too,' said Su bitterly.

Dai seemed to accept the rebuke with equanimity. 'Let us hope the Wise Ones will not be displeased. Follow me.'

They followed him to the centre of the circle, where he arranged them in a small inner ring, a few metres apart.

Then he turned to Adam. 'As Lord of the Manor, Professor, it is your privilege to light the fire.'

Dai signalled to one of his Disciples, who walked forward and handed his torch to Adam.

He glanced at Dai. 'Now?'

'Now.'

As he applied the torch to the pile of wood, and as flames and sparks started to fly upwards into the night, the crowd began to chant, louder and louder...

'Anger of fire... fire of speech... breath of knowledge... render us free from harm... return to us the innocence that once we knew... complete the circle... make us one with nature and the elements...'

CHAPTER NINE

AT THE HOSPITAL, DOCTOR Hancock was 'scrubbing up'. The anaesthetist appeared out of the operating theatre, looking worried.

'The patient's had an adverse reaction to the anaesthetic,' he said. 'We nearly lost him.'

Hancock dried his hands. 'That's odd. His father told me he's never had a problem with anaesthesia before. Recheck his renal function.'

Meanwhile Matthew took his place in the students' gallery above the operating theatre and placed the icebox on the bench beside him. Luckily, there was no one else there to ask awkward questions.

He stared down through the window at the inert figure lying under a sheet on the operating table, wondering how he could go on living if anything went wrong. How would he pass the long, lonely, guilt-ridden days, knowing that he had failed both as a husband and a father?

His mobile rang. It was a text message from Su: *Tree nearest the manor.*

He put the phone back in his pocket, praying that nothing would go wrong.

Back in the inner circle, Su's stomach was churning. She looked up at the stars, wondering from which direction the Wise Ones would come, and what it would feel like to have one's mind taken over by them.

Dai strode over to them. But it was no longer Dai: the voice that came out of his mouth was the strange metallic one that she had heard before. 'Have no fear,' it said. 'I am one of the seven Wise Ones, sent ahead of the others to prepare the way.'

'So what is your real name?' asked Adam.

'That is of no consequence. The Sumerians called me Ea, son of Anu. I am a member of the Grand Council of Apsu. We come in peace.'

Adam didn't seem at all shocked or surprised. 'But *why* have you come? What's this reckoning all about?'

'It is about justice, Professor,' said the metallic voice. 'That is all you need to know.'

'Who is Jarman?'

'He is the son of my brother Enlil. The Sumerians called him Ninurta.'

Adam frowned. 'My granddaughter has a theory that during your first expedition to Earth, Ninurta killed your leader. And when the rest of you went back to your own planet he was left behind as a punishment.'

Dai/Ea glanced at Su, the ring of flaming pitch-torches reflected in his dark eyes. 'Your granddaughter is a very intelligent young lady, Professor.'

Sandra looked stunned. 'So the legend is true?'

'Yes, doctor. Anu, son of Anshar, was killed by Ninurta, his grandson. That is why we left him here when we returned to Apsu five thousand years ago.'

Su stared at him, unsure whether she had heard him correctly. '*Five thousand years!*'

'I realise you must find it hard to believe, Miss de Courville. But Ninurta – the criminal you know as Jarman – is much older than that. He was five thousand years old when our expedition first arrived on your planet, which is still relatively young for our species. Some of us live for twenty thousand years.'

There was silence for a moment, except for the night breeze rustling through the grass.

'Was it Anu that you buried under the obelisk?' asked Adam.

'Yes.'

'So this reckoning is some kind of trial, to decide whether to let Ninurta go home?'

'No, not a trial, Professor, because his guilt has already been established. This is a special convocation of the Wise Ones, to consider whether he has now expiated his crime.'

'Like a court of appeal?'

'Indeed.'

'And what part are we expected to play?'

'You and your family will be the hosts for the other members of our Grand Council.'

'What d'you mean – "hosts"?' asked Sandra nervously.

'For the duration of the reckoning, they will share your minds and speak through your mouths.'

'*Share our minds!*'

'You will come to no harm, doctor. Though we all have the gift of thought projection, we use it with care. Rest assured, if there were any danger to your health or sanity, we would not take the risk.'

Su shivered and rubbed her arms, which were covered with goosebumps. 'You mean, there'll be an alien in my head? That's pretty weird. What will it feel like?'

Dai/Ea smiled. 'It will be like having a guest in your house for a short while. You, Miss de Courville, will be the host for my sister Inanna. But do not be alarmed. Though you will be aware of her presence and hear her voice, your mind will still be your own. And the proceedings will be conducted in your own language, so you will understand every word.'

'Why are you holding your reckoning here?' asked Adam. 'Why not on your own planet?'

'For several reasons, Professor. Because this is where Ninurta's crime was committed, and we need human testimony. Also, to take him back to Apsu before we have reached our verdict would be too dangerous. First, we must make sure that he is truly repentant.'

'But why are you using *us* as hosts?' asked Sandra. 'You could have chosen anybody.'

Dai/Ea shook his head. 'No, doctor. You and your family are not just anybody. You yourself are a distinguished historian who will be an important witness.' He moved on to Adam. 'And as for you, Professor, the fact that Ninurta used your grandson as his host gives you the right to see justice done. It is unfortunate that Matthew is not here. It means that Ninurta's father Enlil has no host, and he will have to speak in his own defence.'

'It doesn't sound as if he *has* a defence,' said Sandra, 'but all we're concerned about is Tom. This convicted murderer of yours has obviously gained control of his mind. What will happen to him?'

'That depends on our verdict, and Ninurta's reaction to it.'

Su stared at Dai/Ea in alarm. 'You mean, whatever happens to Ninurta will happen to Tom too?'

'We will try to separate them. The Grand Council will take the boy's safety into consideration.'

Su lost her temper. 'What d'you mean – take it into consideration?' she shouted, her voice echoing round the circle. 'Ninurta's *your* problem. How are you going to get him out of Tom's head?'

'I will not lie to you, Miss de Courville. We cannot guarantee the boy's safety, but we will do our best to guide the surgeon in his difficult task. It is against our laws to misuse another species.'

'But that's exactly what you're doing.'

'No. It is what Ninurta is doing.'

Su glanced at Adam for support, but as none was forthcoming she ploughed on alone. 'Is Tom still at the hospital?'

'Yes.'

'Has he had the operation?'

'Not yet. He is just about to have it.'

'Will he pull through?'

'As I told you, it depends on these proceedings. Which will be erased from your minds at the end of this special convocation, so that you will have no knowledge of what took place here.'

'Why is that necessary?' asked Adam.

'Because humans are not yet worthy, Professor. Perhaps in time, when you have learned to live together in peace, we will teach you the Ancient Wisdom. Until then, it must remain hidden from you.'

Adam glanced round the circle. 'There are still only three of us... plus my son and grandson... and you, Ea. That makes six hosts. I thought there were supposed to be seven members of your Grand Council?'

'The seventh Wise One was Anu, my father, killed by Ninurta five thousand years ago. He has not been replaced.'

Adam frowned. 'This is all very confusing. I take it I'm still speaking to Ea?'

'Yes.'

'And what about the rest of us? Who will *we* be hosting?'

'You, Professor, will be the host for the great Lord Anshar, Anu's father. He is also the senior member of the Grand Council and the wisest of the Wise Ones.'

'Sounds like good casting,' said Adam, giving Su a comforting hug.

'And what about Jarman?' asked Su. 'I mean Ninurta. If Tom's having an operation, who will *he* speak through?'

'He will appear when I call him – as what you call a hologram.'

The night suddenly became colder, and Sandra rubbed her arms. 'Who will be speaking through me?'

'Nintu, Anu's widow,' said Dai/Ea. 'But only to record her verdict. For most of the time you will be required to speak for yourself – as a historian.'

'And what about me?' asked Su. 'Nobody will want to share my mind, will they? My thoughts are rubbish.'

'You will not be doing the thinking, Miss de Courville. I have chosen you to be the host for my sister because she, like you, is wise beyond her years. She will have to choose whether to support me or my brother Enlil, Ninurta's father.'

'And what will be your function?' asked Adam.

For the first time, Su thought she detected a deep anger in Dai/Ea's metallic voice. 'Anu was my father. I will therefore be Ninurta's prosecutor. And I intend to call for the maximum penalty.'

'What's that?'

'Elimination.'

Su's stomach started churning again. Surely this couldn't mean what it sounded like? And if it did, what about Tom?

Doctor Hancock stood by the operating table, scalpel in hand, thankful that his young patient's long scaly body was covered by a sheet.

He glanced at the anaesthetist, who was watching the electrocardiograph. 'Stable?'

'Yes.'

'Then I can start?'

The anaesthetist nodded. In the gallery, Matthew turned his head away as Hancock made the first incision on Tom's forehead.

Dai/Ea, scanning the star-studded sky, suddenly turned to the ring of disciples and villagers. 'It is time!' he said in his mechanical voice. He turned to Adam, Sandra and Su. 'Prepare to receive the Wise Ones. Close your eyes and allow them to enter your minds.'

He looked up at the canopy of stars and opened his arms as if he was embracing them. 'Come!'

The crowd began to chant again, softly at first, then louder and louder: 'Fire of speech... breath of knowledge... render us free from harm...'

Su pretended to close her eyes, but only half-closed them. Through the narrow gap, she saw what seemed to be a shower of tiny meteorites fall from the darkness onto the others and turn them momentarily into balls of brilliant light. Then she felt a pleasant warmth suffuse her own body, which gradually turned to heat. Her skin began to tingle as if she had just come in from the cold...

Matthew watched tensely from the students' gallery as Doctor Hancock, bent over the operating table, probed into Tom's brain.

'There's been an alteration to the white matter,' he told the anaesthetist. 'I've never seen anything like it before...'

The anaesthetist was watching the heart and blood pressure monitors. 'Pressure's dropping. Down to eighty.'

Hancock had his own concerns. 'I can't stop the bleeding.'

'Down to sixty. He's gone into VF.'

Hancock snapped at one of the nurses. 'Defibrillator! Now!'

The nurses rushed the defibrillator trolley to the operating table and switched it on. Hancock picked up the paddles. 'Clear!'

The nurses stood back, and he applied the paddles to Tom's chest.

The boy's body jerked with the shock of the discharge.

Su opened her eyes and glanced round the circle. Everyone looked the same: Dai, her mother and grandfather were standing in the same positions. Even the Disciples didn't seem any different, though their torches seemed to be burning more brightly.

Yet the others *were* different. They seemed to have acquired an inner strength; a serene dignity which hadn't been present before she closed her eyes. The crowd seemed to sense it too: they waited in a respectful silence for whatever was to happen next.

What happened next was a soothing girl's voice speaking inside Su's head. 'Do not be alarmed,' it said. 'I am Inanna, Ea and Enlil's sister. I will not intrude into your thoughts. Try to forget that I am here.'

The voice was so loud and clear that Su was surprised no one else had heard it. 'How can I forget you're here when you *are* here?' she told it crossly. Then her curiosity got the better of her. 'Do you look like a fish?'

'How I look is not important, Khonsu. We have come to decide Ninurta's fate. Watch and listen, but do not interfere.'

She watched and listened as Dai/Ea stepped forward and bowed to Adam. 'Except for Enlil, the Grand Council is now assembled, Lord Anshar,' he announced.

'Why is Enlil not here?' demanded Adam/Anshar in another metallic voice that sounded even older than Ea's.

'His host is not present, great lord.'

'Why is his host not present?'

'He is at the hospital. His son is very ill.'

'Is this Ninurta's doing?'

'I believe so.'

'It will count against him when we consider our verdict.'
Anshar turned to the crowd. 'This special convocation of the
Grand Council has been called to decide whether or not
Ninurta has purged himself of his crime. As you know, the
original sentence imposed by us five thousand years ago was
provisional, and we therefore have three verdicts open to us. If
we believe that he is truly repentant, we can end his
banishment. But if we believe there is still evil in his heart, we
can either vote to prolong his exile or to eliminate him.'

Su stared at Anshar, aghast that such terrible words were
coming out of her grandfather's mouth. Didn't he realise that
he might also be condemning Tom to death? Or didn't he
care? Was this the Wise Ones' justice – to make an innocent
boy suffer for someone else's crime?

Anshar thought for a moment. Then he moved up to
Sandra. 'Nintu – you will remain silent while I address Doctor
de Courville... Doctor – You are both a historian and a
physician, are you not?'

'Yes,' said Sandra.

'We know nothing of human anatomy. In your opinion, do
your physicians have enough knowledge to separate Ninurta
from the boy?'

'No.'

Except for the crackling of the fire, there was total silence
in the circle while Anshar remained lost in thought for a
moment. Then he turned to Ea.

'Summon Ninurta.'

Ea turned to the east and opened his arms. 'Ninurta, son of
Enlil,' he called into the darkness. 'Come!'

Matthew stared down at the electrocardiograph, which was
pinging at an alarming rate. The anaesthetist felt Tom's
forehead.

'The patient's sweating,' he said to Hancock, 'and his pulse
is increasing. We have an emergency, George. You have to
arrest the bleeding.'

Hancock turned to one of the nurses. 'Draw up ten
milligrams of vitamin K.'

Matthew held his breath while the nurse took an ampoule out of a box and drew the contents of it into a syringe. Then she plunged the syringe into Tom's arm.

Su watched spellbound as a cloud of mist began to form in the centre of the inner circle and slowly shaped itself into a transparent figure of a very old man.

She knew instantly from the virtual reality construct on Tom's laptop that this was Jarman, but why was he transparent? Did his appearance as a hologram mean that his physical self was still in Tom's head?

The hologram glanced contemptuously round at his judges. For a moment, his eyes settled on Su, and she had the uneasy feeling that he wanted to eat her for dinner.

Anshar turned to Ea. 'You will speak first, Ea.'

Ea moved to the centre of the inner circle and, standing next to the hologram, addressed the crowd.

'Five thousand years ago, we made a grave error,' he said in his automated voice. 'According to Apsu law, the penalty for murder is elimination. But to our shame we decided to be lenient: in the hope that Ninurta would repent and turn away from the path of wickedness, we merely sent him into exile here on Earth. And how has he repaid our leniency? By adding to his catalogue of crimes, for which he has shown no remorse. Now he is even using a young boy to cloak his iniquity...'

He walked slowly round the inner circle, speaking to each judge individually. 'We must not make the same mistake again. This time, he must cease to exist...'

'Ugh!' said Hancock. 'Come and look at this.'

He moved away from the operating table, to allow the anaesthetist to take his place. As he did so, Matthew glimpsed the inside of Tom's brain. There seemed to be something that looked like a tiny white octopus clamped over it, with its long, thin tentacles reaching in every direction.

Matthew felt sick. He rushed out of the gallery and into the toilet on the other side of the corridor, reaching the handbasin just in time...

'To help us reach our decision,' Anshar was saying, 'we need evidence from a human historian.'

Su watched tensely as he moved over to her mother. 'Nintu – I wish to question Doctor de Courville. You will again remain silent while I do so.'

She wondered what evidence her mother could possibly give. But if the aliens thought it was important, it could only be good news for Tom: her mother would never support Ninurta's elimination if there was any chance that it would put Tom's life in danger.

Then she remembered that it would not be her mother who would be voting, but an alien with her face. And she would have to make an agonising choice: if Tom was to be saved, they would also have to save a murderer.

'As a distinguished historian, doctor,' Anshar went on, 'would you say that your species has become more civilised or less civilised in the last five thousand years?'

'It depends what you mean by civilised,' said Sandra quietly. 'Our artists, writers, composers and architects have left us some priceless legacies... and our doctors and scientists have discovered many cures for previously terminal diseases. Also, there are more and more organisations devoted to the reduction of poverty, famine and disease...'

She hesitated, as if she had more to say but decided not to say it.

Anshar also seemed to have noticed her hesitation. 'But you have also had many more conflicts, have you not, doctor? More murders? More wars? More cruelty?'

'I'm afraid that's true,' said Sandra. 'Throughout our history, there have been far too many examples of our inhumanity.'

'And did this inhumanity increase while Ninurta was living here?'

'Yes. We seem to find it hard to live in peace. There have certainly been many more deaths in battle.'

Su was becoming more and more alarmed. Didn't her mother realise that her evidence was putting Tom's life in danger? That he might have to share whatever sentence the Grand Council imposed?

'How do you explain this increase in fatalities, doctor?' asked Adam.

'Well first of all,' said Sandra, 'there are many more inhabitants on this planet than there were five thousand years ago. And our weapons have become much more lethal. A spear kills one man, but a machine gun kills hundreds, and a nuclear bomb kills thousands. There has always been conflict on Earth – but it's humans themselves that are the killers, not their weapons.'

'So you do not hold Ninurta responsible for teaching you how to kill?'

'No. We have free will, so we must answer for our own actions.'

Ea could contain himself no longer. 'Do you believe in evil, doctor?'

Sandra hesitated. 'I don't know. Yes, I suppose I do.'

'You have a character called the Devil in your mythology, do you not?'

'Yes.'

'And is it not true that humans blame this creature for encouraging them to commit evil deeds?'

'That was often the case centuries ago. Nowadays, only the superstitious hold such beliefs. In most countries on our planet, anyone who commits murder is held accountable for it by law. To blame it on the Devil is no longer an acceptable defence.'

'So you don't believe he exists?' Ea pointed to Ninurta's hologram, still smiling his malevolent smile. 'There he is, doctor – the devil from Apsu on whom all your primitive myths are based: the serpent in the Garden of Eden, the Minotaur of Crete, the one-eyed Cyclops. He is not a myth. See how he smiles, revelling in his infamy. We must put an end to him once and for all.'

The hologram began to flicker like a faulty light-bulb...

Matthew had moved down to the ground floor of the hospital and was watching tensely through the operating-theatre window as Hancock gently prised the tentacles of the white octopus from Tom's brain. When it was finally free, he held it up with a forceps and examined it closely as it wriggled and squirmed like a freshly-caught fish.

The anaesthetist moved to his side. 'What on earth is that?'

'No idea,' said Hancock. 'I've never seen this kind of tumour before. I'll take it to the lab for analysis.'

Matthew rushed in. 'I'll do that,' he said, grabbing the forceps and dropping the octopus into the icebox. Before Hancock or the anaesthetist could stop him, he rushed out again.

'Ninurta will now speak in his own defence,' said Anshar.

Jarman/Ninurta turned to face the crowd, appealing directly to them in the rasping voice that Su had heard coming out of Tom's mouth when he was angry. But she noticed that it was considerably weaker.

'I am accused of misusing another species during my exile here on Earth,' he said, 'but if you believe I am guilty, then the Grand Council must share my guilt, because you abandoned me here without any supervision. You had no right to use this planet as a prison, without a thought for the inhabitants. You call yourselves the Wise Ones, but you acted without wisdom. Now you have a chance to redeem yourselves by allowing me to return to Apsu, so that the humans may live in peace.'

'They would also live in peace if you were eliminated,' said Dai/Ea venomously. 'And so would the rest of the galaxy.'

Su glanced at her watch: it was a quarter to twelve. And there was still no sign of Matthew.

Matthew was speeding over Salisbury Plain in the hired car, with the icebox on the passenger seat beside him.

He was suddenly dazzled by a blinding light in the rear-view mirror: another car was coming up fast behind him, its headlights full on.

He glanced at the speedometer: he was doing ninety-five, so the other car must be doing well over a hundred. He slowed down to let it pass, but then he saw the blue light on the roof.

Cursing his luck, he pulled into the side of the road, and the police car pulled up behind him. In the rear-view mirror, he watched a man get out of the passenger seat and saunter over to him, taking his time.

He rolled the window down, and the policeman poked his head inside. 'This your car, is it?'

'No,' he told him. 'I hired it at Heathrow.'

'Let's see your licence.'

Matthew opened his wallet and handed him his American licence.

The policeman studied it by torchlight. 'Foreigner, eh? Well we don't appreciate visitors to these shores using our roads as racetracks...'

'I'm not a foreigner – I'm British. And my son's very ill in hospital...'

The policeman sighed. 'If I had a quid for every time I've heard that one...'

'Look,' said Matthew desperately, 'Why don't you call Jim Browning at Wiltshire CID. He'll vouch for me.'

'Got influence in high places, have you? I've heard that one before too...'

Matthew suddenly snatched his licence back and stamped on the accelerator. The car shot forwards, sending the policeman flying backwards onto the road. He turned all the car's lights off and peered into the impenetrable darkness ahead, trying to find a side road he could use as an escape route.

At the next village, there was a signpost pointing right and left. It was too dark to read, so he turned right and stopped. A moment later, the police car raced past and disappeared into the night.

Su glanced anxiously at Adam, wondering if he'd noticed that Ninurta's hologram was solidifying and growing larger as he continued to speak in his own defence. His voice was becoming younger and stronger too.

'You seem to believe that the humans were perfect before I arrived on their planet,' he was saying, 'but they were not. They were primitive savages, and it was not I who taught them to hate and steal and kill – they knew those things already. The only crime I will admit to is the killing of Anu, for which I have no regrets. He was unforgivably weak, and as I said at my trial, a leader must be strong. In any case, I have now served the sentence you imposed on me. And during my exile, the humans have benefited greatly from my presence among them.'

'Perhaps you would give us an example of your benevolence?' said Anshar.

'I can give you many examples, some of which I placed on the boy's computer as visual evidence of my good deeds. It was I who gave many young people the gift of music, and I who saved the life of Queen Marguerite of France. I also helped Noah build the Ark, so that he and his family could escape the Big Flood. I guided Moses and the Jews to the promised land, and it was I who revealed the secret of relativity to Einstein. And when I learned of the holocaust, I tried many times to have Adolf Hitler assassinated.'

There was a long silence, with each of the Wise Ones waiting for the others to speak. Anshar turned to Sandra. 'And what do you say to that, Doctor de Courville?'

Su wondered how her mother could possibly disprove Ninurta's claim. But she didn't even attempt to disprove it.

'What Ninurta has told you may be true,' she said with quiet authority, 'but it is not the whole truth, because the results of all these actions were catastrophic. Many scholars believe that the Great Flood was a punishment for Noah's drunkenness. Einstein's theory of relativity led directly to the nuclear bomb. And as for Queen Marguerite of France, if the attempt on her life had been successful, perhaps thirty thousand French Protestants would not have been massacred. The same could also be said of Hitler. Seventeen people tried to assassinate him between 1939 and 1945, some even before that. But they all failed, usually because Hitler cancelled an appointment at the last minute.'

Anshar frowned. 'You believe he had prior warning?'

'Either that, or he was extremely lucky. And I don't believe in that kind of luck.'

'But if it was Ninurta who warned him, how could he have known the terrible consequences to the human race of saving his life?'

'I can't answer that,' said Sandra. 'But I believe he did know. Hitler consulted many astrologers, and Ninurta could well have been one of them.'

'There!' said Ea triumphantly, turning to Anshar. 'We have all the evidence we need, great Lord. Let us be rid of him once and for all.'

Su, who had been listening to the debate with mounting alarm, opened her mouth to scream 'WHAT ABOUT TOM?' at them, but nothing came out. Instead, the girl sharing her mind seemed to sense what she was about to ask and spoke for her. 'If we vote for elimination, what will become of the boy?'

Another contemptuous smile spread across Ninurta's face. 'A good question, Inanna,' he rasped. 'Remind these pompous fools that they cannot eliminate me without eliminating us both.'

'It is time to take a vote,' said Anshar. 'Nintu – as Anu's widow, you have the right to vote first. Which is it to be – mercy or vengeance?'

Su held her breath, waiting for the alien inside her mother's head to answer. 'Ninurta must be eliminated,' said the emotionless metallic voice. 'To kill my husband, a senior member of the Grand Council, was a heinous crime, for which he should have paid the ultimate price five thousand years ago. Now I demand justice. A life for a life.'

'I too vote for elimination,' said Ea. 'Ninurta is plainly a danger to the whole galaxy. It would be irresponsible of us to let him live.'

Su couldn't believe what she was hearing. 'WHAT ABOUT THE DANGER TO TOM?' she wanted to scream. But again, when she opened her mouth, nothing came out of it.

'Two votes for elimination,' said Anshar. Su found herself staring into a pair of wise old eyes that didn't belong to her grandfather. 'Now you, Inanna.'

Su had no alternative but to keep quiet and pray that the girl inside her head was more forgiving.

'It is better that a hundred guilty ones go free than an innocent one be punished,' she was relieved to hear Inanna say. 'If we cannot separate Ninurta from the boy, we must release him.'

'With no safeguards?' demanded Anshar sternly. 'What if he causes more deaths on some other planet? We will never be forgiven.'

'And I will never forgive myself if I vote for the death of an innocent young human.'

'What about you, great Lord?' asked Ea. 'You also have a vote.'

Su waited for Anshar's reply, confident that Tom was now safe. Surely the wisest of the Wise Ones couldn't vote for Ninurta's elimination, knowing that he would also be condemning Tom to death?

But to her horror, his answer was uncompromising. 'It is my duty to weigh the life of one boy against the millions who will probably die if Ninurta is free to contaminate the whole galaxy. So by three votes to one, the decision of the Grand Council is...'

'Haven't you forgotten something, Anshar?' rasped Ninurta. 'I am still a member of the Grand Council. Therefore I too have a vote.'

Ea glared at him. 'A judge cannot vote when he himself is being judged.'

'Why not? There is no law that forbids it.'

The judges glanced at each other uneasily. 'That is true,' said Anshar. 'We never considered such a law would be necessary. I assume you are voting for your release?'

Ninurta nodded. 'You would hardly expect me to vote for my own extinction.'

'It makes no difference. By three votes to two, the verdict is elimination.'

'The decision is invalid!' rasped Ninurta, whose voice seemed to be getting deeper and stronger. 'My father is not here, and he would certainly vote for my release.'

Anshar hesitated. 'We will wait five minutes for Enlil, no longer. After that, the sentence will be carried out.'

Matthew turned off the main road and sped down the Avenue towards the village. On either side of him the stones flew past: dark, primeval shapes against the midsummer moon.

He glanced at the icebox beside him, wondering whether Adam had thought his plan through. To introduce iron into a solenoid, even in such a small quantity, could be extremely dangerous, because it would dramatically increase the strength of the magnetic field. Instead of trapping Jarman in the field, the energy in the stones might well nourish and rejuvenate him. Had Adam taken that into consideration?

At the end of the Avenue, the main circle came into view: a circle of fire, illuminated by the ring of flaming torches. In the centre, next to the dying embers of a bonfire, Matthew could just make out Adam, Sandra, Su… and, towering over them all, a colossal figure which could only be Jarman. His worst fears seemed to have been confirmed.

He parked the car by the side of the road, grabbed the icebox from the passenger seat, and raced round the circle, trying to find a way through the crowd of onlookers. But they were staring fearfully at the giant in the centre and wouldn't let him through…

'The five minutes is up,' announced Anshar. 'Ninurta will now be eliminated.'

'Then I will make sure that you also eliminate the boy,' said the giant, his deep voice booming in the still night air. 'If I cease to exist, so will he.'

'No!' cried Su, running to him. 'Please – let him go. Take me instead. I'm expendable, Tom isn't.'

Jarman looked amused. 'I do believe this is what you humans call love,' he boomed. 'Another weakness! No, little girl. I have no intention of letting your friend go. He and I will travel together into oblivion.'

Matthew was crawling through a forest of legs, dragging the icebox after him. People were treading on him, kicking him, but he managed to fight his way through to the front of the crowd. As soon as he was sure he was inside the circle, he opened the lid of the box… and watched in amazement as a cloud of iron filings flew out, heading for the centre of the circle…

Su backed away from Jarman/Ninurta as a swarm of what looked like tiny black insects flew out of the darkness and attached themselves to him. He shot up into the air like a bullet and started to stretch and shrink like a piece of elastic as he was caught by the strong vertical field above the circle...

Meanwhile Matthew was crawling around the base of the tree where, according to Su's text, Adam had hidden the battery. The onlookers took no notice of him, because they were gazing in awe at the extraordinary object which was careering around the night sky above their heads, constantly changing its shape. One moment it elongated into a thin piece of string: the next, it flattened out into a large CD.

Matthew scrabbled desperately round the roots of the tree, cursing himself for not bringing a torch. At last, his fingers closed round one of the cables. He followed it to the battery and quickly pulled it out, breaking the electric circuit running round the stones...

...and high above the crowd, Jarman was torn apart by the conflicting magnetic forces of each stone and, with a scream of agony, exploded into a million brilliant fragments that lit up the darkness for a moment before cascading gently down onto the grass.

There was complete silence from the crowd. Then, as it started to disperse and drift home, Adam and Matthew met in the centre of the circle.

'So much for science being a delusion,' said Adam with quiet satisfaction. 'I'd say that was one-nil to the scientists, wouldn't you? Pity we won't remember it.'

As they walked back towards the Manor, the cluster of tiny meteorites was already ten light years away, speeding back to Apsu.

Chapter Ten

Tom's rapid recovery was astonishing. Every day for the next two weeks, when Matthew and Su visited him at the hospital – sometimes accompanied by Adam or Sandra – there was a marked improvement. Two days after the operation, he was sitting up in bed. Within a week, he was jogging up and down the corridor and sneaking down to the café on the ground floor for some chocolate-chip muffins. He caused so much trouble that the senior nurse, who had strict instructions that he wasn't to be allowed out of the Special Care Unit, had to station a colleague outside the door.

The X-rays confirmed that the operation had been an unqualified success. Doctor Hancock confided to Matthew that he had never known a patient recover from major surgery so quickly. But he insisted that Tom should be kept under observation at the hospital for at least another week.

Sandra was preoccupied with the thought that now there was a hint of autumn in the air, Matthew would soon be leaving. Though she had only known him for two summers – thirty years apart – she had begun to realise that she would miss him dreadfully. And though he had never said anything, she knew he felt the same. The way he smiled at her, the way he would quickly look away when she caught him staring at her, the way he had clung to her for a moment after he had helped her over the fence – all the signs were there.

But they didn't have much time: if he didn't make a move soon, there might not be another chance.

One evening, as they were having coffee in the drawing room with Adam, the phone rang. Sandra answered it, and an American voice asked to speak to Professor Matthew Brake.

'Who's calling?' she asked.

'Joseph Lowry. I'm head of his department at MIT.'

With a sinking heart, she handed the phone to Matthew and listened to his side of the conversation. His British accent suddenly became transatlantic.

'Hi, Joe... No, never heard of him... But why can't he visit during the fall semester – it's only ten days away... Well it's not very convenient, Joe. My son's just had a serious... yeah, I realise it's a lot of money... Okay, give me a couple of hours and I'll call you back.'

He put down the receiver and pulled a face. 'Some billionaire wants to endow a new space lab. Seems MIT's the front runner, but he insists on meeting all the lecturers before he makes a final decision. So I've got to go back and make a presentation.'

'When?' asked Adam.

'Next weekend.'

'What about Thomas?'

'He's out of danger. And I'll only be away a couple of days. I can fly back.'

Sandra thought of offering to bring Tom over to the States when he was well enough to travel, but said nothing. The first move had to come from Matthew.

But it was Adam who made the offer. 'No, don't worry, old chap. Soon as Hancock gives me the nod, I'll bring him over.'

The move, when it came, was disappointingly ambiguous. That evening, as Matthew and Sandra walked back from the pub, he asked her if she fancied a trip to Boston. Next time Adam came over, maybe she and Su could come with him?

She was unable to hide her irritation. 'Maybe we could,' she said coolly, 'if we're not too busy.'

He seemed to realise that the invitation had sounded rather half-hearted and tried to make amends. 'It's just that our kids seem to get on so well. And it'll be easier for you to get away than me.'

'Why?' she asked, bristling. 'I have a job too, you know. Two jobs, actually. You think your work's more important than mine?'

'No, of course not. I'm sorry. It's just… I'm not sure when I can get away again.'

'Neither am I.'

They stared at each other, both waiting for the words that would break the log-jam. But the words never came, and they walked back to the Manor in silence, thinking wistfully of what might have been.

The following evening, having booked his flight, Matthew drove to the hospital to say goodbye to Tom, and to give him the new smartphone he had bought so they could keep in touch.

'I don't know if they'll let you use it in here, Tommo,' he told him. 'But you can take it into the garden when you're well enough.'

'I'm well enough now,' said Tom grumpily. 'Can you get me out of here, Dad? This place is like Alcatraz.'

'Well at least it's not surrounded by water. So you won't have to swim for it.'

He moved to the door, but Tom called after him.

'Hey, Dad. What happened on Midsummer Night? Did you go to Dai's shindig?'

'Yes.'

'What happened?'

'To tell you the truth, I don't remember much about it. Dai and his Disciples did their thing in the circle. Burning torches, incantations to the moon – that sort of thing. Complete garbage, of course.'

Early the next morning, Matthew threw his suitcase into the hired car and went back into the house to say goodbye.

Adam was standing in the hall, staring up at Margaret's portrait. 'It's very odd,' he said thoughtfully. 'It's three years since she died, yet it suddenly seems like yesterday. She's always in my thoughts, of course, but she's never felt so close to me.'

Matthew put an arm round his father's shoulders. 'Perhaps she's been looking after us, Dad. Helping us to come through this… whatever it was.'

'I'd like to think so.'

'It's the same old question, isn't it? What the hell was it all about?'

Adam smiled. 'Don't ask me. I'm just an ignorant old scientist. Maybe your grandchildren will be able to tell you.'

Mrs Crabtree appeared, carrying a paper bag which she thrust into Matthew's hands. 'Sandwiches for the journey. Tell Master Matthew not to worry – there's no meat or fish in them.'

Matthew was about to tell her that she'd got the names muddled up again, but thought better of it.

'Thanks, Mrs C,' he said, kissing her cheek. 'It was good to see you again. Have you seen the ladies this morning?'

'They must be still abed. I'll wake them up for you.' Before Matthew could stop her, she crossed to the dinner gong and gave it a thwack that hurt his ears.

A moment later, Su came tearing down the stairs in her pyjamas and flung herself into Matthew's arms. 'Bye, Matt. Don't worry – I'll look after Tom for you.'

Sandra had followed her down the stairs wearing a white robe, her hair tousled with sleep. He moved up to her and kissed her cheek.

'Bye,' he said awkwardly.

She gave him a wan smile. 'Safe journey.'

Neither of them could think of anything else to say.

Outside, Matthew and Adam embraced. 'See you soon, Dad. Keep me posted about Tom.'

'Of course. Bring him back next year.'

'I'm not sure how he'll feel about that.'

Adam glanced back at Su, who was standing in the doorway with Sandra. 'I think you'll find he won't be able to keep away.'

Matthew climbed into the car and drove off. He caught sight of Sandra in the rear-view mirror, disappearing into the house. Was it too late to turn back, apologise for his crassness and tell her he loved her? Yes, it *was* too late. There was a tide in the affairs of men... and he had missed it.

He stopped at the crossroads and glanced up the lane towards Hawthorn Cottage. Dai was shaking hands with his disciples as they filed into a battered minibus. Kevin climbed into the driver's seat, and the minibus rattled towards Matthew in a cloud of thick black smoke that would have had the environmentalists on the warpath.

Just before it turned right into the Avenue, Kevin leaned out of the window and called to him. 'See you, Matt. Next time, let's hang out together, okay?'

Matthew left the car by the side of the road and walked up the lane to the cottage. Dai, about to close the door, saw him and met him at the gate.

'What's going on, Dai? Your disciples deserting you?'

The old man grinned. 'I've resigned as their icon. They wanted me to come to Glastonbury, but I can't stand that dreadful music. And I can't leave the circle, as you know.'

'Now don't start all that again. You can leave the circle whenever you like.'

'You'll see, Matthew, you'll see. *You* won't be able to leave either.'

'Just watch me.' He held out his hand. 'Goodbye, old friend. See you next year, eh?'

'If I'm still upright.' Dai pointed to the cannabis plant. 'Want to take some of that with you?'

'No thanks. If I need to forget my troubles, I'll stick to alcohol.'

'You're getting middle-aged, Matthew. You want to take the Welsh bard's advice. "Do not go gentle into that good night".'

Matthew walked back down the lane, thinking about what Dai had said. Was he getting middle-aged? If so, he must fight against it. Life, as Joe Lowry was fond of saying, was not a rehearsal.

As he reached the car, he glanced back at the cottage. Dai was still standing by the gate, waving to him. He waved back, realising that this might be the last time he would ever see him. By next year, the old man could well have gone to the great poaching ground in the sky.

As he drove down the Avenue, the stones on either side of him seemed to share his melancholy mood. It was as if they had finally bonded with him, as if he had passed some sort of test. Maybe now they would stop haunting his dreams. But he knew he would never entirely escape from them, wherever he was in the world. Though they had caused him so much grief, they had played a big part in his life. And part of him would always be trapped in their magnetic field.

As the car approached the edge of the circle, he remembered Dai's prophecy that he wouldn't be able to leave the village. He gripped the steering wheel tightly and held his breath... but the car passed smoothly through the invisible barrier. With a sigh of relief, Matthew hit the accelerator and headed for London.

Back at the Manor, Sandra was standing at the drawing room window, staring forlornly at the garden, basking in the early autumn sunshine. Adam appeared beside her.

'I'm sorry it didn't work out,' he said gently.

She turned to him. 'I don't know what you mean.'

He kissed her cheek. 'Yes, you do.'

Later that morning, Su was sitting on the riverbank where Adam had tried to teach Tom how to tickle trout, watching a flotilla of ducks floating downstream in search of food. The summer was almost over, she thought disconsolately: soon Tom would be going home, and she would have to go back to school. How could she get through the days, weeks and months till she saw him again? Perhaps she could persuade her mother to take her over to the States at Christmas, but even that was an eternity away.

She lay back on the grass, covering her eyes with her arm to shield them from the blazing sun. There was nothing to look forward to – no mysteries to solve, no heart-to-hearts on Glastonbury Tor. Just an empty wagon in the courtyard.

'Hey! How's my girl?' It was Tom's voice. She sat up, to see him coming up the path, carrying a paper bag. The bandages round his head made him look like a wounded soldier returning from a war.

She jumped to her feet and ran to him. He picked her up, held her high in the air and brought her slowly down until their mouths were level with each other. Then he kissed her – a long, lingering kiss that made her whole body tingle.

'So they let you out?' she asked breathlessly when they came up for air.

'No, I escaped. Caught the bus back here.'

'Escaped? But they'll come looking for you.'

'No, they won't. I checked in with Grandpa. He's calling the hospital to tell them where I am.'

She stared at him with concern. 'You'll get into terrible trouble.'

'It's worth it.' He pulled her down onto the grass and opened the paper bag. 'I brought us a picnic. Fish and chips. And a couple of hamburgers.'

Back at the Manor, Adam was on the phone in the hall. Sandra sat on the stairs, listening as he tried to placate an irate Doctor Hancock.

'Oh I quite agree, Doctor,' he was saying. 'It's highly irresponsible. I'll bring him back myself straight away... What?... Well, if you're sure?... Yes, of course. I'll ask Doctor de Courville to keep an eye on him.'

He put down the receiver and turned to Sandra. 'Hancock says young Thomas might as well complete his convalescence at home. Apparently he's been making such a nuisance of himself at the hospital, they're glad to get rid of him.'

'But this isn't his home,' said Sandra.

'He seems to think it is. Rather gratifying, isn't it?'

That night, at dinner, the phone rang. Sandra disappeared into the hall to answer it, and was away a long time. When she came back, red-eyed, she sat down at the table, put her head in her hands and burst into tears.

'Who was it?' asked Adam in alarm.

'It was Matt. He's asked me to marry him.'

'Well there's no need to cry about it. I take it you accepted his proposal?'

'Of course.'

Su and Tom high-fived each other. 'So when are we going over, Mum?' asked Su excitedly.

Sandra dried her eyes on her napkin. 'We're not going anywhere. Matt's on his way back here. He said Dai was right – he couldn't leave the circle after all.'

Towards midnight, after Matthew had returned and they were still celebrating his engagement to Sandra in the drawing room, the doorbell rang.

'See who that is, will you, Thomas,' said Adam, who was slumped on the sofa. 'All this champagne seems to have rendered me immobile.'

Tom went into the hall and opened the front door. A tall, thin man stood outside, his face hidden in the shadow of the porch.

'Sorry to bother you, young man,' he said. 'I was wondering if this house was for sale?'

'No,' said Tom.

'Pity. You don't by any chance know of any other property in the village that's on the market? I'm a geologist, you see, and I want to spend my retirement in this village, investigating the stones.'

'Sorry, I haven't been here long. But my grandfather might know. You want me to ask him?'

'No, don't bother. I'm sure I shall find somewhere suitable very soon. Happy Day.'

The stranger turned and walked away down the drive.

Also available from

fantom
publishing

Raven

by Jeremy Burnham and Trevor Ray

THE ORIGINAL NOVEL INSPIRED BY THE TELEVISION CLASSIC

The ancient underground caves are in danger, with plans afoot
to use them for the disposal of atomic waste. But forces are at
work to save the sacred ground – forces from another time.

Why do the caves contain mysterious symbols and how
does the legend of King Arthur connect with them? What
power does Professor Young, the archaeologist, have to save
the cave complex? And why does the merlin suddenly appear?

Raven, on probation from Borstal, finds himself caught up
with these strange powers, and begins to realise that the future
of the caves depends on him…

ISBN 978-1-78196-114-8

Available in hardback from
www.fantomfilms.co.uk